DEEP WATERS
OF
Destiny

**CALUMET
EDITIONS**

Minneapolis

First Edition May 2022
Deep Waters of Destiny. Copyright © 2022 by Pete Carlson.
All rights reserved.

This is a work of fiction. All of the characters, names, incidents, organizations, and dialogue are either the products of the author's imagination or are used fictitiously.

Printed in the United States of America.
10 9 8 7 6 5 4 3 2 1

ISBN: 978-1-950743-83-4

Cover and book design by Gary Lindberg

DEEP WATERS
OF
Destiny

PETE CARLSON

**CALUMET
EDITIONS**
Minneapolis

Also by Pete Carlson

Ukrainian Nights
Tearza

Chapter One

Gunner looked at his watch and frowned. Rizzo, the head of the largest mafia organization in Sicily, hated people who were late. Gunner rushed to change clothes and ordered one of his crew to take him ashore in a speedboat. A young man in a black suit, open-collar white leaned against a Mercedes, smoking a cigarette. He threw the butt away when he saw Gunner step out of the boat and walk down the pier. Gunner nodded. The man placed Gunner's carry-on inside a black sedan.

Gunner tried to relax during the drive from Monaco to Eze, a seaside village high above the pristine southern coast of France. He had received two unsettling messages late last night—an urgent message to meet Rizzo early the next morning and one he'd have to deal with later.

Gunner reflected on his last three years as captain of Rizzo's three-hundred-foot yacht. Even though he'd been to Rizzo's home many times, he didn't know the man on a personal level. Their meetings were always business, not social. Of course, Gunner knew Rizzo's connection with the mafia before he accepted the job, but the opportunity to become a captain on one of the most expensive, ultra-luxury yachts in the world was tantalizing. During his interview, he was impressed with Rizzo, finding him charming and intelligent with a quick sense of humor. His passion for food and wine and his pride for the people of Sicily were contagious. But a dark side lurked behind Rizzo's smiling façade, a volatile temper directed at anyone who challenged his point of view or failed to follow orders.

1

Gunner arrived at Rizzo's compound fifteen minutes later. After armed guards opened the gate, the sedan moved up a long driveway to the main house. Another guard stood next to the front door and nodded for Gunner to walk up the stairs.

"Gomez, your soccer team is going down in the 1996 US Cup this year," Gunner teased.

"Ahh, the Americans! They are all talk."

"Twenty Euro we beat you by two goals."

"Done!" Gomez smiled and opened the door. "Enjoy your stay."

Rizzo's assistant, Maria, rushed up to greet Gunner.

"How's my girl?"

She blushed as she took his bag.

"Do you have a recent photo of your beautiful daughter? She must be five, no?"

"Yes, yes, but later. You're late, and I was told to take you to the pool as soon as you arrived." She led him through a living room with a vaulted fresco ceiling that opened to a huge deck and an infinity pool overlooking the ocean a thousand feet below. Maria offered a fresh espresso while he waited for Rizzo. Gunner sat down at a table on the edge of the patio and checked his cell phone messages, wondering what was behind the urgent meeting. He hoped Rizzo wasn't firing him.

A sliding glass door opened from an office next to the living room, and Rizzo walked out to greet Gunner with a smile and extended his hand. "Good to see you. Thanks for coming on short notice. How was the trip from Palermo?"

"Uneventful. Your ship's in perfect condition."

"Any other problems?"

"We lost two crew. They got in a fight at the Monte Carlo Casino last week. They were arrested, and I'm in the process of replacing them."

Rizzo shook his head. "I'm glad you manage these idiots." Rizzo sipped an espresso. "How are you? Damn, you always look good. I wish I had your genes."

Gunner relaxed—no pink slip this time. "Maybe you should try exercising once in a while."

Rizzo laughed. "Exercise is overrated." He turned and looked out over the ocean. "Another beautiful day. I love this time of year."

Gunner smiled and dipped a chocolate biscuit into his espresso. "Early summer is always full of possibilities."

Rizzo grinned. "You're a funny paradox. Speaking of opportunities, that's why I wanted to meet." Maria stepped out of the house with a large tray of food. "Maria, please hold all my calls." He broke off a piece of fresh baguette and laid a large slice of soft cheese on it. "How long have we known each other?"

"Hmm, I think it's been almost three years."

"Have you enjoyed our time together?"

"Of course. You gave me a wonderful opportunity. The Destiny is one of the top yachts in the world."

Rizzo paused and yelled at Maria again. "Can you bring us a bottle of champagne? You know the vintage I like." He pointed at a bowl of tiny strawberries called *Frais des Bois* meaning strawberries of the woods. "Other than good caviar, nothing tastes better than strawberries with champagne." He settled in his chair and nibbled on prosciutto and olives. "Tell me about yourself."

Gunner chuckled. "About me? Why? I have no intention of dating one of your daughters."

Rizzo laughed. "Fair enough. Other than you're one of the top captains on the water, I want to know more about you."

Gunner looked toward the ocean, amazed that he had not covered this basic information before. "Not much to tell. Raised in Maine. Went straight to Vietnam after graduation in 1970. Started working at a yacht club in Miami after my tour. Kept my head down and worked my way up—and here I am."

"And..."

"And what?"

"Why didn't you return to Maine after your tour?"

"There was nothing for me back there."

"What about your parents?"

Gunner squirmed in his chair. "As I said, there wasn't a reason to go back."

"Where did you learn to sail?"

"My father loved to sail. We belonged to the local yacht club, and I cut my teeth sailing dinghies and sunfish sailboats around the bay. My dad dreamed of retiring on a sailboat and sailing the world. While I was in high school, we built a forty-nine-foot sloop in the backyard. We called her "Rainbow." Finished her just before I left for Vietnam."

"So what happened? Did your father follow his dream?"

Gunner played with a strawberry. "It's a long story. Best for another time."

They ate in silence for a minute.

"What about you? You've never told me your story," Gunner said.

Maria stepped out of the house carrying a bottle of Krug Clos D'ambonnay on a tray with two flutes. Rizzo unwrapped the foil and slowly eased the cork out to preserve the bubbles. He poured two glasses, raised his glass and said, "Salute."

Gunner took a sip, and his mouth exploded in foam from tiny bubbles followed by layers of flavors that changed the longer he rolled the wine in his mouth—first a creamy mousse, then a touch of apple, followed by a luxurious finish of nutty cocoa. He closed his eyes for a second and let them linger. When he opened his eyes, Rizzo was smiling.

"First time with this particular champagne?"

"Wow." Gunner leaned forward. "Crazy. I've had champagne before, but never like this. Reminded me of my first kiss with Babby Larson. She was seventeen, and I was sixteen. She tasted like bubble gum and made me just as dizzy."

Rizzo chuckled as he took another sip and then held the flute up to the sunlight. "Love this stuff. Although I'll never admit to my friends in Sicily that I prefer French Champagne to our Italian sparkling wines."

"Do you suppose a case could find its way to my cabin somehow?"

"Do you believe in miracles?"

"I do now."

"Then you never know," Rizzo said as he refilled Gunner's glass.

"Were you born in Palermo?" Gunner asked.

"Yes. I'm glad you asked because that's in part why I wanted to meet with you. You see, my family has lived in Sicily for over a hundred years. I want to take you to see my home and our operations in Sicily after we finish breakfast. Do you have any other plans for today?" Gunner shook his head. "Good, I have my helicopter ready to fly us to Palermo. I want you to see where I grew up and where most of my extended family still resides."

"This sounds serious. Are you proposing marriage or planning to adopt me?"

Rizzo smiled, then he grew serious. "I want to bring you into the family because I trust you. I have a business proposition."

Gunner frowned. "I'm not much for family."

Rizzo ignored his comment and refilled their glasses. "Here's to the Destiny and the Rainbow. May they take us to beautiful places and give us many great adventures." They clinked glasses and looked each other in the eye. "As you know, our family business has been exporting olive oil for generations. We also own sea salt farms, dozens of olive farms and wineries around the island of Sicily. We've been looking for ways to expand our markets, and I have the opportunity to create a new partnership to distribute our products to the United States. The relationship is still very preliminary. I have various business terms to work out, but I think this agreement will come together soon."

"Good for you." Gunner sipped on his glass of champagne. "But how would that involve me?"

"I need someone I can trust to protect me."

Gunner frowned. "I don't do bodyguard work."

"Not physical protection. I can take care of myself. What I need is someone to protect my interests from others." He leaned forward. "My goods will be shipped from Sicily to Aruba. From there, my new partners will transfer my products onto their container ships and transport them to the Dominican Republic. At that point, the product will get divided and transported into smaller vessels and shipped up the eastern seaboard of the United States." Rizzo paused to let his plan sink in.

"My question is the same. Why do you need me?"

"You know all the harbor masters, customs officers and local politicians. You have a unique network of important people along the entire shipping route through the Caribbean to the United States. You also own a yacht club in the Dominican Republic, a major port where the goods get divided into smaller transports bound for the east coast of the United States." He stared at Gunner. "I need someone I can trust to make sure the shipments end up where they are supposed to."

Gunner shook his head. "I'm a simple captain. I don't have any experience with stuff like that."

Rizzo waved his hand in the air. "Your contacts throughout the islands are invaluable. You are exactly what I need to protect my valuable investment.

Gunner placed his glass on the table, stood and walked several feet away to the railing on the edge of the cliff. He gazed at a sailboat in the distance. Without turning around, he asked, "How valuable?"

Rizzo joined him at the railing. "Let's just say I'm not doing this for practice."

"What's the value of your first shipment when it gets to the States?"

Rizzo smiled. "Should net about fifty million in US dollars after expenses."

Gunner wasn't a fool. He knew this was a low estimate and understood this was not about olive oil and salt. Jett, his best friend with contacts in the pentagon intelligence department, had given him a full report on the Rizzo family. They were the oldest and largest mafia family in Sicily. Gunner believed that as long as he stayed in his lane as captain of the yacht, he'd be safe from any criminal activity. This was different. What Rizzo was asking crossed a line, and they both knew it.

Gunner whistled. "That's very valuable olive oil."

"Some say it's the best in the world."

"How many shipments do you plan in a year?"

"We'll start with one and hope to increase that to three in the future if everything works out."

Gunner did the math in his head. He assumed they were transporting heroin from eastern Europe, Russia and the countries around Afghanistan. Aruba made sense because the Venezuelan and Columbian cartels had been slowly taking over the Aruba harbor and buying off politicians and police.

"How big is the container ship?"

"Five hundred containers."

Gunner figured Rizzo would hide heroin inside about 10 percent of the containers and fill the rest with olive oil, sea salt and wine. At the current market rate of $3,000 per kilo of cocaine, the money involved was staggering. Gunner didn't know the net market price for heroin, but if it were anywhere near cocaine, one shipment could net Rizzo approximately half a billion dollars.

"Come on, Gunner!" Rizzo said. "This is a terrific opportunity."

"I have to think about this."

Rizzo smiled. "Give me a ballpark number?"

"It's not about the money."

Rizzo frowned as his jaw tightened. "I'm doing this deal because I can use the money for good reasons."

Gunner grunted. "So, nothing is as it seems?"

They locked eyes for a moment until Rizzo clapped his hand together. "That's why I like you. You're a very savvy guy."

"Ok, let's see this country you're always bragging about."

* * *

It was a short helicopter flight from Eze to Palermo, Sicily, following the western coastline of Italy. Along the way, Rizzo gave Gunner a history lesson on Sicily. He was a proud man who loved his country and was extremely bitter about how Northern Italy had gutted Sicily of its wealth and governance over the last fifty years. He pointed to Sicily in the distance. "Most people don't realize that Sicily was at one time the star of Europe and the Mediterranean. We're geographically located at the crossroads of the major commercial trade routes that moved back and forth from Europe, Africa, the Mediterranean and the Middle East for centuries. The downside is that we've been conquered by every major empire. The upside is that we have a rich, diverse culture unlike any other."

As they approached Palermo, Rizzo continued his history lesson. "Look at the port. Imagine how for centuries that bay was filled with ships from all over the world." He moved his mic closer to his mouth. "After World War II, the parliament, which was controlled by the wealthy families of the northern regions—Rome, Florence and Venice—voted to rebuild northern Italy by taking money out of our treasuries. Even though we're the largest regional state in Italy, they refused to provide anything but token money for us to rebuild, and they ignored our needs for basic infrastructure and social support services. The government essentially abandoned us. As a result, we've gone from one of the richest states of Italy to now, in 1996, becoming the poorest." Rizzo gritted his teeth as he continued. "We've been on our own ever since."

The chopper landed a short distance from the city center. They departed and walked to a black Mercedes. "I want to show you something in Palermo," Rizzo said. "It will not take long." On the way into the city, the car stopped near a park next to the palace and several government buildings. Gunner expected to tour the beautiful palace grounds, but Rizzo led him quickly into a maze of narrow streets in a poor area of the city.

After a ten-minute walk, Rizzo stopped in front of a mostly destroyed building and pointed at a wall that still showed the remnants of ancient columns. "Look at this!" he said. "Our city is filled with priceless architecture and art, yet there's no money for restoration. No money for medical clinics, hospitals, social services, education. Our young people have no job opportunities. They have to leave home and go to Europe or the US to obtain a job. It's pathetic."

"What can you do?" Gunner asked.

"My family has been criticized as the devil by the puppet government and the church, but we're the only ones that help our community. We provide the only jobs that pay a decent wage. We're the ones who fund the clinics and hospitals. We're the ones who provide loans to local businesses because the banks won't. We're the ones who fix the roads and provide money for basic utilities."

Rizzo stopped and turned in a circle. The narrow streets were crowded with people selling wares and trying to make a living. "These are the people I love."

Gunner looked at the run-down buildings and inhaled the stench of garbage that lay in piles for the lack of sanitation services.

"Now you understand why I want to develop this new business relationship," Rizzo said. "I need the money to provide better services for my people. Our organization provides social, health and business assistance throughout Sicily."

Gunner nodded.

Rizzo stepped into a small restaurant. "Buon Giorno," he said to the waiter who greeted them. The waiter slapped his hands together, kissed Rizzo on both cheeks and yelled toward the kitchen. The owner emerged and rapidly shook Rizzo's hand. At the same time, the majority of the patrons stopped eating and clapped as Rizzo sat down at a community table. Waiters quickly brought out baskets of fresh bread and large pitchers of red and white wine. For two hours, multiple courses were passed around family-style until Gunner couldn't eat another bite.

Rizzo pleaded for mercy as two older women tried to hand-feed him more ravioli and then turned to Gunner. "It's time to go," he said. "You need to see two more things before you spend the night at my house in Taormina."

They flew south from Palermo to Marsala along the western coastline until the helicopter began hovering above the salt pans that produced some of the richest sea salt in the world.

Rizzo said, "Those dikes form a patchwork of pans. The water is periodically drained from one pan to another until the seawater evaporates enough to rake and dry the salt in the sun. This produces some of the richest sea salt in the world. Our family has owned these salt pans for a century."

Gunner had been quiet on the flight, but the salt pans provoked a question. "Are you planning to ship this sea salt to the States along with your special olive oil?"

"Yes, we need better distribution for our salt, olive oil and wine. The middlemen have become greedy in Europe and take too much money."

After twenty minutes, they landed on top of a tall hill overlooking the beautiful town of Taormina. His house was perched on the edge of the cliff. The staff carried Gunner's bag as Rizzo ushered him onto a deck that wrapped the length of the house. On the far end was an infinity pool with a breathtaking view.

Rizzo pulled up two chairs alongside the pool. The staff brought out a glass of white wine for Rizzo, a gin and tonic for Gunner and two Cuban cigars. They sat in silence for several minutes as the sun set on an orange horizon.

"Do you feel it?" Rizzo asked.

Gunner nodded and blew out a cloud of smoke.

Rizzo pointed his cigar at Gunner. "You and me. We're not so different. We each have had to fight all of our lives for what we believe—for what we know in our hearts is worth sacrificing for. I know how you have silently supported friends like Cody and Jett. I also know you took a second mortgage out on your yacht club to buy the land in Virgin Gorda so you could develop it. Should I go on?"

"I'm impressed. You're very thorough."

"I need to be, but don't take it personally." Rizzo leaned forward. "We're outliers here. I don't like authority. Neither do you. We do the things we have to do. People think they know us, but they don't."

This comment didn't seem to require a response, so the two men sat in silence another few minutes, perhaps a sign they were growing more comfortable with each other. Finally, Gunner said, "I love your place."

Rizzo nodded. "I come here whenever I have a difficult decision to make. I have clarity here that I can't achieve anywhere else."

Gunner looked at Rizzo. "Is that why we're here? For clarity? Are you having second thoughts about your new business opportunity?"

Rizzo made a slight smile. "It's not without substantial risk. As I hope you can appreciate after our tour today, it's not just about making more money for the family. I have more money than we will ever need, but our economy is getting worse. My people are suffering more every day, and there's no one else who can help them. That's why I wanted you to be involved—to ensure this new venture will be successful." He lost his smile. "Now, please, tell me if we are getting married or just dancing."

Gunner shifted uneasily in his chair and looked out over the ocean. "Look... I know you intend to put the money to good use. It's just... I don't think this works for me."

Rizzo leaned forward. "Come on, Gunner. As I said, I don't need the money for myself. This new venture will raise millions to help my people."

Gunner rubbed his chin as he considered his current status. His marina was underwater. Jett had two unsold spec homes in Colorado. In addition, he had purchased vacant land on Virgin Gorda to help Jett get out of Colorado. He was strapped financially, and Rizzo knew it.

"Speak to me, my friend," Rizzo said. "This could be good for both of us. What do you need to make this worthwhile?"

Gunner turned to Rizzo. "I need to think about it a little longer."

The seduction continued with a six-course dinner ending with red snapper encased in a thick shell of sea salt and then almond granita with an ice-cold aperitif glass of homemade limoncello.

After dinner, Rizzo looked at his watch. It was after midnight. "Think about our conversation today. We'll return to Eze in the morning."

Gunner nodded. "I'm going to take a dip in the pool and then turn in. Thanks for the great dinner and the tour."

Rizzo gave a "don't mention it" wave and started up the stairs to the second level.

Gunner grabbed a bottle of wine and walked to the infinity pool, which shimmered in a luminescent blue light a thousand feet above the calm sea. A full moon reflected off the ocean. He sat in a lounge chair, sipped his wine and closed his eyes.

What a day, he thought. They say you only have five pivots in your life. He had counted four already, so he knew this could be one of his last life-changing decisions. The house was dark now except for a light coming from Rizzo's second-floor master bedroom and a floodlight illuminating the deck. Everyone was asleep, so he threw off his shirt and shorts and dove naked into the pool. Alone, he swam to the far end, where he rested his arms on the edge and watched the lights flickering below.

A woman's voice startled him. "It's an amazing view, especially on a night with a full moon."

Surprised, Gunner turned around and trod water while squinting at the shape of a woman backlit by the floodlight at the far end of the pool. She was carrying a wine glass and reached for the bottle he had set on the table.

"May I?" she asked with a slight Russian accent. "Rizzo always drinks great wines."

"Be my guest."

Gunner glanced at his glass on the table and then at his clothes.

The woman smiled. "You seem to have a dilemma."

Gunner swam closer to the edge of the pool and noticed that she was quite beautiful—a typical Eastern European face with high cheekbones, full lips and deep, black eyes.

"I don't think so." He grinned. "I think it's you that has to make a choice. Either you take your clothes off and join me, or you can refill my glass and hand me a towel."

"Hmmm, that is a problem." She smiled at him. "Since we just met, I'll take the latter. However, I may change my mind next time."

Gunner swam to the edge of the pool. "You never know—there might not be a second opportunity."

She filled his glass and threw a towel at him. "I'll take my chances."

As he pulled himself out of the pool and dried off, the woman caught her breath at Gunner's athletic body. She also noticed several scars on his chest, back and legs.

Gunner didn't bother to dress but sat on the chair with the towel across his lap. He picked up his glass and looked at the mysterious woman.

"What should we drink to?"

She licked her lips. "Endless midnight swims under full moons."

"I'll drink to that," he said. "Back home, we call it skinny dipping."

"And where's home for you?"

"A long way from here."

They drank their wine and looked at the moon for a minute.

"I should introduce myself," the woman finally said.

"I know who you are."

She looked surprised but quickly recovered. "And how do you know that?"

"Rizzo talked fondly of you." Gunner leaned back in his chair. "Not too many women would wander out after midnight to check on a naked man in their pool. It's Nika, isn't it?"

She nodded and brushed her long, dark hair behind her ears. "Do you know that he lost his wife while giving birth to a baby boy? It crushed him to lose them both at the same time. He had three beautiful young girls who saved his life. He always wanted a son but couldn't bring himself to marry again." She shifted closer to him. "What do you think of Rizzo?"

"An interesting man."

"Let's see. I believe you've been his captain for two—"

"Three years this June." Gunner picked a fresh cigar out of the humidor Rizzo had left.

"Care for one?"

"Of course. Rizzo prefers the Cubans and has them flown in regularly."

"I like you already. I'm surprised we haven't met before."

"That may change soon. Rizzo wants me to oversee the new business opportunity."

Gunner reached for the lighter. As his hands held the lighter to her cigar, their faces were less than a foot apart. Nika's eyes were fixed on Gunner's.

Gunner smiled. "I enjoy a woman who knows what she wants."

"And I enjoy a man who isn't intimated by a woman."

They leaned back and watched the moon for a few minutes.

13

Gunner looked over at Nika. "Nice to share the evening without the need for conversation."

"I thought you might have had enough of that on the tour today." She poured more wine for both of them. "Have you thought about his proposal?"

"Not much. This is the first time he's mentioned his new deal. Is that why you were sent out here? To persuade me to get involved?"

Nike shook her head. "Rizzo didn't send me."

"Then—why are you here? Certainly not just to see a naked man in a pool."

She played with her cigar. "I felt the need to have a conversation before you make your decision. I was in your shoes about five years ago. I'm well aware of your financial stress, and I know why it exists. Admirable, but your sense of responsibility to others is also your weakness. Right now, you are considering the opportunity to solve the problems of people you love and are tantalized by never having to worry about money again. But you are realistic about the risks and the consequences of saying 'yes' to Rizzo." She puffed on her cigar. "How am I doing so far?"

"Keep going. You've done your homework." Although he was listening, he couldn't take his eyes off the way she crossed her long legs. *This is one dangerous woman,* he thought. *She knows exactly what she's doing, and she's enjoying it. Game on.*

"You're a smart man. Do you understand what agreeing to Rizzo means?"

Gunner played dumb. "Please tell me."

"Rizzo is one of the most amazing men I've ever met. He is brilliant, a great judge of people, charming, loves his family and the people of Sicily but demands loyalty. He's generous, but never forget how cruel he can be when it matters. The first time I met him was in his corporate offices in Palermo in 1991. His office was two thousand square feet overlooking the harbor, decorated with paintings and sculptures from all over the world. He was dressed in a black suit and white, open-collar shirt with a sliver of hair combed back and flowing almost to his shoulders. He looked like a famous actor in a classic movie. He had a cigar in one hand and a phone in the other. Almost a cliché. His feet were crossed on top of his desk, and he was laughing and talking with a broad smile. I was working for another successful man then, and we were here to discuss some business. My Russian employer was not comfortable with his English or Italian, so I was there to translate."

"How did you come to work with Rizzo?"

Nika paused. "At the time, I was in a very dark place with few options. I had become friends with Rizzo through many conversations and negotiations with my employer. Over several months, I was translating more for Rizzo than my boss. At some point, he asked me to come to work for him. Choices have consequences. And some consequences you can't take back."

"How did you get a job with the Russian?"

"We had a mutual acquaintance, and I have several talents he needed. I was in a compromised situation at the time, and he bailed me out."

"Literally or figuratively?"

"That's a story for another time." She stopped and filled her glass with the last of the wine. "Do you understand what I'm trying to explain to you?"

"I'm trying, but it's a little hard to concentrate watching you..." Gunner smiled, glancing at her short skirt and long legs... "drink what's left of my wine."

"Rizzo is very sensitive. You are either with him or against him."

"What are you saying?"

"You will be fired the minute you say anything but yes to him."

"I know."

"I made that choice five years ago."

"Do you have any regret?" Gunner asked.

Nika stood. "Good luck with your decision." She took one more sip of her wine and walked away.

Gunner stretched out in his lounge chair. What other choice did he have? If he refused, he'd lose his job on the Destiny, lose the marina and the land development he'd funded. As he reached for his glass, he saw that the lights to Rizzo's bedroom were off. He also saw the reddish glow of the end of a cigar in the shadow of the balcony.

* * *

The next morning, Gunner joined Rizzo for breakfast next to the pool. Rizzo asked, "Did you sleep well?"

"No, I never sleep well on land."

Rizzo sipped on his espresso and said, "Nika told me this morning that you had a nice visit last night after I went to bed."

Gunner nodded.

"She was impressed."

"By what? My financial dilemma?"

Rizzo smiled and bit into a fresh croissant. "She's important to me. Invaluable over the last five years. She runs a major part of my family's operations. Did you know she speaks five languages? She has particular expertise in money management."

Gunner shook his head slightly and leaned back in his chair. "It was obvious she has many talents." He smiled. "What is her role in your new business?"

"She was the negotiator on the deal terms of the new cartel. Now she is planning the trip to Aruba to celebrate the arrival of our first shipment. You'll like working with her. She has a temper, though, and an edge that's hard to describe." He paused. "She isn't the most diplomatic of people when things don't go her way. But she's a brilliant negotiator, probably because she's so beautiful that men underestimate her."

"I'll try to remember that," Gunner said.

"Did you make a decision? Are we getting married? What's the price?"

"Five million. In gold bars. Delivered to the Rainbow before the first shipment leaves the port."

Rizzo smiled. "That's quite a wedding gift."

"And the use of your private jet anytime, anywhere, no questions asked."

"You must be joking. Five million? Not a chance. I'll give you half that amount."

Gunner didn't blink as he looked into Rizzo's eyes. He believed he could always tell when a man was lying or bluffing. "Then we can pretend we never had this conversation."

"Let me ask you something. Do you like running the Destiny?"

"Come on, Rizzo. I'm not a fool. I understand the threat. You are welcome to replace me anytime you want."

"You drive a hard bargain. Let's shake on three million and move on."

"No—it's five. And then I'm yours."

Rizzo played with his cigar for a minute. Finally, he smiled. "I agree to your request, but I need to discuss this with my partner."

Gunner frowned. "You never mentioned a partner. I assumed this was your operation."

Rizzo waved his arms in the air. "No worries. It's a minor detail."

"Why do you need a partner?"

"I can't supply all the, uh, olive oil from my sources. I need to bring in enough to fill the shipment."

"Who's your partner?"

"Trust me. It doesn't matter."

"I need to know, or I'm not your guy."

Rizzo hesitated, then said, "A man named Bykov."

Gunner clenched his teeth. "A Russian?"

"Yes."

Gunner loved the Italians but hated the Russian elite. The oligarchs that he'd met over the years on various yachts were volatile and dangerous. They did not have a moral compass and were capable of anything. This news changed things.

"I'm out."

"Don't be silly."

"I don't trust the Russians."

"I will maintain complete control."

"Have you done any business with them in the past?"

"Yes, enough to believe this could be an outstanding partnership."

Gunner pointed to the newspaper on the table. The headline read: Osama Bid Ladin declares war on the US. "Do you think this will affect your partner's ability to source the heroin from Afghanistan? Also, I heard that Boris Yeltsin is expected to be reelected again as president of Russia."

Rizzo waved his hand in the air. "I have been assured that neither of these events will affect my partner's ability to deliver the heroin."

Gunner rubbed his head. Finally, he responded, "Given the involvement with Bykov, my fee is now ten million. I'll help you monitor the first shipment delivered from Aruba to the Dominican Republic. Once the pipeline is confirmed, you won't need me anymore, and I can go back to running your ship."

Rizzo shook his head. "Bullshit. There's no way we're going to pay that."

"Then we don't need to continue our nice chat."

"Why do you need to double your fee?"

"You know why."

"You're a funny man." Rizzo scanned Gunner's face for any clue if he was bluffing. "I can make $7.5 million work, but that's it."

Gunner nodded. "Oh, one more thing."

Rizzo's smile left his face.

"Who's your partner once the shipment is delivered to Aruba. I want to know who I'm babysitting until they deliver to the Dominican Republic."

"The main cartel is from Columbia with a minor involvement of a family in Venezuela."

"Is it Castillo and Perez?"

Rizzo's eyes widened. "How did you know?"

"That's why you're paying me the big bucks."

"And possibly one more guy, Ortega," Rizzo added. "He controls the largest Mexican cartel."

"Wow, the three stooges. I heard they're making a big push to expand their cartel." Gunner went back to the table. "So you and your buddy, Bykov, are forming a new cartel? Something like east meets west?"

"You're smarter than you look," Rizzo said.

"Now, that's a compliment I can understand." Gunner played

with his glass. "Tell me—why the Columbian cartel? Isn't Europe enough?"

"We need to expand. Our European markets are saturated."

Gunner smirked. "Ah, and your ships don't return empty."

"Simple, old-school trading. Just as my great-grandfather did when he sailed wooden ships around the world."

Gunner knew this was the point of no return—his last chance to take care of things.

Rizzo glanced at his watch. "We have to get back to my house in Eza. I have an important meeting later. We can talk more after that. I want you to discuss with Nika the logistics of making the first shipment successful." Rizzo stood and placed his hand on Gunner's shoulder as he walked past. "This will be fun!"

* * *

Once they landed the helicopter in Eza, Gunner had Rizzo's driver take him back to Monaco. He needed to check on the yacht and start planning the trip to Aruba. On the way back to the harbor, his phone buzzed with a call from Miami, which he didn't pick up.

Gunner waited until he was back in the Destiny cabin to return the Miami call. He stared at the number on his cell phone for a moment, then took a deep breath. He remembered other times when his life was altered by new information from a phone call. He touched the call button and waited.

A woman answered. "Hello, how can I help you?"

"This is Gunner, I'm returning her call."

"I'll see if she's available."

Gunner doodled on a piece of paper while he waited.

"Hi Gunner, I'm glad you called. Where are you now?"

"Monaco."

"We need to see you."

"Why?"

"You know why."

Gunner flinched. "Are you sure?"

"Yes."

Gunner sighed and set the phone on his desk for a second. He could still hear her faint voice.

"Gunner, are you still there?"

He picked up the phone. "I'll have to make some arrangements, but I think I can get to Miami later this week. We have to keep this information very—"

She cut him off. "I know. Don't worry."

There was a loud knock on his cabin door.

"I have to go," he said, "but I'll let you know when I confirm my flight."

Gunner picked up a photo of a reunion on the Rainbow with his best friends. The trip in 1991 had been arranged to celebrate the twentieth anniversary of their return from the Vietnam War. He stared at the photo for a long time as fond memories of that trip lingered.

* * *

Back in 1991, their reunion was long overdue, but life had gotten in the way. This was their third attempt to make a reunion happen. The banter and teasing resumed as if they had seen each other yesterday. The water lapped against the side of the Rainbow, gently rocking the forty-nine-foot sailboat in Bitter End Cay. The sun was just touching the horizon, spreading out its red, yellow and orange rays like a peacock.

Gunner emerged from the galley with three tall glasses filled with rum, fresh lime juice and a splash of sweetened coconut milk. He handed one to Cody, sat down in the cockpit and pointed at Jett. "I'm not giving you one until you tell me the name of the bar where we got hooked on this drink," he said with a big smile.

Jett loved that smile. He had watched it charm the pants off too many girls to count. Although Cody and Jett had aged, Gunner had hardly changed in the past twenty years. In a swimsuit, his tan body was brown and taut from years of hard physical work. His long, dark brown hair was tousled and the same length as in the seventies. But it was his eyes that Jett always noticed first, always the eyes. Piercing blue, they seemed to make women dizzy from across the room or instantly put a man on notice. Gunner cast a spell on everyone that met him.

Jett paused, thinking back over the last twenty years. "I can't remember the name of the bar, but I certainly remember the girl. She was beautiful and smelled like a gardenia. Weren't we in Nassau?"

Cody shook his head. "You guys are pathetic. It was the End of the World bar on Bimini.

"Yeah, that's right," Jett said. "And what about Jimmy, the bartender? That guy was crazy!"

"We were all crazy back then, weren't we? Remember sitting at the bar and we made a bet on who would still be alive?" Cody asked, looking at Gunner.

"I remember," Gunner said quietly. "I guess I fooled you. Neither of you thought I'd be here, did you?"

Finally, Gunner handed Jett his drink. "Let's make a toast," He raised his glass. "To us and..." Gunner stopped.

Cody and Jett glanced at each other. Gunner was distracted, his mind on a private journey somewhere in his past. After a moment, a smile broke out. "To us and the Rainbow. She has always kept us together."

They clinked their glasses and turned to the south to watch the sun reflect on the rain from a small squall passing in the distance to create a rainbow. *Perfect,* Gunner thought. It felt good to be back on the Rainbow with Jett and Cody. She had aged well; forty-nine feet of love, sweat and tears had gone into building this boat with his dad in their backyard. This was the first extended reunion since Gunner and Cody left the States and moved to the Dominican Republic. Jett had left his father's law firm to develop luxury, single-family homes in Telluride, Colorado. Gunner had become one of the top captains in the Caribbean on luxury sailboats and motor yachts, while Cody was running Gunner's marina in the Dominican Republic.

They watched the sun dip below the horizon. Nobody spoke for a long time.

The next day they sailed from Virgin Gorda to Martinique, a paradise with low mountains and clear, cobalt blue water. The breeze was starting to pick up. Gunner turned his face to the morning sun and sniffed the air. "No rain. It's going to be a good day. Cody, let's get the anchor up."

"Aye aye, captain," Cody answered.

Cody and Jett moved across the deck in unison. No need for words. Like riding a bicycle, Jett was amazed at how quickly they remembered their familiar roles. Gunner was born to sail, born to be a captain. He commanded instant respect.

Cody raised the anchor while Jett untied the straps holding the mainsail to the mast and began attaching the main clips in the track. After a few minutes, the mainsail was ready to be hoisted.

"Cody, climb the mast," Gunner said, then glanced at Jett. "You take the bow and walk us through the reef." Once Cody had reached the top of the mast, Gunner yelled, "Talk to me every fifty feet. Watch for the big coral heads." Gunner pointed to the bow. "Jett, grab the depth stick and sound every twenty yards. I want to know if we get less than fifteen feet. Once we clear the main reef, remember there's one more reef off to the starboard. We'll have to tack once before we can run free."

Cody looked concerned. "What about the wind? It's swirling."

Gunner looked up and smelled the breeze. "We'll be all right for now. It's still early. The wind hasn't picked up enough to worry about yet." Gunner's eyes were ablaze. They all sensed the change.

As they cleared the last reef unscathed, Gunner cut the engine. Cody pulled up the main, and as the sail caught the first whiff of wind, the boat groaned as she started to heel over. They shifted their weight to re-balance as she began to pick up speed and work her way to the deep water.

The Rainbow rode the ten-foot swells as if on a gentle rollercoaster. The sail was full but luffing slightly. Cody and Jett glanced back at Gunner on the helm, waiting for him to decide how he wanted to set the sails. Cody was on the mainsail while Jett held the steel crank, ready to adjust the jib once the mainsail was set. Gunner's hands were strong and steady on the wooden wheel of the helm as he waited patiently for the boat to settle. They had been through this so many times over the years that they knew he was waiting for the negotiation to finish with the boat and for Gunner to become one with the water and the wind. Long ago, he had tried to explain how to *feel* the ocean, how to *feel* the wind, how to let go and stop being "what we used to be." But Cody and Jett never understood it the same way Gunner did.

Cody smiled at Jett and nodded toward Gunner.

Gunner suddenly yelled, "Jett, come back here."

Confused, Jett wondered what was wrong. It had been a while, but he didn't recall missing anything on the prep.

"Take the helm," Gunner ordered. "I want to see if all those years with your nose in a book have ruined you."

He stepped aside and put his hand on Jett's shoulder. Jett was surprised because Gunner had never done that. Physical touching was something Gunner was never comfortable with. His parents loved him dearly, but they had rarely hugged him. Because he was adopted, they never experienced the bond that came from natural childbirth.

Jett placed his hands on the wooden wheel and instantly felt the boat move through his arms and into his legs. As the Rainbow caught the breeze, she heeled over and started to swing downwind to the port. They quickly changed their stance to correct their balance.

Gunner smiled. "Here we go. Let's see what you remember, smarty pants."

Jett yelled at Cody over the wind, "Crank the main in a little."

"Not yet," Gunner gently said. "Let her settle first."

Jett yelled again, "Cody, wait on the sail."

Cody laughed at the confusion. Holding a large metal crank, he put his hands on his hips. "What the hell? Make up your mind, will you? We don't have all day!"

Gunner pointed at Cody. "Hold the main where she is and then crank her in when Jett gets his line."

Cody waved. He understood.

Gunner smacked Jett on the back of the head and yelled, "Don't you remember anything I taught you? Stop looking at the sails, shit. Forget what you see. You can't sail by sight. You have to sail by feel. The Rainbow will tell you. You can't think. That's been your fucking problem since I met you."

Jett bristled for a second but knew he was right. Gunner was also the only person Jett knew who could insult people with the F word and make them feel good about it.

As they moved away from the reef, the water turned into a deep, violet blue. The swells began splashing over the bow as the boat crested the top of the bigger waves.

"Ready?" Gunner leaned close and whispered, "Hold her steady for a second and close your eyes."

"What?" Jett asked. "Are you kidding? Then I can't see what I'm doing."

"Exactly. You have to trust her before she'll trust you."

This made Jett think of Sky, his ex-wife, back in Colorado. Trust, or lack of it, killed their relationship. Maybe he'd tried to hold her too tightly.

The boat swung sharply to the port. Gunner scowled. "Are you listening to me?" He shook his head. "Now wait, she'll tell you what to do. You'll feel which way to turn the helm."

"But what about trimming the sails?"

"Don't worry about Cody, he'll know how to adjust the sails once you get there."

Jett closed his eyes again and waited. He tried to relax and fight the temptation to open his eyes and turn the wheel. The boat bucked and rocked like a horse that could sense someone strange trying to ride her. For an instant, Jett panicked and started to turn the wheel but then felt Gunner's hand on his arm.

"Loosen your grip," Gunner calmly instructed.

It helped. Jett could now feel the boat wanting to turn starboard, the exact opposite of what he thought he should do.

"There you go," Gunner said. "Now trust her."

Jett was barely touching the wheel now. Then it happened. He felt the boat settle. The speed increased, and both the boat and he started to move smoothly in harmony with the wind and waves instead of fighting them. Jett opened his eyes.

Cody didn't need to wait for any orders. He knew what to do and was already cranking the sails to take out the last of the luff. He grinned at Jett as he cranked fast to set the sail just right.

"Feel it?" Gunner said to Jett from behind. "She's accepted you."
Jett blushed. "That was incredible."

Gunner slapped him on the back. "Next time, leave your fucking brain at home." He moved forward on the deck to help Cody finish setting the jib.

They had a 554-kilometer run ahead with plenty of time to talk and enjoy the day. The sun glistened off the bronze, sweaty backs of Cody and Gunner as they moved around the deck and trash-talked to each other over the howl of the wind. The breeze felt good on Jett's face. He realized how much he loved these guys.

After dinner, Jett was on the first shift alone with Gunner. Neither spoke for several minutes. "I have a question for you," Jett said. "What's your first memory of water? Nobody loves the water more than you do."

"Mom teaching me to swim at the lake," Gunner said. "I must've been two or three, but I remember it so clearly. Water is my happy place." Gunner looked down at his glass and played with the rim. "Water has the same magical draw for everyone."

"I wonder why."

"Because we were born in water. The womb was our first home."

Gunner started to say something but then stopped. Finally, he shook his head. "It's really good to be with you guys again." He stood up and walked to the bow. Watching the horizon, he thought about his childhood and his first memory of water.

* * *

Gunner was only two when his mother, Kate, had walked into the water with him until they were chest-deep in front of their lake house. Kate worked hard to hold onto him as he squirmed to escape her grasp. She slowly lowered him into the water and then let go. He panicked at first, sinking and kicking wildly as he held his breath. He looked at the fuzzy outline of his mother's swimsuit above him. As he sank into the summer water, he felt completely different. For the first time in his life, he was free, weightless, wrapped in a warm blanket of water. The lack of sound comforted him.

Suddenly, his mother grabbed his arms and yanked him out of the water. "Sweetie, you can't just lay underwater like that," she told him. "You have to kick and move your arms."

His father, Tom, yelled from the dock, "You can't just let go of him." He dove in and swam to where they were standing. Staring at Gunner, he said, "Kate, did you notice how he struggled at first but went limp after you let go of his hands?" He scratched his head. "Weird! That's the first time since he was born that he wasn't acting like he was on a double dose of Ritalin."

Kate frowned. "Tom, stop it. Don't talk like that." She looked at Gunner, continuing, "You're always saying there's something wrong with him."

"That's not true. It's just that he seems a little odd. You remember how different he behaved than other babies his age."

"He's not different!" she insisted.

"You know what I meant."

Gunner's parents had spent years debating whether to have children, and the indecision put a strain on their relationship. They each had grown up in a small family in rural Vermont. After they'd married and moved to the coast of Maine, they tried for three years to have a child but failed. Adding to Kate's feeling of inadequacy, her mother often complained that she was the only woman in town who didn't have a grandchild. Then Tom learned that he was infertile and took it as a personal failure. They had never talked about children again.

Tom worked as an architect for a local company based in Seal Bay, a small town nestled on the Maine coast. A quiet, gentle man who was short and pencil-thin, he preferred to read books and spend time in his garden, although his main passion was sailing. He had taken an architecture job in this small town because the pace of work was slow. Designing an occasional church, library, house or office building didn't consume his life. More importantly, his job gave him time to work on his life-long dream of designing and building a sailboat. He planned to eventually retire and sail with Kate around the world.

Their house was set inland on the shores of a lake about three miles from the ocean. When the wind was right, he could smell the sea and feel its pull on his emotions. Neither Kate nor Tom was much for conversation. They lived together but, in many ways, led separate lives, especially after they found they couldn't have children. Kate taught physics at the local college. When not playing her violin, she spent most of her time inside a small library Tom had built in their house.

One evening late in the fall, Kate's sister called while Tom was pulling the dock out and winterizing the boat.

"Kate, are you sitting down?"

"No, why?" Kate asked.

"Please sit down. I have something wonderful to tell you."

Kate could hear her sister breathing hard into the phone.

"What's so important?"

"I found you a baby."

"What?"

"I have a baby for you."

"Are you crazy?"

"You said you wanted kids someday."

"No, Tom said that." She sniffed. "I've never been sure about motherhood."

"But what if?"

"Not interested."

"Why not?"

"Because... that's all."

Kate never told Tom that a baby was available for adoption, but that option tantalized her for several months. One spring evening, as Kate and Tom were having dinner on the porch, Tom looked up and sniffed the air. "Smell the ocean?"

"I do."

"I love that smell."

"I know," Kate paused. "I have something to ask you."

"Sure, anything."

"Do you still want a child?"

"What?"

"You know that I've resisted having children, but I've changed my mind. I know how much you'd enjoy raising a child."

"You don't like kids. Why bring this up now?"

Kate smiled, reached across the table and touched his hand. "Because you need someone to help you build that sailboat of yours."

* * *

Six months later, the adoption agency told them their baby would arrive in two weeks. It was a boy. They were surprised and scared. They assumed it would take months, even years, for the agency to find a baby. Tom worked every night fixing up the baby's room, finishing just before the baby's scheduled arrival.

They were so nervous the day they picked up their new son from the agency. The adoption process took hours because there were dozens of documents to fill out. Finally, the director held the last form in her hand. "I need his name. What are you going to call him?"

"Gunner Thomas," Kate said. "Gunner was my grandfather's name."

A young woman entered the room holding the baby. Kate reached out for her son but looked terrified. After an awkward moment, the young woman helped Gunner snuggle into Kate's arms.

"Relax, you're not going to drop him," the aide said. "Just be careful to hold his head. They are all bobbleheads at this age. In a month, he'll be strong enough to hold his head up." She started to walk away. "Good luck."

The baby yawned and quietly stared at his new mom and dad.

"Look at those marble eyes," Kate said, looking at Tom.

Tom peered closer. "Damn, it feels like he's looking right through me." He rubbed Kate's shoulder. "Everything's going to be fine."

"What if he doesn't like us?"

"He'll love us." Tom looked over to the adoption director for help.

The director patted Kate's arm and reassured them. "It's normal to have these feelings. I've been doing this for twenty-five years, and in a few days, you'll wonder how you ever lived without him."

* * *

From the bow, Gunner glanced back at Jett in the cockpit. He was glad they had found the time for a reunion. He smiled as Jett got up and moved about the deck of the Rainbow, securing the various hatches as they sailed into deeper water. Gunner thought about everything they had gone through since their childhood in Maine. Jett was Gunner's best friend. They had grown up two houses away from each other. Jett was short for his age and walked with a slight limp because he was born with one leg slightly shorter. Gunner savored fond memories of their childhood, particularly one morning in June when Jett had walked to Gunner's house.

Jett had waved at Gunner's mom, who was at the kitchen window. "Is Gunner home?"

She jerked her thumb toward the back. "He's at the lake."

Jett walked around the house and joined Gunner sitting on the dock.

"Are you excited about your birthday tomorrow?" Gunner asked.

"Not really. Mom's throwing a big party because I'm turning eighteen. It's embarrassing."

"I wish I had even one birthday like yours," Gunner muttered.

"Why do you say that?"

"Nothing—your mom's the best." Gunner dangled his feet in the warm water and surveyed the horizon. "Have you checked the weather for tomorrow?"

"No, why?"

Gunner pointed at a long string of clouds feathered high above them. "See the cirrus clouds" They always show up before a change in the weather. I hope it doesn't rain for your party."

Jett laughed. "You may have a little trouble with school, but you're the only person I know who can identify any cloud in the sky or name any bird or constellation.

"According to my parents, that kind of knowledge isn't going to get me into a good college." Gunner frowned. "They don't know I don't want to go to college. I may not be smart in school as you, but I'm good with my hands. I found that out helping Dad build a sailboat.

Jett turned to Gunner. "You're plenty smart. Don't ever let people make you think differently. Look, we're almost done with our senior year. Let's make the most of it."

"Thanks," Gunner said. "It's hard sometimes. Hard to pretend to be someone I'm not."

They sat in silence for a minute.

Gunner turned to Jett and shielded his eyes with his right hand. "You look tired."

"I didn't sleep very well last night."

"Why not?"

"My folks were fighting again," Jett explained.

"About what?"

"The usual." Jett swirled his feet in the water. "Dad's gone all the time because of work, and Mom hates it. She hates that Dad was the oldest son and has to run the family business and support all his brothers and sisters."

"You're the oldest son. Aren't you expected to run the family business someday?"

"Never." Jett shook his head. "I hate what that company has done to our family. I hate all the family fights."

"But you'll be rich. Set for life."

"I don't care. I'll never agree to take over the business." He stared out over the water. "Besides, my younger brother is much better with numbers than I am."

"Do you have a choice about it?"

Jett ignored the question and jumped into the water. Gunner followed, and they swam to a raft thirty yards away. Suddenly, they heard someone running down the dock. Cody performed a full somersault as he reached the end of the dock and landed with a huge splash. He quickly swam to the raft and joined them in a game of water tag. Gunner always won. He could hold his breath longer than anyone and could swim as fast as a porpoise underwater. Exhausted, they lay on their backs on the warm deck of the raft.

"Hard to believe we graduate next week," Jett said to no one in particular.

"I can't wait," Cody said. "I hate school."

Cody lived two blocks away. His father was a mean man and beat his mother regularly. Tragically, the only time he ever touched Cody was in a rage while hitting him with his fist or a belt. His mother left them when Cody was seven, and he never heard from her again. She had mental health issues that scarred Cody as a young child. Psychologists say that lack of touch and emotional abuse are far worse than physical abuse. Fortunately, his dad became sick with Hepatitis C and died a few months after his mother disappeared. An elderly, widowed aunt moved into his house to raise him. She tried her best, but the damage was already done to Cody.

Cody was a skinny boy with black bangs that always hung over his sullen, dark eyes. Gunner befriended him when they were young. That was Gunner—he always had a soft heart for the wounded. However, it took Jett more time to get used to Cody's wild mood swings before accepting him as a friend. Cody had a short temper and a mean streak that surprised them at times. Gunner always made excuses for him because he understood his pain. He knew better than anyone what it was like when you don't belong. Over time, Cody eventually became a permanent part of the threesome.

"Hey, Gunner, what do you want to be after you graduate?" Jett asked.

"A cloud with nothing to do but float around the sky as high as I can be."

Jett laughed.

Gunner placed his hands behind his head. "What about you, Jett? If you don't want to run your dad's company, then what would you like to do?"

"Maybe work at an aquarium such as Sea World, or maybe a marine biologist. I don't care as long as I'm near the water."

They lay quietly watching a flock of geese pass over, then they made a tight circle, set their wings, and landed on the lake about twenty yards away.

Jett looked at Cody. "What about you?"

"Not sure, but I know one thing. Whatever I decide to do will be a long way from here."

Gunner pointed at Jett. "Should we tell him?"

Cody nodded. "Might as well. He'll find out soon enough."

Jett sat up. "What are you saying?"

"Cody and I enlisted last weekend. We haven't told anyone yet. We plan to wait until after we graduate."

Jett gasped. "You're kidding, right!" He glanced back and forth between them. After neither responded, "SHIT! You can't do that. Have you seen the news? The Vietnam war is getting worse."

"Too late now," Cody said. "We signed the papers. The government owns us."

Jett pleaded with Gunner, "There must some way to get out of this. You can't be serious. Why?"

Gunner shrugged.

Jett laid back down on the raft. "Your parents are going to freak out."

"Not for me," Cody said. "My aunt doesn't care. Maybe for Gunner."

Gunner leaned on his elbow and looked at Jett. "I have to leave here and find out who I am. I'll never know if I don't do this."

They sat in silence for a long time before Jett spoke. "Let's grab the boat and go fishing."

Gunner frowned. "I can't. Have to go to a cousin's birthday party."

"Bummer."

"I hate it," Gunner said.

"Hate what?"

"Spending time with these people. They're so different from me."

"Different how?" Jett asked.

Gunner shook his head. "There's nothing about me that is remotely like them. I feel like an alien from another planet when I'm with them." He looked at his friends. "Not like when I'm with you knuckleheads."

"That's too bad. I love getting together with my cousins," Jett said.

Gunner shook his head. "But you have a normal family."

Cody said, "We all want to be like Jett."

"I better get going," Gunner said.

That was the end of their childhood. The year was 1970, and the Vietnam war was expanding. Their future plans were put on hold because all three enlisted.

Six months after they graduated, they were walking knee-deep in rice paddies. The daylight was fading, and they had lost two men earlier in an ambush. Tired and scared, they prayed to arrive safely at their landing zone for a pickup before dark.

* * *

The phone's buzz snapped Gunner out of his daydream. Looking at the photograph of their last reunion made him lonesome for his best friends. He set the picture down and glanced at the year on his desk calendar—1996. How fast the last five years had passed since their reunion. Growing up in Maine seemed like a century ago. He had just turned forty-four and vowed to schedule another reunion on the Rainbow as soon as he finished the trip to Aruba.

The call was from Rizzo. Gunner thanked him for the tour of Sicily. "Did you get confirmation of our deal from Bykov?"

"We're all set," Rizzo said. "I want you to work with Nika on the itinerary for the first shipment. The container ship will leave Odesa, Ukraine, in less than three months. I have business in St. Thomas before it arrives, but I want us to meet the shipment when it gets to Aruba. You pick the route, but I want to be there for the transfer of goods between our ships and theirs."

"I can make all the arrangements," Gunner said.

"How far is Aruba from St. Thomas?"

"Southwest about 850 kilometers."

"How long to make the trip?"

"We typically average around twelve to sixteen knots. Should take about two days, depending on the weather. How many guests will I be accommodating?

"Plan on Bykov, but I don't know the size of his entourage."

"Understood," Gunner said. "By the way, I need to take a few days off and see some friends on Virgin Gorda. I want to use the jet."

"No problem. I appreciate that you've agreed to help me."

Gunner didn't answer but slowly hung up. From inside his cabin, he looked out over the harbor in Monaco, filled with amazing yachts from all over the world. He loved his job and knew he would miss it.

His next call was to Bonita at his yacht club. They still needed to hire new crew members, and he was confident she could fill the positions on short notice. She agreed.

Next, he dialed Jett. "Hey buddy, how's it going?"

"Hi, Gunner," Jett said. "How's Monaco? How much money did you lose in the Monte Carlo casino?"

"Came out about even. Paid for my gin martinis, but that's about it. I have some time off before we sail to St. Thomas. Thought I'd fly over to see you and Addie."

"Perfect," Jett said. "How long can you stay?"

"Not long. I need to get ready for a trip to Aruba. See you soon."

Gunner hung up and called Marco, his first officer. "Rizzo has scheduled a trip to St. Thomas and then to Aruba," he explained. "Meet me on the bridge. I'm going on a short vacation to Virgin Gorda, but I have a list of things I need you to accomplish while I'm gone."

Chapter Two

Gunner arrived in Virgin Gorda late the following afternoon. His taxi dropped him off at Addie's tropical house tucked on a hill with spectacular ocean views. As he stepped out of the vehicle, he heard a yelp from inside, and the door flew open. Addie ran over and stood on her tiptoes to hug him. Addie was only five-foot-two but full of energy.

"I'm so glad to see you," she said.

Gunner kissed her on the cheek. She smelled sweet from the white gardenia in her hair just above her ear. Barefoot and wearing a light blue summer dress, she didn't look sixty even though her hair had turned snow-white since her husband died. Her tan skin was still smooth, which belied her real age. She had sparkling blue eyes that matched the color of her dress and a shy smile that made you want to kiss her.

"Addie, you look beautiful. How is it that I look older every year, and you never age?"

Addie blushed. "I don't believe you, but you're sweet to say that."

"Where's Jett?"

"He's on the deck waiting with a gin and tonic." Addie laughed as they

"He's been like a little kid waiting on Christmas morning to open presents."

"I don't know how you put up with him."

Jett yelled from the open patio. "I can hear you!"

Jett lounged in a chair facing the sunset. "Perfect timing," he said as he reached into a cooler and pulled out a pre-mixed gin and tonic in a tall frosty glass. He waved at Addie and Gunner to take their places on lounge chairs positioned along the edge of a pool high above the ocean.

"Hurry up. The sun will set in twenty minutes," Jett barked.

Gunner raised his glass and said, "Doesn't get any better than this."

They made small talk for a few minutes, and then they all gasped as the sun exploded with one last burst of reds and oranges. Dozens of multi-colored rays shot out from the flaming orange ball that hung on the edge of the sea. Even though Gunner had witnessed thousands of sunsets on the ocean, he was always amazed at how fast the sun disappears once it hits the horizon.

"You know what I like about the sun?" Gunner asked.

Addie turned her head. "What do you mean?"

"The sun is unconditional. It's something you can always count on. It doesn't ask for anything. It gives us the same beautiful sunshine every day, no matter if we deserve it or not." He paused. "I can't say that's true about people."

Addie and her husband, Jack, owned the large tract of land surrounding their classic island home. They had retired from Canada years ago and built a large home that reminded him of a huge treehouse. Over the years, Gunner had become close to Addie, Jack, and Paz, the governor. They made a point to always have dinner whenever Gunner stopped in Virgin Gorda on his frequent client trips. It became more difficult, though, when Jack was diagnosed with ALS, Lou Gehrig's disease. His healthcare had taken a terrible toll on Addie. It was a blessing when he finally died.

After the last hurricane had flattened Virgin Gorda, Gunner had the idea to get Addie involved with the governor to help the locals rebuild the island. He also suggested that she sell off her excess land to him. He told Addie about his friend, Jett, who developed high-end, luxury homes in Telluride, Colorado, and convinced Addie that she would love Jett, the perfect partner for the project. The sale would provide Addie with a substantial income and guarantee her long-term security. It would also assure her that the development would be done by someone she trusted. Gunner's other motivations, however, were to surround Addie with four homes so she wouldn't be so isolated and lonely and to help his best friend, Jett, get out of Colorado.

"Who's cooking tonight?" Gunner asked.

Addie jerked her thumb toward Jett.

Gunner groaned. "Oh no, the last meal he made for me was hot dogs and microwaved macaroni."

"Gunner, why don't you freshen up from the trip while I help Jett start dinner?"

An hour later, Gunner emerged from his casita wearing a tropical island—a short-sleeved shirt covered with bright colored flowers—and white cotton pants with drawstrings and sandals. He walked into the kitchen and found Jett alone making dinner.

"What's that great smell?" Gunner asked.

Jett pointed to the oven. "Paz brought fresh Mahi-Mahi for me to cook tonight," Jett said and then pointed. "He's out on the patio with Addie. Why don't you join them while I finish in here?"

"I'll join them in a minute." Gunner leaned against the kitchen counter and watched Jett pounding fresh conch into patties. "How's everything going?"

"Great, I've had several inquiries from potential buyers on both houses closest to the beach. I recently submitted the plans for permitting on the other two home sites."

"That's great, but not what I was asking."

Jett pretended to ignore him.

"How do you like Virgin Gorda? I know it's only been seven months, and this is a long way from Telluride."

Jett nodded. "Seems like yesterday when you invited me to come here. Still can't believe you called while I was standing over Stevie's grave, and you were three thousand miles away."

"Distance doesn't define us, my friend. We learned that in Nam, remember?"

Jett rubbed his eyes. "Why don't you go outside and catch up with the governor and Addie?"

Gunner put his hand on Jett's shoulder. "We can chat later. Yell, if you need anything." He grabbed his drink and walked toward the open patio doors.

Jett was shucking oysters when the oven alarm went off. His mind drifted to the day seven months earlier when Gunner called as he was standing over the grave of his son, who had died of leukemia at ten. He had selected this particular gravesite because it had a view of a tall waterfall cascading from a box canyon. He shuddered as he recalled Stevie's last day and how they had lived in an ICU unit for six months, praying the last bone marrow transplant would work, hoping for one more day. Even after all these years, he could still smell the latex on his hands and feel the scratchy paper gowns and masks that were required in isolation.

* * *

The beeping IV unit jolted Jett out of sleep. In the dim light, he could see Stevie sleeping in his hospital bed. Sky, his wife, was curled up in a lounge chair, her face covered by a spray of dark hair.

Stevie's favorite nurse, Anna, entered the room with a syringe and a bag of blood. She turned off the alarm and reset the IV monitor. The commotion stirred Sky, who pushed the hair away from her eyes and pulled the blanket up to her chin.

Anna's eyes were moist with tears as she injected another dose of morphine into Stevie's IV port. Jett watched her adjust the drip flow on two IV bags. One was used for a continuous blood transfusion, and the other provided a cocktail of chemo in a desperate attempt to keep him alive.

Stevie opened his bloodshot eyes when he sensed Anna's presence. "Thank you," he said, his words slurring.

"You're welcome."

Stevie motioned for her to lean in. "I need to tell you something."

She wiped his forehead with a damp washcloth and said, "Can I get you anything else? Water? Ice chips?"

"Can you come closer?" Stevie whispered.

"Honey, what is it?"

He whispered, "I'll miss you."

"Don't talk like that. You're not going anywhere," she lied. Anna looked at Jett and pointed to her mask. They both knew the end was near. Jett nodded, knowing what she meant without saying it. Anna leaned over, took her mask off, and kissed him gently on the cheek. She smiled, touched her lips with her finger, and placed the kiss on his lips. "You're my hero."

Anna's beeper vibrated. "Stevie, I have to leave, but I'll be back to check your vitals and bring you some breakfast."

Stevie watched Anna as she stopped at the doorway and looked back at him. He tried to sit up and wave but slumped back into his pillow.

Jett lightly patted his hand. "Stevie, hang in there, buddy. The morphine will take effect in a minute."

Stevie nodded behind closed eyes. Sky looked on helplessly as Stevie writhed in pain. The painful hemorrhaging under his skin made hugging him impossible.

A few minutes later, two nurses in white isolation gear entered to change the plastic sheets. Stevie was losing blood from his rectum faster than they could replace the loss. Jett knew the end was only a matter of time.

Stevie's breathing slowed as the morphine kicked in. He opened his eyes while motioning for Jett and Sky to come closer. "How are you?" he asked.

"Fine," Jett said as he rubbed Stevie's left hand. "We should be asking you that question."

"That's not what I meant. How…are…you?" he asked again.

His parents looked at each other, confused.

Sky leaned closer and ran the back of her finger down his cheek.

Stevie whispered, "You need to know that I'm going to be fine when this is over."

Jett started to protest, "Don't talk like that."

"I know where I'm going. You don't have to worry about me."

"That's crazy talk," Jett insisted.

Stevie looked back and forth between Sky and Jett. "I'm worried about *you*."

"Stop it," Sky said, squeezing a ball of tissue in her hands while fighting back tears. "You're going to get through this."

Stevie ran his tongue over his blistered lips.

"Do you want some water?" Jett asked.

Stevie nodded. Jett held the straw up to Stevie's trembling lips. He only took a little sip before he slumped back into the pillow. "I'm so tired," he said and then suddenly tried to sit up.

Sky leaped out of her chair and tried to make him lie down. "What are you doing?"

But he wouldn't lie down. And Sky noticed that his eyes were clear—back to the pretty green of his father, not the cloudy grey look of the last couple of days.

"Take off your gloves," he asked.

They thought he was dreaming or hallucinating. Taking off their gloves could endanger their son in this maximum isolation room.

"Please take off your gloves," he pleaded.

Jett and Sky slowly removed their gloves.

"Hold me," he said, struggling with each breath. "I'm cold."

Jett and Sky looked at each other with a silent scream of denial— *no, no, not now, not yet*— and then gently climbed into bed with him, one on each side. After they were settled in, Stevie's breathing slowed down, and Jett recalled the many nights he had watched Stevie peacefully sleep like a baby. As they lay together, a calm that Jett and Sky would never be able to explain gradually replaced their fear. Finally, Stevie took three deep breaths and was gone.

* * *

Standing next to Stevie's grave, Jett wiped away tears and let the cool mountain air calm him. It had taken years for Jett to realize that Stevie had taught him how to die. The student had become the teacher.

Sky and Jett never fully recovered from their loss, and over time it became an invisible wedge between them. They sometimes talked about having another child but couldn't bring themselves to replace

40

Stevie. Eventually, they tried counseling, but by then, it was too late to restore their relationship.

Jett wished he could explain to his friends how seeing death up close helped remove the fear of it.

Jett's cell phone buzzed. He looked at the number and smiled. "Hi, Gunner."

"Where the hell are you right now?"

He choked for a second and looked away from Stevie's grave. Before he could answer, Gunner yelled into his ear.

"Get your ass down here. I have to finish a run to St. Lucia, but after I drop off four couples at the end of the week, I'm flying to Virgin Gorda to pick up the Rainbow and Cody. We're long overdue for a reunion on my sailboat."

Jett shook his head. "You always had a knack for timing."

"Why?"

"I'm standing over Stevie's grave." Neither spoke for a moment until Jett added, "It's still hard to believe he's gone."

"This will be good for you, Buddy. Pack your European marble bag and your toothbrush and fly down here."

"I wish I could. I need to submit plans to the town staff for a new build-to-suit home."

"Who's the client?"

"A wealthy man from Mexico."

"Screw that. I insist that you fly to Virgin Gorda at the end of this week."

"You don't understand. Cash is tight. I need this client. The residential market in Telluride has slowed, and I have two spec homes sitting empty. It's killing me."

"I have a real estate development opportunity to show you down here. I'll pay for your ticket. Come on, we need to catch up anyway."

"I don't know."

"If you don't say yes right now, I'll call Sky for permission." Gunner laughed. "I doubt you want me to do that."

"Okay, I'll talk to her tonight and catch a flight out on Saturday. But I can only stay for a few days. Not like last time. I gotta go."

Before he hung up, he asked, "Hey, one last question. Why did you call me today—I mean right now?"

"Because it's the twenty-first." The phone went silent for a moment. "I always remember."

Jett slowly took the phone away from his ear.

"Jett, are you still there?"

"You're an amazing friend. Thanks for remembering Stevie."

Jett knelt, set flowers next to Stevie's gravestone and smiled at the small angel sculpture from Anna, Stevie's guardian angel. He walked slowly back to the car, debating how to tell Sky he was leaving for Virgin Gorda and not coming back.

That night, Jett shivered as he stepped from their bedroom onto a patio dusted in snow. The house was perched mid-mountain, high above Telluride. The small ski town lay asleep at his feet. Hundreds of tiny white lights twinkled throughout the valley. The high mountain air, so crisp, so clean, gave him clarity for the first time in years.

He heard the slider open and quickly flicked his cigarette into the snow.

"I thought you quit." Sky said.

"Don't start with me."

She stepped beside him, looking at the moon. "Can't you sleep?"

He shrugged and zipped a black fleece higher around his neck. "Probably the last snowfall of the season."

Wrapped in a white robe, Sky tightened the ties around her waist. "It's four o'clock. Come back to bed."

"Give me a couple of minutes."

"What's wrong?"

"I'm fine."

"Bullshit."

Jett thrust his hands into his pockets.

"Spit it out," she scoffed. "For once, be a big boy and say what you're thinking."

He had learned years ago it was useless to argue with Sky. She was so sweet when they first met, but now, even when he was right, she found a way to twist his words and make him feel like a loser.

"You wouldn't understand. I just needed some fresh air."

"Worried about Virgin Gorda?" she asked. "I overheard Gunner tell you that he purchased the property, and everything's set for you to start the new development."

Jett nodded.

"How long will you be gone?"

"Not sure. A couple of days," he lied.

"That's what you said last time."

"I need to meet Paz, the governor of Virgin Gorda, and his planning staff, and then I'll return."

Sky shook her head.

"Does it matter?" Jett said, "You have your clique of beautiful people to keep you busy."

"At least I have friends."

Jett turned, debating whether to respond. Without make-up, she looked older in the moonlight. Over the last year, there was a sense of desperation in her efforts to avoid the inevitable changes that occur when a woman reaches forty. She had spent a fortune on tight clothes, hair color, yoga and a personal trainer. All for her business, of course. Jett wondered what she saw when she looked into a mirror—that tanned young woman in the prime of her life when they'd first met or some dreadful image of herself in the future. Anything, it seemed, but the reality of a woman who was finding her first grey hairs. Although Jett hadn't met Sky until his late twenties, he had always wondered why Sky was attracted to a young, average-looking lawyer-turned-residential-developer. Sky could've married anyone.

Sky glanced back and forth between the mountains and Jett, who continued to stare at her. "What are you looking at?" she asked.

"Just thinking about when we first met."

"Don't. You always do this when we argue."

Neither spoke for a long minute, each avoiding the obvious. Each struggling with how to end a marriage that was over a long time ago.

Jett broke the silence. "I feel like having a drink. You want one?"

"No. It's almost dawn."

He nodded to himself. "Well, I've decided to have one."

"What time do you leave?"

"After I meet with Lopez."

"When do you close on the house you built for him? He told me he was going back to Mexico at the end of next week."

"Next Monday. He owes me $250,000 for custom changes I made on a handshake because he's one of your private ski school clients." Jett glanced sideways at Sky. "Does he know I have two other spec homes that haven't sold?"

"Probably. They're listed on MLS."

"I don't trust a man that wears more gold than most women own."

"Lopez was asking Susan a lot of questions about the market. She's the best broker in Telluride." Sky frowned and crossed her arms. "I don't know why you didn't hire her for our projects. They'd be sold by now."

"You know why."

She put her hands on her hips. "You've never even tried to like any of my friends."

"You call those people *friends*? They could care less about you. All they talk about is money and who has the bigger house and about their friends behind their back."

"What a joke." She put her finger on her chin. "Let's see… your friend Tom's an alcoholic ski patrolman. Jimmy will never be more than a teacher in middle school, and Bobby's barbershop teeters on closure every year."

"Do you want to know the difference between my friends and yours?"

"Enlighten me."

"They're happy." Jett paused. "They're not perfect, not fancy, but kind people trying to make a small difference by thinking about something besides themselves. Do you know what I like the most about these ordinary guys?"

Sky looked away.

"They know what it means to love one another." He shook his head. "Something you or your friends will never understand."

And there it was, finally out in the open—the deep canyon that had been separating them since their son died. Jett fought back tears as he watched the lights of two snowcats grooming a ski run high above them. Some days he wished he could start over. He'd drive a snowcat, smoke pot all night and sleep like a baby.

Sky sensed the change and then announced softly, "I've decided to accept Lopez's invitation to meet his family in Chile in July and continue our ski lessons."

"Are you asking or telling me?"

"Both."

"That's funny."

"What?"

"Never mind," he said, staring over the valley. "I knew you'd go."

"It's only for a month."

"Sure, only a month."

"You'll be working all the time anyway. It's your busiest time for construction."

"That's not the point. When you became his exclusive ski instructor, you knew the rumors that he was part of the Mexican drug world."

Sky bristled. "That's all gossip. After spending most of the ski season with Lopez and his family, I found him to be a sweet man who happens to own several successful companies."

"And a major player in the Mexican cartel."

"You're just jealous."

Of course, I'm jealous, Jett thought. *What decent man would allow his wife to spend the winter as a private ski instructor for a handsome, wealthy man? And what kind of man would agree to his wife traveling to Chile with a drug dealer for a month?*

It was irrational, he knew, but he wanted to hurt her for turning away from him after Stevie had died and for her various affairs. Hurt her for leaving him for a wealthy, younger man who could provide her with a lifestyle he could never give her.

She was waiting for a response.

"Do whatever you want," Jett said, avoiding eye contact. "I don't care."

"Fuck you." She walked into their bedroom and locked the slider.

Sky was asleep by the time he entered the house through the garage and returned to bed. Jett shut his eyes and tried to turn off his mind. Monkey brain, his mother called it. He rose again and finished packing in the basement. He'd be meeting Lopez in twenty minutes at the job site to pick up the check. Gunner would have a private jet ready and waiting for him.

Jett picked up a framed picture of Stevie and him fly fishing together. With moist eyes, he carefully wrapped the frame in a sweater and set it inside his suitcase. Twenty minutes later, he drove away, glanced into the rearview mirror and regretted how his marriage had fallen apart.

* * *

The oven alarm snapped Jett out of his memories.

Gunner walked into the kitchen. "We heard the alarm. Paz and Addie are worried that you'll burn our dinner. Need any help?"

"You can grill the pineapples and oysters while I slice the tuna and scallops for sushi."

"I'll take them to the grill in a second. But first—are you happy?"

"It's been a challenge at times, but I love it here. This island is paradise. I can snorkel or scuba dive almost every day." Jett started to mix the conch meat in a bowl with lime juice, various seasonings and a homemade lemon aioli. He set the knife on the cutting board. "Funny, I always thought I'd have a big family, lots of kids, a dog and live quietly in the suburbs. I don't think I could ever risk having children and losing one again."

Gunner slapped Jett on the back. "So be it... we can become old bachelors together."

Ten minutes later, Jett walked out on the patio with a platter of hot conch fritters. "What are we talking about?"

"Addie, of course," the governor said.

They each grabbed a chair and a plate of fritters.

The governor took a bite and licked his lips. "Jett, I've lived here my entire life and never had conch fritters this good." He turned to Gunner. "So, what's it like working around the rich and famous?"

Gunner laughed. "They can be high maintenance, but I have staff for that."

"Tell me about the man who owns the Destiny."

"Rizzo's from Sicily. His family is old money. They've produced olive oil, wine and salt for generations."

"I heard he's the head of the mafia that runs Sicily."

"I wouldn't know about that."

Paz pointed his finger. "You should be a politician."

Gunner smiled back. "I don't care what he does. There isn't anything I haven't seen working luxury yachts. I'd never have lasted a week in this business if I judged the people who owned these yachts."

"Is he like the Godfather?"

"You've watched too many movies. I don't interact with him very often, but he always treats me with respect, which is not how some of my previous clients have behaved. What's keeping you busy these days?"

"Some new characters on the island are causing trouble. I hear the same thing from my counterparts throughout the Lesser Antilles." He sighed. "It's not good. What do you hear?"

Gunner shifted in his chair.

Paz continued, "There's talk about the Venezuela and Columbia cartels pushing their influence north. They used to be satisfied with staying in their backyard, but that appears to be changing."

"I'm heading to Aruba in three weeks. I should get a better read down there."

They spent hours talking as dear friends do. Finally, Paz looked at his watch. "Thanks for the amazing dinner, my friend," he said to Jett and then hugged Addie.

Jett shook his hand and said, "I'll walk you out."

After Paz had left, Gunner motioned to Addie. "Can we sit for a few more minutes? I want to catch up with you. You look happy."

"I'm always happy when I see you."

"No, you look a different kind of happy."

She shook her head. "I don't know. It was hard to be alone after Jack died. I was depressed for months."

"What happened to change that?"

She smiled. "You."

"What do you mean—me?"

"If you hadn't suggested I sell that property and bring Jett here, I'd still be paralyzed. Thank you. It's been lifesaving to have him around. He helps me with all the things that Jack used to do." She smiled again. "We've become very good friends."

Gunner stared at the fire pit next to the pool. "Did Jett share his story with you?"

"He did."

"And the loss of his son, Stevie?"

She nodded. "We had a lot in common. As you know, Jack and I couldn't have children. I miscarried during the first year of our marriage. I was pretty far along when it happened. We had already selected a name for our boy. When the doctor examined me after the miscarriage, they found I had ovarian cancer, so they did a full hysterectomy. That ended my chances of having a baby. The worst part was we didn't have time to grieve because I had to fight cancer." She stared out at the ocean. "Losing our child almost ruined our marriage. Jett and I have gone through much of the same things."

"I know Jett is very fond of you. He said you were an 'old soul.' Anything else you want to tell me?"

Addie blushed. "It's not what you're thinking."

Gunner laughed. "Sure. Anything you say."

"You look tired," Addie said.

Gunner shrugged. "It's complicated."

"I'm glad you brought Jett here. As you know, Jack could be difficult."

"More like abusive."

Addie nodded.

"Jett's wife used him their entire marriage," Gunner said. "When Stevie died, they lived in the same house but had different lives. She never deserved him. Love was not part of their relationship. Sex, maybe, but not love."

"I understand. Jack was an alcoholic and married me to make babies. It was after my cancer, and we were told I couldn't have children that he became abusive." She paused. "I was so naïve when we married. Sex is easy, but intimacy is hard."

Their gaze turned to the fire that was dying down.

She touched Gunner's hand. "So the answer is—yes, I am happy now. And I want you to have the same thing."

Gunner shook his head. "Don't."

"But—"

"Love you, Addie."

Addie rubbed his arm. "Love you, too."

"Take good care of our buddy while I'm gone."

"I promise."

Gunner flew back to the yacht early the next morning before anyone woke.

Chapter Three

Palmer jumped at the sound of a loud crash from the kitchen close to her table in an open-air café. In the night air, she took a sip of wine to calm her nerves and watched Viktor Petrov, her contact, walk away from their meeting. She was tired, hated Ukraine and couldn't wait to finish this mission.

After two years undercover, she had gained twenty pounds, picked up smoking and begun drinking more than was good for her. *It's not like in the movies*, she often thought. *They don't tell you about the stress when you're in training at the Academy.* Although she and Viktor had met secretly on a regular basis over the last year, Palmer sensed something was wrong. Viktor had seemed nervous and kept looking at his watch. He was the best informant she had cultivated in Ukraine but was paranoid, insisting on a different location each time they met. Palmer was unfamiliar with this café in an old Russian neighborhood near the seaport where Viktor worked.

Palmer took out a small notebook and wrote down the information he had provided about a large drug shipment from Odesa to Aruba sometime in the next couple of months. *Finally,* she thought. *This is the big break I've been waiting for.* Although Viktor didn't know the exact schedule for the shipment, his information meshed with the DEA's recent intelligence regarding an expansion of the main port in Aruba to accommodate large container ships.

She paid and walked to the bathroom located in the rear of the café. Out of habit, she chose the last of four stalls. A minute later, the lights went out. She froze and waited while her eyes adjusted to the moonlight illuminating the room through small windows. She quietly pulled up her pants as someone opened a stall door, then closed it and moved to the next one.

Trapped, she knew the puny lock on her stall door wouldn't protect her for long. Knowing she only had a few seconds, Palmer searched her purse for a special pen made of carbon steel with a very sharp point. She swore at all the unessential things cluttering her bag. When she graduated from the Academy, the Agency had given her the inconspicuous pen/weapon because, in many circumstances, it was too risky to carry a gun or knife. As the door opened to the stall next to her, two years of training flashed through her mind.

Out of good options, she carefully lifted the latch to her stall door and braced her feet against the toilet. As the door opened, she launched against it, using the door as a weapon. The door slammed against her attacker, knocking him off balance. Palmer dropped him with a powerful leg kick to the chest. She attempted to run past him, but he grabbed her right ankle. She twisted and stomped his wrist, breaking his grip. Their eyes met in the dim light for a fraction of a second, but then she caught a silver glint in his left hand. She watched the knife plunge into her left leg but oddly felt no pain. At the same time, Palmer saw his exposed neck. The sharp pen entered just under his left ear, and the man gasped. Before he could react, she jammed the pen into his neck two more times. The man slumped to the floor, blood spurting from his neck.

Palmer slid to the floor against the bathroom stall, fighting the urge to cry out, worried there might be others outside. Blood oozed from beneath the knife grip stuck into her thigh. She took a deep breath, pulled out the knife and tied her scarf above the wound as a tourniquet. Gritting her teeth as the pain surged up her leg, she reached for her cell and punched in a number. A man answered.

Palmer gasped, "Bird down."

She knew they'd locate her using the GPS on her phone. She dragged herself behind the entrance door to the bathroom, the best place to defend herself if another attacker came. She was grateful for all the time she'd spent in defense training. Even though she was of average height, she was strong and athletic. Resting her head against the wall, she hoped she wouldn't bleed out before rescue came.

Fucking Viktor, she cursed while gripping the bloody phone. *I'm not dying here, not now.*

Palmer passed out before the DEA team recovered her and transferred her to a safe house. She opened her eyes as the doctor was finishing the last stitches.

"You were lucky," Boris said. He was her team leader in Ukraine. "Missed a major artery by a miracle. You should have a full recovery."

"Where am I?"

"A safe house. We have a jet waiting to fly you to New York within an hour."

Palmer shook her head. "No, I want to stay and finish this. We're so close."

"Not going to happen. You're still on the Russian mafia's Most Wanted list. We found out a few minutes ago they killed your informant after he left the café."

Boris leaned close to Palmer's ear and whispered, "We have a mole. This operation is compromised, and we're shutting it down. I talked with Bob Davis at headquarters, and they've already reassigned you to Miami. The Italian mafia is making a big push into Florida."

She didn't like it, but this made sense. Before she'd been assigned to Odesa, she had operated undercover to track the Italian and Russian mafia as they expanded their heroin trade from Russia and Ukraine to New York. The majority of the heroin coming out of eastern Europe was controlled by two men, Rizzo, an Italian, and Bykov, the Russian leader of an equally large and dangerous criminal organization. The DEA had recruited an informant that supplied updates on a new club in Miami the mafia used as a front for their criminal operations. The club, Tiger Eye, had quickly become a favorite of celebrities as well as the small and big players involved with a variety of criminal activities.

Once her leg had healed, Palmer was inserted as a waitress at the Tiger Eye club. Everything about the club was over the top, from the Cuban décor to free champagne in the women's lounge. Tuxedos and long dresses were common. Over the next three months, she noticed more known members of the Italian mafia from New York City and new faces from Russia coming to the club. She observed several meetings between the Italians and Russians. Palmer didn't know what these meetings were about until one evening when a table of drunk Russians bragged too loudly about a new business deal and made vague references to a large shipment.

As Palmer served their table throughout the evening, she overheard them talking about the ports of Santo Domingo and Rio Haina in the Dominican Republic and about expanding the port of Aruba. Palmer quickly recognized the significance of this information and requested a trip to Santo Domingo to follow the lead.

* * *

Four days later, Palmer stepped out into the bright sunlight from a jet parked on the tarmac of the Las Americas airport in the Dominican Republic. The summer heat and humidity hit her like a blast furnace as she walked down the steep stairs and followed the other passengers to the terminal. After clearing customs, she took a taxi to a small hotel in the heart of Santo Domingo. She marveled at the paradox between the Dominican Republic, one of the most prosperous countries in the Caribbean, and Haiti, the other country that shared the island, which was by far the poorest. She had orders to gather any information about a new club, Wahoo, which was run by the same mafia group that owned the Tiger Eye in Miami.

Once settled in her hotel, Palmer called her boss, Bob Davis, to confirm her arrival. "I'm staying at the Blue Ocean Hotel," she told him. "Any update from our informant in Sicily?"

"We think Rizzo and Bykov are cutting some kind of deal with the Columbian cartel."

"This situation gets worse every day. Are you thinking what I'm thinking?"

"Yes." Bob paused. "If our intelligence is correct, we're looking at the creation of the largest criminal drug cartel in history."

"How sure are you about the Columbian involvement?"

"We need to confirm, but so far, the info looks legit. This would produce a disastrous expansion of drug traffic in the US and we already have a drug crisis. Can you find out how active the Columbians are in Santo Domingo and the rest of the island?"

"Yes. I'm going to the Wahoo Club tonight. I doubt the timing and strategic location of this new club was just a coincidence."

"Be careful," Bob cautioned. "Remember what happened in Odesa."

"Thanks, but I can take care of myself." Although she sounded confident to Bob, she worried about the risk that someone she knew from the Tiger Eye in Miami would recognize her at the Wahoo. The odds were low, but she knew the possibility was real.

An hour later, Palmer took a walk to find an outdoor café for a late lunch. Along the way, she wandered through an outdoor market filled with dozens of small vendors. The air was filled with the smells of various meats and seafood sizzling on metal grills. She watched couples holding hands as they browsed from table to table but then looked away, regretting that her choice of career made such everyday, intimate moments almost impossible. Since the DEA moved her location frequently, she never made real friends. Fortunately, she had a gift for languages, a useful talent during previous assignments in Russia, Ukraine, Italy and France.

When operating deep undercover, her sole lifeline was Bob, her boss. Unfortunately, Bob was an arrogant, insecure man who had almost no experience in the field. Even worse, he was intimidated by Palmer, having quickly realized she was much smarter than he was.

Having an exceptional memory and high intelligence was both a blessing and a curse, particularly for a woman. She was confused when some students ostracized her for being so smart. She never got over the pain of classmates calling her a freak, nerd, smarty-pants and worse. Eventually, she resorted to underperforming at school to avoid the resentment and bullying, especially from boys. Unfortunately, college wasn't much better. If she challenged her professors too much, grades declined.

When she was approached about working for the DEA, she

immediately agreed but became easily frustrated when her peers, mostly insecure men, couldn't see or understand what was so obvious to her. Her managers, however, quickly realized how smart she was. Instead of mentoring Palmer, they used her intelligence to promote their careers. Facing regular discrimination as a woman working in a male-dominated organization, she was furious about how they would take the credit for her ideas and excellent work while rarely recommending her for the promotions she had earned. When she had the opportunity to pivot from a staff job to working undercover, she jumped at the chance. She'd have more control of not only *what* she did but *how* she did things.

Halfway through the market, Palmer spotted an outdoor café. The small tables were less crowded and the food on them looked good.

A young man holding a menu rushed out to greet her. "Please, please, join us. We have the freshest seafood in the city."

After he pulled out her chair and let her settle for a moment, he started to hand her a menu but hesitated. "My name is Manuel, but my friends call me Manny." He stepped close enough that Palmer could smell his strong cologne. "Americano? I can switch the menu to English."

"*Yo hablo Espanol.*" She reached for the menu in his hand. "This will be fine."

Manny smiled. He was handsome, with long black hair combed behind his ears. He appeared to be about her age and wore a white shirt with black pants. Palmer liked the small gold ring in his left earlobe and matching gold cross that swung from his neck as he poured her a glass of water.

"What can I get you to drink?" he said with an infectious grin.

Palmer pointed at her water glass. "I'm fine."

He wagged his finger at her. "It's such a beautiful day, you must try one of our Mamajuanas."

Palmer laughed. "You must be kidding. You make a drink with marijuana?"

It was Manny's turn to laugh. "No, the drink is called *Mamajuana*. It's a local drink. Rum, red wine and honey to soak in a bottle with tree bark and herb. You must try it. If you don't like it, I'll replace it with something else, no charge."

Palmer couldn't tell if he was kidding or serious. "Sounds terrible, but I'll take your word for it."

He placed his hand on her bare arm. Palmer didn't move. The last time a man touched her was in Ukraine.

"I'll be back to take your order after I bring your drink." He turned to walk away and added, "I promise that you'll love it."

Palmer glanced around the café while Manny made her drink. Couples and friends filled half the tables, while the rest were occupied with families. She hated eating alone. It was the worst part about working undercover in foreign countries.

Manny returned with her drink.

Palmer took off her sunglasses and picked up the glass filled with the ruby-colored cocktail. "Salute," she said and took a sip.

Manny waited for her response. "Well? What do you think?"

"*Muy bueno.* Love it," Palmer said.

She ordered lobster, and by the time it came to the table, most of the customers had already departed.

Manny grinned and said, "May I ask—are you here on business or vacation?"

"Do you have a minute, Manny? This is my first time in Santo Domingo, and I have a couple of questions."

Manny pulled out a chair and sat down. "How can I help you?"

"I'm here on vacation and want to experience the nightlife. The taxi driver suggested a new club called the Wahoo. What do you think?"

"Sí, the Wahoo is the new hot club." He studied Palmer. "It attracts a very fast crowd. Are you sure you want that?"

Palmer winked. "I'm a big girl."

Manny grinned. "I don't doubt you."

"Tell me about the club. What type of people go there? Who owns it?"

"A couple of Americans opened it six months ago. I heard they have a similar club in Miami. Santo Domingo has become an international city. We have a large population of wealthy people from Columbia and Venezuela who have bought property and vacation here."

Palmer played dumb. "Why here?"

Manny glanced around the empty café. He lowered his voice, "Our country has become a major gateway for goods to the United States." He smiled and waved his hands. "All kinds of goods." He leaned forward. "Do you understand?"

"Yes." Palmer played with her salad. "Back to the Wahoo. I came here to have some fun."

"Do you have a husband or a boyfriend with you?"

Palmer sighed. "No, I needed a break from work and had two weeks of vacation. I came by myself."

Manny shook his head. "I don't think a nice woman should go alone to this club."

Palmer frowned and squinted hard. "Why do men always underestimate women? It pisses me off."

Manny quickly raised his hands in the air. "I don't mean to offend you. It's not like clubs you have in the States. Trust me, this is a different world down here." He crossed his arms. "Don't get mad, please."

They sat in silence for a long minute, and then Manny leaned toward Palmer.

"Look, we don't know each other, but I could take you if you wanted to see the club. I know many of the regulars."

Palmer stared at Manny for a moment, calculating the offer and the risk. He seemed sweet and could be a potential contact here.

"Can we go tonight?"

Manny grinned. "*Sí*, the Wahoo doesn't get busy until around ten. I can pick you up at your hotel at ten o'clock, and we can have a nice dinner. The music and dancing don't begin until eleven or twelve." He stopped. "Is that too late for you?"

Palmer took a large gulp of her drink. "As I said, I'm a big girl."

Manny tapped the table with his right hand. "Great. I'll see you later tonight. He was several steps away when he slapped his forehead a walked quickly back to the table. "I don't know your name or which hotel you're at."

Palmer chuckled. "My name is Palmer Olson. I'm at the Blue Ocean Hotel."

Manny bowed. "Thank you, madame. I'll see you tonight."

Palmer returned to her hotel excited to report her new connection with Bob. Manny could turn out to be an ideal source of information. *What a coincidence*, she thought. *And I've only been here a few hours.*

It had only been six months since she'd killed a man in Odesa. She never learned why the mafia had put a hit on her. She had a perfect undercover alibi acting as an executive of an oil drilling company looking for new business in the untapped Ukrainian oil and gas fields. Her assignment was to learn more about the heroin drug trade that originated in the Afghanistan region and used Kyiv as a distribution point to Western Europe. Unfortunately, it only takes one informant to go rogue and create havoc in these operations.

After a short nap, she called Bob Davis. "I'm back at my hotel and made an interesting contact today at lunch, she said, explaining what she had learned about the Wahoo.

"I'm impressed," Bob said. "You've only been there since this morning. I'm glad you'll have an escort to the club. but are you comfortable with this guy Manny?"

"Yes, my radar has gotten better spotting bad guys. I believe he's harmless."

"Harmless is good, but is he handsome?"

Palmer laughed. "Fuck you."

Bob added, "As your safety director, I had to ask."

"Hey, don't blow it. For a second, it almost sounded like you cared."

"I care enough to give you some late-breaking news that's consistent with what Manny described and the influx of Columbians and Venezuelans buying large residential and commercial properties there. We thought they were doing it to get money out of their countries in the event of a political crisis. But our people have seen a dramatic increase in the money they're investing throughout the Dominican

Republic in the last few months. We've also seen major upgrades to the main port in Santo Domingo. This country has always been a big gateway for cocaine and marijuana to the US, but this is different. Up to this point, the Columbians controlled the majority of the drug trade, but the CIA has picked up chatter about an expansion in the Caribbean. Get this, Aruba is expanding their main port to accommodate container ships and—"

Palmer interrupted him, "Of course—this all makes sense. Rizzo and Bykov are getting in bed with the Columbians. They'll ship heroin to Aruba and then transfer their load onto ships operated by the Columbians. The Columbians will transport the drugs to the Dominican Republican to be divided into smaller boats and planes that will transport the drugs to the Florida Keys and other remote areas."

The pace of Palmer's words accelerated as she talked and paced around her hotel room. "Rizzo and Bykov will benefit from expanding their heroin market to the United States in greater volumes using the Columbian's existing pipeline." Palmer paused. "Wow, this is brilliant! I'm sure that Rizzo and Bykov's ships won't return to Europe empty—they'll be filled with cocaine and marijuana supplied by the Columbians." She switched the phone to her other ear. "Good God, Rizzo and Bykov will flood Western and Eastern Europe, along with the Ukraine and Russian markets, with a huge, cheap supply of cocaine." She stopped pacing. "Do the boys at Interpol know what we suspect?"

"Yes, they've been monitoring Rizzo's activity for months and suspect the same thing. Bykov is a newcomer, and we don't have as much intel on him yet."

Palmer resumed her pacing. "We have to find a way to stop this."

"Agreed, but the Columbians are already in control of everyone who has authority over customs and shipping at the main port in Santa Domingo. The Columbian cartel has used a combination of bribery and threats to make sure their shipments are not confiscated. Unfortunately, they've now accomplished the same thing in Aruba. The Columbians are using Aruba as the launching point for the drugs that go to the Dominican Republic. It looks like Aruba is the primary port the ships will use to exchange their loads."

"Bob, we need someone to infiltrate Rizzo's organization and find out if this is true and what their specific plans are."

He laughed. "This is why I hired you. Palmer. We want you to get close to Rizzo."

"I'm in—but how do we do that?"

"We know that Rizzo's spending more time on his yacht, the Destiny. At some point, we assume they'll sail the yacht to Aruba so they can be there for the arrival of the first shipment. We're convinced Rizzo will be on board when they depart."

"But how do I infiltrate the ship?"

"Interpol informed us that two of the crew members from the Destiny started a fight in the Monte Carlo casino. They'll need to hire new staff, and we think you'd be perfect because you speak Italian, Russian and Spanish. We also know that Gunner, the captain of Rizzo's yacht, owns a small business in the Dominican Republic called the Dolphin Yacht Club, close to the main port in Santo Domingo. This guy also has a good brokerage boat business as well as a unique reputation for finding crew for yacht owners. Several major marine brokerage offices in the Mediterranean, including the marina that Gunner owns, posted ads online to fill the two vacant crew positions on Rizzo's yacht."

"That's a crazy coincidence!"

"This may be a great break if we can get you hired on his yacht."

"What about my cover? They'll ask a lot of questions about my previous jobs and experience."

"Our staff is working on it right now. We should have a new life story and job experience for you by early tomorrow. We've already booked an appointment for your job interview. The man managing the marina is Cody, but the person you should talk to at the yacht club is a woman named Bonita. She's been there since Gunner purchased the club years ago."

"Tell me about Cody."

"He grew up with Gunner. They served in Vietnam together and worked at a large marina in Miami after that. We're in the process of preparing a dossier on Gunner and Cody."

"What does this Cody look like?"

Palmer could hear Bob leaf through papers. "I'm looking at his picture. He's a skinny, short man with straight black hair. Has beady eyes and looks like a spooky guy that just crawled out of a hole. We want you to continue identifying the major players in the Dominican Republic and if there's any new chatter about this new deal."

Palmer pulled out a pad and started to make notes. "Bob, are you sure you can pull together a credible cover this quick? These are really bad guys."

"Got a team working it."

"I know a fair amount about Rizzo from previous briefs. I recall that he employs a woman named Nika, who runs a large part of his operations. From what I remember, they described her as very tough and extremely thorough." Palmer paused. "My cover has to be air-tight, or I'm a dead woman."

"We understand. Trust me," Bob said.

She didn't trust Bob but didn't have a choice. "I'll be ready when you are."

Palmer terminated the call and reached for a carbon steel case containing her computer. She input a code to unlock the case and pulled out her computer and several briefs. She was tired but exhilarated at the same time. The thought of penetrating Rizzo's organization by working on his yacht was exciting. He was a big fish, and this could really help her career at the DEA.

She glanced at her watch—four o'clock. She could work for two hours and still have time for a nap before getting ready for Manny.

* * *

Manny was right on time. Palmer greeted him in the hotel lobby.

"*Buenas Noches*. You look beautiful."

Palmer rolled her eyes. "You didn't need to say that. We're not on a date."

Manny feigned disappointment. "I'm crushed."

The Wahoo Club was only a short walk from the hotel. As

they approached the main entrance, Manny waved at two large men stationed at the door in black tuxedos and earpieces. Palmer glanced at the long line of people inside a roped-off sidewalk.

"It's early." Manny nodded toward the crowd. "Looks like you picked a good night."

He took her arm and walked past the line. The two security men greeted Manny with bear hugs.

"Carlos, Jose, I want you to meet Palmer. She's on vacation from the States."

"Welcome to the Wahoo Club," Carlos said. "We have a nice table waiting for you." Carlos nodded to Jose, who opened the door and spoke into the mic attached to his earpiece. Carlos leaned toward Palmer. "Enjoy your evening. You have an interesting escort, but he's harmless."

Manny laughed. "Thanks for the vote of confidence." He grabbed Palmer's arm and steered her through the door. "Carlos is a gentle soul, but Lord helps the guy that steps out of line in this club."

As they stepped inside, Palmer asked, "How do they know you?" Manny grinned. "Cousins."

The maître d' rushed up to Manny. "*Buenas Noches*. Your table is waiting. This way, please." He led them to a prime table just off the dance floor facing the band, which was scheduled to start later.

As they settled into their seats, the maître d' snapped his fingers, and a waiter picked up a bottle of champagne from a silver bucket on a stand next to their table. As the waiter unwrapped the foil, the maître d' handed them menus. "The grouper is excellent tonight. The chef is baking each fish in a mixture of herbs." As the waiter poured the champagne, Manny pointed to Palmer, "Antonio, this is Palmer, here on vacation. Her first time in the Dominican Republic."

Antonio bowed. "Welcome. I hope you enjoy your time with us tonight." He smiled and placed his hand on Manny's shoulder. "Just make sure he pays."

Palmer laughed. "Any other suggestions?"

Antonio crossed his arms and placed a finger on his lips. "Let's see—"

Manny interrupted him. "Antonio, love you, but you talk too much." He lifted his glass of champagne. "I've become quite parched listening to you try to impress this young lady."

Antonio laughed. "Pablo will be your waiter for tonight. Let me know if I can be of any further assistance."

"Thanks, Antonio. Did you say the champagne was on the house?"

Antonio shook his head and walked away.

Manny raised his glass for a toast. "Salute, here's to your health and to my good fortune that we met today."

Palmer clinked her glass and took a sip. "Thank you for your kind offer to bring me here." Their eyes met for a brief second. "Antonio appears to know you."

"Antonio's my brother-in-law. I tried to talk my sister out of marrying him, but as you can see, I lost the argument." He chuckled. "One thing you'll learn about the Dominican Republic is that we have large families."

Palmer surveyed the room decorated in tropical themes like the famous clubs in Havana's heyday and the more modern clubs in Miami. Dozens of tables were filling rapidly with a variety of people dressed for an evening in an exclusive club.

Throughout dinner, Manny talked about his family and childhood. He was charming and seemed to know everyone. A steady stream of men and women stopped by their table to say hello, and, of course, they all wanted to know the name of his date. Such visibility was dangerous. Palmer prayed that no one from the Tiger Eye was in this club tonight.

"You're very popular."

Manny grinned. "My café business depends on regular clientele. So, I must make many friends."

As they finished dinner, Palmer decided it was time for work.

"This club is great. Tell me the story behind it."

"It opened several months ago by some guys from Miami."

At that moment, they were interrupted by a group of loud young men and women as they crossed the dance floor to a private room on the other side of the floor. Palmer recognized that two of the men were speaking Russian. They were followed by a group of young Latino men and their women. The young women wore skirts so short and tight they could barely walk. Antonio appeared flustered and rushed ahead of the group to open large double doors revealing a private room.

Manny pointed to the obnoxious group. "There's part of your answer."

"I don't understand," Palmer said, pretending that she was confused.

Manny leaned forward. "You're not a reporter or something like that, are you?"

Palmer laughed. "Of course not. Do I look like a reporter?"

Manny smiled. "No, you don't." He sipped on his drink. "What exactly do you do for work?"

"I'm a boring consultant. I sit at a computer all day and conduct research for clients."

Manny lowered his voice. "Without going into all the details, my beautiful homeland is quickly becoming invaded by Columbians and bad Russians. We hate them because they have turned our seaports into a major gateway for drugs passing from Columbia to the United States."

"What's their connection to Miami?"

Before he could answer, the band started to play, and the group emerged from their private room to dance. Manny pointed to the two Russians.

"They're far worse than the Columbians. They showed up several weeks ago. Antonio thinks they are disgusting and dangerous."

"Do you know why they're here?"

Manny's eyes darted to the dance floor. "Those two guys are nothing but dumb thugs, but their boss ordered them to get control of our two main ports—and to use any means to get the job done."

"How can they do that?"

Manny frowned. "Bribery and threats. To prove they're serious, they've already killed the man in charge of customs and the head of our local police." Manny paused. Without pointing, he nodded toward the dance floor. "The tall Russian with a tattoo on his neck is Kazlov, and the one wearing the pink shirt with the five pounds of gold hanging from his neck is his sidekick, Fedorov. The other two men doing the Salsa with the girls, who should be home with their mothers, are Columbians." Manny shook his head. "Your lucky night. This is like your Super Bowl of bad guys in one place." Manny nodded to a dozen men stationed around the room in tuxedos. "Don't make it obvious, but look around at their bodyguards."

Palmer slowly turned her head and studied the men.

"Friendly looking bunch, aren't they?" Manny said.

"Is there anything that can be done to stop them?"

Manny shook his head. "How do you fight against guys like these?" He turned his head toward the dance floor. "Oh boy, this will make the night interesting. See that skinny guy wearing a Hawaiian shirt that just joined them on the dance floor? He's one of the local wannabes. His name is Cody. He's been thrown out of here more times than I can count. Antonio wanted to ban him, but the owners kept making excuses for him. He's a weasel and runs a small yacht club down the coast. I don't know any of the details, but I've heard he's supplying the Russians and Columbians with 'go-fast' boats whenever they need them, which is quite often."

"Go-fast boats?" Palmer feigned ignorance.

"They call them 'go-fast' because they can run up to ninety-five miles per hour on calm seas and have a very low profile that makes them invisible to most radar. Once they drop off the drugs in the Florida Keys or other remote places, they try to return for another load. But they lose a few boats every month because the Coast Guard intercepts them, engine trouble, or they just abandon them because the pressure of detection is too great. They have amazing communication technology, so they know exactly where the Coast Guard is operating and how to avoid them." Manny shook his head as he stared at Cody dancing like a fool. "That's why they need Cody. He's a slime-ball, but he has contacts in Miami that can produce as many boats as they need."

Palmer shivered. She couldn't believe the coincidence of Cody showing up tonight. Tomorrow, she would be in the yacht club's office to interview for a crew position.

Manny asked Palmer. "Do you want to dance?"

She yawned. "I'll take you up on the offer another night. I'm a little tired from my travels."

"No problem."

After dinner, which Palmer insisted on paying for, Manny dropped her off at the hotel with a suggestion. "The evening's still young. And you are on vacation." He pointed to a bar next to the hotel. "I happen to know the owner."

"What a surprise. Who don't you know in this town?"

Manny shuffled his feet in a shy way. "They make excellent drinks."

Palmer hesitated for a moment. "I appreciate the offer. Maybe another time."

She was honest with Manny—she was tired and went to her hotel room. The next thing she knew, her cell phone vibrated off the nightstand onto the hard floor. She rolled out of bed and reached for the phone.

"Hello."

"Good morning, Palmer," Bob said. "We have your new cover ready. I'll send it to your computer in the next ten minutes."

"Good timing. My interview is scheduled for this afternoon."

"Worried?"

"No, why?"

"Did you get to the club last night?"

"Yes. I'll file a report when I return from the interview. I was shocked, but my new friend Manny knew everyone in town. He confirmed everything we suspected."

"Good luck today."

"Thanks. I'll keep you posted."

The cover story arrived ahead of schedule. Palmer ran through it repeatedly. Having an exceptional memory was a great advantage. Finally, she closed her computer and locked it in her carbon steel case.

The Dolphin Yacht Club was about ten miles from the hotel. As her taxi passed the main port, Palmer wondered how many of the ships had drugs hidden in the cargo. As Palmer stepped out of the taxi at the marina, her radar went off when she noticed a black sedan with tinted windows drive slowly past the parking lot. She turned her face away to avoid any photos taken by the occupants and walked quickly toward the entrance. She knew the risk she had taken going to the Wahoo Club. She'd need to be careful in case her cover had been blown already.

The Dolphin Yacht Club building looked more like a beach house than a traditional marina headquarters. The central office was an open room with high ceilings and large windows that overlooked the small marina. The walls were covered with various sea-related decorations—a large blue marlin, fluorescent blue-green Mahi Mahi, a sea turtle, lobsters and dozens of framed underwater photographs of fish. Near the entrance, a pretty young woman sat at a desk piled with stacks of papers.

Palmer waited patiently in front of the desk and smiled as the young receptionist finished a phone call. At last, the woman said, "Hi, my name's Bonita. How can I help you today?" She wore a pink tube top and white shorts with a fresh white gardenia tucked into her black hair.

There was something about the woman that made Palmer instantly like her. Maybe it was the way she smiled with her eyes. She was a natural beauty with no make-up. A gold cross on a necklace glistened against her smooth dark olive skin. Palmer guessed that she and Bonita were about the same age and noticed Bonita's ring finger had no ring.

"I'm here to interview for the position you posted for a crew member on the Destiny."

Bonita smacked her forehead. "You must be Palmer, I'm so sorry. I got your email confirmation but forgot about your appointment. I was delighted that you were here on vacation. Perfect timing. I much prefer to meet candidates in person, but that doesn't happen very often."

Bonita pointed to a couch on the far side of the office facing the ocean. "Let's talk over there so I can avoid the phone while we chat. Can I get you some water or coffee?"

Palmer nodded. "I've had too much caffeine already, but I'd love some water." While Bonita grabbed two bottles of water out of a nearby refrigerator, Palmer reflected on how quickly the staff at the DEA and CIA had spotted the help wanted ad and arranged an interview.

As they settled into the couch, Bonita asked, "How much do you know about the job?"

"Not much more than what was described in the job posting—typical crew position, vague list of duties, minimum two years of experience and a current passport."

"The job description is vague for a reason," Bonita explained. "You have to agree that no job is below you. You'll be performing numerous tasks that will change daily depending on the needs of the captain."

"No problem with that. I've crewed on several yachts." Palmer pulled out an Agency-created resumé she had printed at the hotel and handed it to Bonita.

Bonita scanned the document. After a few minutes, she set the resumé in her lap and cocked her head.

"Wow, that's quite a resume. We don't usually see people this qualified. Most of the candidates I interview for crew positions are a mix of people off the grid either looking for something or hiding out." She paused. "Which is it with you?"

Palmer shifted her position on the couch while buying an extra moment to think of how to respond. "That's so interesting," she said, smiling. "Do you ask everyone this question or just me?"

"I've placed hundreds of people on yachts. This question saves me a lot of time. Depending on your answer, I can tell if I want to offer you the job or not."

Palmer stared at Bonita for a second. She had underestimated this cute, innocent-looking woman. She leaned toward Bonita. "I have to confess—I'm both hiding something and looking for something."

Bonita sat up a little straighter. Palmer could see she hadn't expected that answer.

"Please don't tell anyone this," Palmer said, pretending to look carefully at the room. "I'm *hiding* the fact that I'm a secret undercover agent on an assignment."

Bonita laughed. "I can't wait to hear what you're *looking* for."

Palmer's expression changed as she gazed out the window at the blue ocean dotted with several sailboats anchored off their marina. "What I want..." She stopped for a moment before continuing. "I mean...I'm *looking* for the perfect beach on the perfect island where I can fall in love with the perfect person who loves me only for who I am—nothing more—and nothing less." Then she added wistfully, "And, of course, to live happily ever after."

Bonita's eyes swelled as she glanced at the closed office in the far corner of the room. "Tell me more about yourself."

Palmer briefly discussed her background and experience, as stated in her resume, and then waited.

Bonita nodded. "That's all nice, but I meant—tell me about *you*."

Palmer took a deep breath. "I'm thirty-two years old, smarter than most, but get bored quickly. I have a wicked temper, and I don't like men who try to push me around—which is probably why I'm not married. I love to read and write. But my true love is for the sea. Sailing on the open ocean in the deep water is where I feel at home and find true freedom. Away from anyone's expectations. Away from the regular discrimination we experience as women. The sea is my first and only true love—at least so far."

Bonita looked at Palmer with her mouth open. "That's quite an answer."

They sat in silence for a moment.

Palmer placed her hand on Bonita's arm. "Now it's your turn."

Bonita shook her head. "I'm a simple girl from a poor family that immigrated from Cuba."

"How did you get here?"

Bonita sighed. "I have a large extended family in Miami. I miss them since we moved.

"We?"

"It's a long story." She glanced at Cody's office. "What about your family?"

"You're lucky." Palmer looked down at her bottle of water. "To have a family must be wonderful. I never had the joy of a real family.

My parents died in a car accident when I was very young. Spent the rest of my childhood moving from one foster home to another."

"My God, I'm so sorry. That must've been terrible."

Palmer nodded. "You mentioned earlier that you could tell if I was right for the job after I answered the question. So what do you think?"

Bonita laughed. "Unless it's true that you're a bad-ass secret agent, you have the job."

Palmer clapped her hands together. "Thank you!"

"I need you to fill out some paperwork. And then we can continue our conversation." She stopped. "One question—the Destiny is anchored in Monaco, France. We don't cover airfare. Can you find a way to get there?"

"Sure—one of my girlfriends works for Air France. She can probably provide me with a ticket to Nice. Monaco is an easy drive from the airport."

"Nice friend." Bonita jumped up from the couch. "Wait just a minute. I need to call the captain to make sure they haven't hired anyone yet."

While Bonita was on the phone, a man walked in wearing a Panama hat and a flowered shirt. He glanced at Bonita, ducked into the office and closed the door. Palmer recognized him from the club—Cody. Last night, he'd been drunk and the loudest person on the dance floor. It had been pathetic to watch how the harder he tried to get peoples' attention, the more they ignored him. In the dim light of the club, he had the pale look of someone that just crawled out from under a rock, but he looked even worse in the daylight.

As Bonita continued talking on the phone, Palmer wondered if Cody was the "we" that Bonita was referring to earlier. She hoped not.

Bonita set the phone down and walked back to Palmer.

"We have a little challenge." She chewed on one unpolished fingernail. "Normally, I can hire and fire for my clients, but for some reason, they want to interview you in person. I've never had this happen before. I told them that I've already hired you, but they insist." Bonita shrugged. "I'm sorry, but I can't do anything about this. I can only tell you that the captain is the owner of this marina. He's an amazing man and has never rejected anyone that I recommend. I'm 99 percent sure this is just a formality." She twisted a strand of hair in her fingers. "It's very strange that they're acting so weird about hiring a new crew member. Something must've happened in Monaco." She shook her head. "They'd like to interview you as soon as possible. What's your flexibility? Can you be there in two days?"

"You mean, fly to France before knowing if I have the job?"

"I'm 99 percent sure."

Palmer nodded. "Well—I have to make a couple of calls. If I can fly out first thing tomorrow, I could be ready the following day for an interview."

"Great. I'll let them know."

Palmer watched Bonita make the call. After a minute, she smiled and gave Palmer the "thumbs up" signal from her desk. Palmer walked over to her desk. "Good news?"

"I was able to get Gunner on the phone, he's the captain, and he assured me that everything would be fine. Gunner does all the interviewing for new hires. He's very particular about his staff. For some odd reason, there's a woman in Rizzo's organization that suddenly injected herself into the hiring process to fill this position. I'm surprised because she never gets involved in this stuff and rarely spends time on the yacht. Gunner sounded irritated but told me not to worry."

"Thanks for the heads up." Palmer nodded and looked at her watch. "I better get back to the hotel and start making my flight arrangements."

Bonita stood and shook her hand. "Welcome to the Destiny team."

As Palmer reached the door, Bonita called out, "Wait a second! Where are you staying?"

"The Blue Ocean Hotel."

"What are you doing tonight? Since you're all alone, would you like to have dinner? I know we just met, but I enjoyed our conversation."

Palmer smiled. "That would be nice."

"Great, I'll stop by your hotel around nine o'clock, and we'll walk to my favorite café. By the way, I already called a taxi for you. He should be in the parking lot waiting for you."

"Bonita, where the hell is my coffee?" Cody yelled loudly from his office.

"Duty calls," Bonita said as she rolled her eyes. "See you tonight."

* * *

Palmer waved at Bonita when she walked through the door of the hotel. She wore a sleeveless, light yellow summer dress. The right side of her shoulder-length dark hair was held up by a pretty turtle shell barrette. The cute, sporty girl in the office had been replaced by a lovely, slender woman with natural beauty.

Palmer rose from the lobby couch. "Wow, you look beautiful."

Bonita blushed. "I don't wear this dress very often. It sits in my closet most of the time."

Palmer hooked her arm under Bonita's and started toward to door. "Well, let's go have some fun."

"Do you like seafood? My favorite café is within walking distance, and it has the best fresh seafood in town. The owner is a good friend."

"Great."

Along the walk, Bonita shared more about the Dolphin Yacht Club and how it had built a nice business with its small marina and boat brokerage services.

"What about the captain? What can you tell me about him?"

"Gunner's very smart. It was his idea to add employment services a few years ago. Yacht owners have a terrible time retaining staff for their boats. Gunner saw the opportunity to fill a strong demand for finding and vetting new crew members. We started out placing crews in the Caribbean, but it quickly mushroomed into a global service once the word got around that Gunner was behind the operation. He has such a huge reputation in the yachting world." She looked sideways at Palmer. "I know that you'll get along great with him."

After dinner, they decided to find another bar for an after-dinner drink. The bar had a small outdoor patio overlooking the bay. Palmer sighed as they sipped straight rum over ice. "This is perfect. What an amazing view."

"Have you been to the Wahoo Club? I heard that it's the hottest club east of Miami."

Bonita frowned. She ran her index finger slowly around the edge of her glass, dipped it in the rum, and then sucked the sweet rum off her index finger. "I hate that place."

"Why? I thought that all the beautiful people hang out there."

"Beautiful is not how I'd describe the crowd. First, it was the Columbians and now the Russians. These are bad people. They're ruining our island."

A yacht passed by decorated with hundreds of lights. The music from the party drifted ashore, and Bonita started to hum along with the song.

Palmer broke the silence. "Tell me more about Gunner? I'd like to know what to expect before I meet him."

"After the Vietnam War, Gunner obtained a job working at a marina in Miami owned by a friend. We met while I was working in the office there. We had our little group—Cody, Gunner and another friend, Jett." She sighed. "Gunner worked his way up the ranks as a captain on larger and larger yachts, always traveling. That was hard on Cody because he relied on Gunner so much. We saw things start to deteriorate with Cody, but he resisted any help and denied he was in trouble. The tipping point came when Cody met some high-flying Columbians. He started smoking pot, snorting cocaine and spending money that he didn't have while trying to keep up with the rich and famous Miami crowd and flashy drug dealers. I begged Cody to stay away from the clubs... but he wouldn't listen."

"I didn't mean to upset you. We can talk about something else."

Bonita shook her head. "I'm fine. Sorry, I don't know what's wrong with me. I haven't shared this with anyone else but Gunner. I'll finish the story, and then we can change the subject."

"Up to you," Palmer said.

Bonita continued, "Gunner had the opportunity to buy the Dolphin Yacht Club and gave Cody an ultimatum. He would have to agree to treatment again and move to the Dominican Republic to help run his yacht club or Gunner would banish him from our lives. So—here we are."

"How's Cody now?"

Bonita turned her face away.

"Does Gunner know?"

"We've talked on the phone. I didn't tell him everything. I keep hoping that Cody will stop hanging out with the Russians and Columbians. He's doing business with them on the side. He won't discuss any of this with me, but I've seen the emails and some receipts. I also know that he's opened a secret bank account in the Cayman Islands. Gunner's going to be furious when he finds out. He only bought this marina to save Cody."

Palmer listened carefully and then asked, "What kind of business is Cody conducting with the Russians?"

Bonita stopped when she realized she was pouring out her heart to a perfect stranger. "Maybe we should go," she said. "It's getting late." Bonita pushed her chair back and reached for her purse. "I'll walk you back to your hotel."

* * *

Palmer was still hungover from last night when she boarded the plane to France. She tried to sleep on the flight, but all she could think about was her night with Bonita. But then her heart ached thinking about her college roommate.

Maeve was her best friend and the first woman she'd ever loved. Palmer replayed in her mind the many times they'd stayed up all night making love and listening to their favorite albums until dawn. She had loved walking endlessly through the streets of Georgetown in the evening while holding hands and sharing their dreams. Maeve was a recovering addict, but they had made grand plans to travel the world after college, and Maeve seemed motivated to stay clean.

Then the tragedy occurred. Palmer had found Maeve unconscious on the floor of their bathroom. She died in Palmer's arms from an overdose of heroin before the paramedics arrived, a classic example of a rich white girl from the Hamptons who had become swept up in drugs in high school. Maeve insisted that she only tried heroin once before she became hooked. She had been clean for three years. Then something had happened, but it didn't matter as Maeve lay cradled in Palmer's arms.

Palmer had rocked Maeve back and forth until the paramedics took her away—and she swore to make the drug dealers pay.

Palmer's thoughts returned to Bonita. There was something special about that woman, yet she was just another person who could never be a friend. As the jet took her away from the Dominican Republic at 430 miles per hour, she fought back the urge to cry.

Chapter Four

Gunner hadn't been back on the yacht for more than an hour before Rizzo called.

"How was your trip to Virgin Gorda?"

"Too short, as always."

"Glad you are back because I need you to fly to Aruba and confirm that everything is in place for the arrival of our shipment. You know the port authority harbor master. Check with him to make sure we don't have any issues with customs."

"No problem."

"Nika told me that Bykov won't join us until we arrive in St. Thomas. I've invited Castillo and his partners for a meeting and dinner on the yacht before we sail to Aruba. There are several outstanding issues to resolve before the first shipment. Plan for an overnight stay. Nika can tell you the exact number in their entourage."

"I'll have the ship ready for departure to Aruba the following day."

It was an uneventful flight in Rizzo's jet to Aruba. The sun was setting on the harbor adjacent to Oranjestad, the largest city in Aruba. Lights from various bars and restaurants along the harbor boardwalk randomly appeared with the emerging stars. Gunner loved this time of night when the strong afternoon trade winds faded, and everything settled for the evening. He sipped a gin and tonic at an outdoor café, wondering if he'd made a mistake taking this job with Rizzo.

For some reason, this decision seemed to have a greater weight.

He thought about the first life-changing decision he'd made shortly after graduation from high school. He knew then that he had to leave his home in Maine; that decision wasn't as difficult as helping Rizzo. At that point in his life, there wasn't a choice. For eighteen years, he had lived his life trying to be someone he was not—struggling to meet everyone else's expectations. He was a guest in his own home. His parents understood he was different from the first minute they held him in the orphanage. As hard as they tried, they knew they were never going to replace his real parents.

It wasn't a surprise when on his thirteenth birthday, they told him he was adopted. His parents were caretakers for those early years, and they knew it. And he knew that he had to leave home and find what was at the end of his rainbow. He knew his destiny was somewhere else—not in Maine.

A seagull landed on the railing of the patio looking for a scrap of food. Gunner smiled and raised his empty hands. With an angry screech, the gull took off for the harbor to find food on one of the boats. *We're not that different,* he thought, *always searching for something we can't find.* The weight of the decision to accept Rizzo's offer was so great because it involved other people, the people he loved and depended on him. He could still back out, but he would need to decide soon.

Gunner's cell phone buzzed, and he saw Rayaan's number on the screen.

"Glad you made it. Can you have dinner tonight?" Rayaan said.

"Sure, I was thinking about the Blue Marlin. I love their grilled grouper."

"No, we need privacy. Can you come to our house for dinner?"

"Perfect, I'd love to see your bride and the kids. What time?"

"Seven. Take a taxi. I don't want people to see us together."

"No problem," Gunner said. "Are you in trouble?"

"We'll talk tonight."

Gunner stopped at a small market along the way and picked up flowers for Rayaan's wife, Alesha, and two chocolate bars for the kids. Rayaan's house faced the beach about twenty minutes from the harbor.

A typical single-level, yellow stucco house with bright blue shutters and trim. Alesha was standing barefoot in the open doorway when Gunner got out of the taxi. Her two little girls hung onto the opposite edges of her ankle-length white skirt. She smiled shyly as she tucked her dark black hair behind her ear.

Gunner waved and walked toward the door. Rayaan brushed past the girls and hugged Gunner. "Thanks for coming."

Gunner knelt in front of the girls and gave each of them a bar of chocolate, then looked up at Alesha. "They're so beautiful. I can't believe how much they've grown since the last time I was here."

"It's been almost a year," she said. "The girls ask about you all the time." She put her arms around his neck and gave a kiss on each cheek. "Come, I have cold drinks and appetizers waiting on the deck." She set plates of seafood ceviche, fried plantain chips and fruit on a table. "Dinner will be ready in an hour."

In the middle of the table was a bottle of dark rum, a bowl of sliced limes and a bucket of ice. Rayaan made two drinks and sat down. "It's great to see you again."

"How long have we known each other?" Gunner asked.

"A long time." Rayaan scratched his chin. "I wasn't married yet and chasing skirts with you from here to St. Lucia."

Gunner pointed to the house. "You're a lucky man. I envy you—you have everything. A great job, a beautiful wife and two amazing kids."

"I know," Rayaan nodded and frowned, "and I'd do anything to protect them."

"So would I." Gunner pulled his chair closer to the table. "Let's talk."

Rayaan reached over and picked up a map of Aruba lying on the seat of a chair. He pushed the rum and food to the side and laid the map of Aruba in the middle of the table. "Things have changed dramatically over the last year. The Perez family from Venezuela has purchased half the island." He moved his finger around a large portion of the map running south of the Oranjestad to the next port city of Barcadera. "We heard that Perez is planning to build a private airstrip and expand the container shipping berths at Barcadera. Six months ago, we had a staff meeting at our Aruba Port Authority office.

Rayaan took a long sip of his drink and held the cold glass to his forehead for a minute in a maneuver Gunner interpreted as stress removal. "The mayor walked in with his assistant and a tall man dressed in a light blue suit and sat at the head of our long conference table. The mayor told his assistant to close the door and drop the shades. Then the mayor spoke. 'There are some wonderful changes about to occur in our city,' he said. 'I want to introduce Mr. Perez. He's the head of one of the oldest families in Venezuela. They own most of the oil refineries and shipping facilities in Venezuela, and they have agreed to become a great partner with Aruba. We have signed a partnership in which they will fund the expansion of our shipping capacity in our ports here in Oranjestad and later at Barcadera. I want you to be of complete assistance to Mr. Perez and his staff.'

"Next, Perez gave a speech. Something like, 'I want to thank you for this opportunity. We believe that Aruba, which is only eighteen miles from our coast, is a perfect location to increase the capacity to handle large container ships. Between our deep-water ports and your two ports, we can dominate the shipping in the western hemisphere. My staff will start arriving in Aruba next month, and they'll direct the port activities going forward.' Then Perez stopped and looked at each of us. Then he ended by saying, 'This may seem sudden, but I can assure you that your responsibilities will not change.'"

Gunner was silent. Rayaan took a long drink and then said, "That was six months ago and the beginning of the end for us at the APA. A dozen of Perez's people showed up a few weeks later and took over our office." Rayaan frowned. "He's a bad man. Mean as a dog with rabies."

"What is their plan?"

"The word on the street is that Perez has paid off the head of police and the military. In addition, the governor has gone radio silent, which means they have him in their pocket as well. As for me and my staff at the APA, it's clear that we're supposed to look the other way and keep our mouths shut. Perez's cronies are now the only people allowed to review cargo shipments coming in or out of the port. We've been told to stay in our offices. I haven't done a physical tour of a container ship for six months. Perez's men give me the paperwork to review and then demand that I approve the shipment." He paused. "Shit, Gunner, I have no idea what's coming or going out of my port. The Columbians could be hiding guns, drugs, money laundering or sex slaves, for all I know.

"Did you mean Venezuelans? You said 'Columbians.'"

"I forgot to mention that in the last four months, a new batch of young thugs came in from Columbia. They're working for a man named Castillo. The original bad boys from Venezuela disappeared and were replaced by Columbians."

Rayaan pointed at the map again. "I heard that most of the cocaine coming out of Columbia is transported to the Mariquetia airfield in Venezuela and then flown to Honduras. From there, it's transported through Mexico into the United States. My guess is they're trying to use the Caribbean routes to expand the distribution of drugs to the east coast of the United States." Gunner rubbed his chin. "It's interesting. Over the last couple of years, Venezuelans have been buying all kinds of real estate in the Dominican Republic. Everything from large estates to commercial businesses. They claim they want to shelter money from their government."

Rayaan reached for a map of the full Caribbean. He pointed to Gunner's port in the Dominican Republic. "Look at this. Once the drugs get into your port, the bad guys can off-load the drugs to go-fast boats or fly small planes all along the east coast. "Have you seen any go-fast boats operating in your port?"

Gunner shifted in his chair. "No, but I'm not around that much."

"I wonder where the bad guys are getting these boats?"

Alesha appeared through the sliding door. "What's wrong? You two look way too serious. Dinner's ready."

Rayaan rolled up the maps and set them on the chair. He slapped Gunner on the back. "Let's go. We don't want to upset our pretty chef. We can finish our conversation after the girls go to bed."

After dinner, the girls insisted that Gunner read them two bedtime stories. They jumped into bed and snuggled on each side of him as he read their favorite books. Alesha watched from the doorway until he was finished reading and put the girls to bed.

Rayaan was waiting for Gunner on the deck. He handed Gunner a cigar and a fresh gin and tonic.

"That is a slice of heaven," Gunner said. "I'd kill to have the chance to put your girls to bed every night."

Rayaan laughed. "You should be around when they fight like crazy and refuse to go to sleep."

Gunner sighed. "I love those girls."

"And they love you."

Alesha joined them on the deck. "Gunner, you're a natural. Why don't you settle down, get married to some sweetie and have kids?"

Gunner grinned. "Oh boy, here we go again. I was wondering when you were going to bring that up."

"It's my duty." Alesha pointed a finger. "Since you are the godfather to our children, I'm taking responsibility for your happiness."

"I don't need any help—but thank you." Gunner glanced at Rayaan for a bailout.

"Don't look at me."

Alesha sat back in her chair and stared at Gunner until he squirmed.

"What?" Gunner said.

"You're a selfish man."

Gunner looked stunned.

Then she added, "And a coward."

Rayaan laughed. "This ought to be good!"

Alesha pointed at Rayaan's chest. "You stay out of this, or you'll be next." She turned back to Gunner, waiting for his response.

"I give up. Why do you think I'm selfish and cowardly?"

"Because your afraid—and a chicken-shit." She flapped her arms and started to crow like a rooster.

Gunner and Rayaan burst out laughing. He looked at Rayaan. "God, do I love your woman."

Alesha leaned toward Gunner. "You're the sweetest man I've

ever met, yet you won't share your heart."

Gunner looked at the floor.

Rayaan put his hand on Alesha's arm. "Let's not…"

"I'm serious," Alesha said. "Find your soulmate. I want you to experience how children are one of the greatest blessings in life."

"You don't understand." Gunner took another sip of his drink. "No woman who desires to have a family would want me."

"Why not?"

"I can't have children. I lost that dream when a mortar landed near me in Vietnam."

Alesha's mouth dropped. "I'm so sorry. I had no idea."

"Don't worry. I'm fine."

Alesha hugged Gunner. "Do you understand that our children are your children?"

Gunner nodded. "I do."

After Alesha left, Rayaan pulled his chair closer to Gunner and began talking as if dinner had not interrupted their previous discussion. "I'm really worried. The island is becoming controlled by the cartels run by Perez and Castillo. They're ruining our lives—threatening our way of life." Rayaan shook his head. "At first, they stayed near the docks and left the rest of Aruba alone. But now, they're extorting money from all the businesses. They claim it's a tax to help expand the ports and bring more business to Aruba. It's hard enough to make a decent living in the Caribbean without having to pay a monthly bribe to the cartel." Rayaan stopped for a second and glanced toward the house. "I'm afraid for my family."

"Why?" Gunner asked.

"Some of us started to push back a little, so the Columbians decided to make an example of one of our dock supervisors. We found him floating in the harbor two months ago." Rayaan threw his hands in the air. "I don't know what to do. We're powerless. Everyone's on the take—the politicians, the head of police, the key military leaders. I heard the cartel is planning some huge deal. I don't know the details yet, but I'm assuming it has to do with a big boost in container shipments of drugs. Something big is going down soon." Rayaan looked at Gunner.

"Have you heard anything? You're sailing all over the Caribbean."

"Not much. Mostly small stuff so far. Local businesses getting the shake-down for money."

"What about the increased shipping capacity?"

Gunner looked out over the ocean. "No, I haven't heard anything about a big deal."

Rayaan hit his hand on the table, which made Gunner jump. "Somebody has to do something!"

Gunner looked at his watch. "It's getting late. I have to go."

"How long are you in port?"

"Just another day, then back to Monaco. Thank your bride for the great dinner. We'll talk again before I leave."

On the taxi ride back to the harbor, his stomach churned from Rayaan's news. Things were worse than he imagined. He didn't like lying to Rayaan, but this was not the time to tell him the truth.

* * *

Gunner flew back to Monaco the next day. After he checked in with Marco and the other officers for a status report, he walked out to the pool where Rizzo was lounging under the hot sun. "You're red as a lobster."

Rizzo smiled. "How was the trip?"

"Everything checked out in the harbor. The port improvements are complete."

"What about the status of the port authorities?"

"We won't have any trouble with them. One of my good friends is the harbor master."

Rizzo took his sunglasses off. "So, what's wrong?"

"I don't have a good feeling about Castillo. Are you sure they can deliver?"

"Bykov and Nika swear this deal is solid."

Gunner grunted.

Rizzo sat up. "What makes you suspicious?"

"The cartel has become very aggressive throughout the Caribbean. I believe Castillo has a lot more ambition than just your deal. Once the first shipment is successful, what's to prevent him from cutting you out and renegotiating with Bykov? How much do you trust Bykov?"

"There's that word again." He frowned. "I don't trust anyone."

"What do you want me to do?"

"Once we start to transfer the drugs from our ship to theirs, have your buddy at the port confirm that the product Castillo promised is fully loaded and accounted for on my ship. I want verification we are getting everything we agreed upon before I return to Sicily. Can you do that?"

"Yes, but what about the risks I just told you about?"

"Thank you for that, but I live with risk every day. This is not my first rodeo."

"But these guys are ruthless."

"Trust me, I know how to deal with people that try to cross me. By the way, your gold is ready. Where do you want it delivered?"

"The Cayman Islands International airport."

"We could make this a lot easier if I just wired the money into your Cayman bank account."

"Thanks, but I want to pick up the gold in person."

"Seems like a lot of trouble when it'll end up in the same place. How long will you be gone?"

"A week or so. I want to catch up with some friends."

"Call me when you get back because there are some things about the new deal that I want to discuss."

"Why don't you review them with Nika? She's been working on the agreement for the new cartel with the Columbians."

"I have my reasons."

"I'm willing to help, but I'm just a simple captain. I doubt I'll have anything of value to add."

"Have a good trip."

Later that week, Gunner called an old friend that owned a small marina on the Grand Cayman island.

"Hi, Max, how's that beautiful wife? Has she left your fat ass yet?"

"Glad you've mellowed over the years."

"How many kids now?"

"Five."

"That you know of!"

"Very funny. What can I do for you?"

"I need to use one of your sheds for some repairs to the Rainbow. I arranged for a friend to sail her to the Caymans. He should be docking the Rainbow in your marina tomorrow."

"No problem. I'll put her on a lift and secure her in building two. When do you arrive?"

"Tomorrow. I'll need some tools and privacy."

"No problem. The building is all yours. How long will you need it?"

"A week, maybe less."

"Need help?'

"No, most of the work is just low maintenance repairs."

"Plan on dinner with us tomorrow night. Margie will make something special for you."

"Deal. See you soon."

The following day, Gunner landed at the Cayman airport using Rizzo's private jet. After loading the locked metal containers from the plane into a rental truck, he drove to the marina to meet Max.

"How are you?" Max asked while shaking Gunner's hand.

"Fine, good to see you. I appreciate setting me up in one of your buildings."

"Why here? Why not do the work at your marina?"

"I need some peace. Bonita and Cody would never leave me alone. I haven't had a vacation in a year and need some downtime. Working on the Rainbow is better than seeing a shrink."

"I'm glad you're here. Let's get you settled."

Gunner drove his small truck to the building, and Max opened the double doors so he could pull in.

"Let me know if you need anything. I'll have a cold one in the fridge when you finish for the day."

"Thanks, Max! You're the best."

Gunner closed the double doors and locked them. He went to

the back of the truck and pulled a tarp off the grey metal trunks. The gold was stacked neatly in each container. He had requested gold in payment instead of money because he could control how to safely secure it without anyone knowing where or what he had done with the bars. He didn't trust the Swiss or Cayman banks because Rizzo had a long reach. If things don't go as planned, Rizzo would do everything in his power to recover the gold.

Gunner wanted Rizzo to believe that he intended to deposit the gold into an account on the island. Instead, he had decided to replace the ballast in the keel of the Rainbow with the gold because he was sure that no one would think to look there. It was hot and stuffy inside the enclosed building, so he took off his shirt and climbed the short ladder onto the Rainbow. He smiled as he surveyed the deck. *She's such a beautiful boat.*

He spent the next four days working. Each day was a catharsis. He loved working with his hands. His mind could let go of everything and focus on the feel of the wood, the energy from power tools, the smell and taste of sawdust in his mouth. At the end of each day, he'd finish with a cold beer while sitting in the cockpit and reminiscing about various trips on the Rainbow.

He also pondered his life. Compared to many people, he felt fortunate. He had survived the war. He'd traveled the globe as a captain on exotic boats. He'd met amazing people. He has a small group of friends of the heart that depend on him and love him. So why did he feel unfulfilled? Why did other people seem so confident, but he struggled with a question he was never able to answer—*who am I?* He sighed, resigned to what he had to do and knowing he was the only one who could do it. He tried to push off any thoughts about the future and returned to daydreaming on the Rainbow.

Gunner finished refitting the boat more quickly than he had anticipated, so he called to have Rizzo's jet pick him up. He also arranged with Max to have one of his employees sail the Rainbow back to his marina in the Dominican Republic.

Chapter Five

Palmer set aside a thick dossier and stared out the window high above the marina in Monaco. The aqua blue water shimmered in the morning sunlight, and pelicans circled above dozens of yachts. In the distance, the Destiny dwarfed all the other boats.

There wasn't any point in reviewing the files again, so she put the documents into a metal case and locked it. Her secure cell phone vibrated. Only one person knew that number, so she picked up a pen and listened carefully to the last-minute instructions from Bob Davis.

Stunned by the intelligence update, she stopped writing halfway through the call, which changed everything. She recognized that her career and probably her life depended on what would happen over the next few months on the Destiny.

Palmer paced her small flat awaiting the time for her final job interview. She wasn't worried about the meeting because Bonita had assured her the interview was a formality, but then one never knows. This opportunity to infiltrate the crew was a coup for Interpol and the DEA. Palmer understood that a lot of eyes were on her.

She glanced at the clock. The shuttle boat was scheduled to pick her up on the pier in forty-five minutes. She kept checking her cell phone for any last-minute messages while pushing an ashtray around on the desk and tapping her fingers next to her espresso. Finally, she closed her eyes, hung her head, and rubbed her hands back and forth on her thighs while using the calming techniques she had learned at the Agency.

Two weeks ago, she had celebrated her thirty-second birthday alone with a bottle of bourbon. *Come on, stupid. This career is what you signed up for. Concentrate. Don't screw this up,* she thought. Even after several deep breaths, Palmer felt the bile rising, and she rushed into the bathroom and vomited. Hovering over the commode, she wiped her face with toilet paper and returned to the sink to rinse the bitter taste out of her mouth.

Staring at her reflection in the mirror, she barely recognized herself. Gone was her long, dark hair, replaced by a short bob-cut that she had bleached blond. Tiny bags under her eyes had not been there six months ago, nor the streaks of grey she had noticed the last time she colored her hair. While undercover, Davis had insisted she use a fake name, Palmer. He had also changed her appearance to someone that, in his words, "should embody an All-American girl," which pissed her off even more. She had always fought against discrimination as a woman and a person of Latino descent, so she was insulted by the insinuation that she wasn't "American" enough.

She glanced at her watch again. *Time to go.* As she emerged from her building, she shielded her eyes from the sunlight and put on sunglasses. Shopkeepers and café owners were busy opening their doors, sweeping the sidewalks and setting out tables and chairs. Palmer returned their smiles as she passed by. It was just another typical day for these folks. This was the life she'd chosen, but Palmer longed to have a day when she didn't have to check to see if she was being followed.

Although the DEA has been monitoring the Columbian cartel for years, the emergence of Castillo as the new head of the Columbian cartel changed everything. He was a ruthless, forty-year-old man who had grown up in the ghettos of Bogota. He had worked his way up the ranks until he'd become part of the inner circle of the Garcia family, who controlled 80 percent of the cocaine and marijuana trade for Columbia and Venezuela.

Castillo was ambitious and had grown impatient with his boss when Garcia rejected a more aggressive plan to expand to Europe. Castillo had recommended that they should buy new go-fast boats to avoid radar detection. He also had explored the acquisition of small underwater submarines to run shipments into the Keys. But Garcia was not interested in expanding the organization. He didn't want to attract more attention.

Last month, the DEA learned that Castillo had killed Garcia and taken control of the cartel. For Castillo, it wasn't about money; it was all about power.

As Palmer reached the marina boardwalk, she carefully surveyed the area for suspicious persons and escape routes before proceeding to the end of the pier. Her biggest worry was that she would make a mistake in her cover story and be exposed. Bob had told her there was zero risk of anyone finding a flaw in her resumé. *Ha! That's what they said before she was almost killed in Ukraine,* she thought.

Walking down the pier, she wrinkled her nose at the sour smell of rotting seaweed, diesel fuel and dead fish. Slowly looking around, she noticed a young man with short, bleach-blond hair waving at her. He was in a white uniform and standing next to a speedboat bearing the name Destiny on a white flag. As she approached him, he extended his hand.

"Ms. Palmer? My name is Luca. I'll take you to the ship. Please, have a seat." Luca jumped into the cockpit and started the twin inboard engines.

The Destiny was anchored two hundred yards outside the main port. She was a mega-yacht commissioned three years ago under the Italian flag. The DEA preparation books had described everything about the yacht and its owner. Palmer visualized the dossier photos of Gunner, a handsome man who looked much younger than his age of forty-four. Gunner had been highly decorated in a special forces unit operating off the grid during the Vietnam War, but even with Palmer's level of security clearance, the description of his heroics was redacted—all of which added to the mystique of this man. Over the following years, Gunner had been in several minor brushes with the law, but most were minor bar fights. The rest of his career was uneventful, although he had a reputation as one of the top captains in the world. The dossier described his personality as enigmatic. He was somewhat of a loner but a natural leader. Charming when he chose to be, but oddly devoid of any known girlfriends.

Palmer ducked to avoid the water spray as the speedboat crashed through the waves. She licked the salty seawater from her lips and felt better once they left the stale air of the harbor. Finally, Luca slowed down and pulled alongside the yacht, then glanced over his shoulder at Palmer. "Give me a second to secure the boat."

Palmer took a deep breath and removed her sunglasses. When the boat was secured, she stepped onto a gangway, glanced up and saw a man in whites wearing a captain's hat and leaning on the railing three stories above. Gunner! He appeared tan and younger than she expected from the photos. He didn't smile or acknowledge her.

Luca jumped out and helped Palmer into the yacht. He pointed toward a doorway.

Palmer took two steps, caught her heel on the bottom lip of the door and stumbled. Her sunglasses flew in one direction and her purse in the other.

Luca grabbed her arm. "Careful, the transition from bright sunlight to the dark hall can be deceiving." He retrieved her purse. "I assume you've been on a yacht like this before. All the exterior doors have a lip to make the door watertight."

Embarrassed by her rookie mistake. "Of course, I know." She quickly recovered. "Clumsy me. Ha! I'm more comfortable in deck shoes than heels. I wasn't sure what to wear for the interview."

Luca pointed to his white deck shoes. "We're pretty casual on the yacht."

They walked up three flights to a lounge that opened onto a large deck facing the stern of the yacht. The bridge was two stories higher than the deck where she stood. A pool occupied a large part of the stern on the second level below. Various lounge sectionals, bars, firepits and soaking pools filled the exterior entertainment spaces.

Luca pointed to a round table near the end of the deck. "Make yourself comfortable. Can I get you anything to drink?" Luca asked.

"No, I'm good, but thanks," she said, then touched his arm. "Do you mind if I ask you a question?"

"Fire away," he said with a toothy grin.

Palmer folded her arms. "How do you like working here?"

Luca shrugged and glanced around the deck. "The ship is fabulous and the pay is great, but—"

"But what?" Palmer asked.

Luca lowered his voice, "I don't know how to describe the vibe around here..." Luca stopped as a young woman walked past them with a tray of fruit. "I have to go. Nika will join you in a few minutes."

"I thought I was meeting the captain?"

"You need to get by Nika first." Grinning, he turned and said over his shoulder, "Good luck," and walked away.

A few minutes later, a tall, young man approached her table from inside the lounge. He was handsomely dressed in the whites of a typical officer. Palmer noticed how he gave each staff member a smile and kind word as he passed by. Palmer started to stand, but he waved for her to remain seated.

"I'm Marco, the first officer of the ship," he said. "I just wanted to say hello before you meet with Nika." Marco crossed his arms. "Our captain said that Bonita raved about you."

Palmer blushed. "She's very sweet. I enjoyed meeting her."

"Just a heads up." Marco's voice grew quieter. "Nika can be very intimidating. She likes the game and thinks she's in charge. Don't rise to the bait. The only person who will decide whether to hire you is Gunner."

"Thanks for your advice."

"I have to go, but I'll see you again."

"I'll look forward to it."

As Palmer waited for the interview, she noticed a short man with wavy, silver hair stretched in a lounge chair on the other side of the deck. He was waving a large cigar and talking rapidly on a cell phone. He wore aviator-style sunglasses and a micro-bathing suit. A young woman in a yellow bikini was gently rubbing oil into his leathery skin. Seated next to him was a tall, attractive woman holding a folder. She frowned and wagged her finger at the man when he suddenly sat up on one elbow, paused his call and yelled at her.

Palmer pretended not to notice, but the whole demeanor of this man made her skin crawl. The woman must have said something irritating because he suddenly jerked off his sunglasses and leaned into her with angry words. Palmer recognized the man as Rizzo, but she wasn't sure about the woman because the sea breeze kept pushing her long hair across her face. Fleetingly, the wind swept the hair off her face, and Palmer recognized the woman as Nika, a key person in Rizzo's mafia organization. Nika was an important person but spent most of her time at Rizzo's house in Eze or his home in Palermo, Sicily.

The argument between Rizzo and Nika continued for a few more minutes and then ended abruptly when Nika stood, pointed at Palmer's table and began marching in Palmer's direction.

Palmer stood and extended her hand, but Nika didn't bother to introduce herself. Palmer quickly removed her purse from the table and sat down. Nika pulled out a chair and opened her folder on the table. She clicked her pen on and off as she scanned Palmer's resumé. Palmer studied the large gold necklace on Nika's neck, the multiple gold bangles on her wrist and the four ostentatious rings on her hands. The rich like to wear their wealth.

Nika looked up and noticed Palmer staring. "Is there something wrong?"

"No, no. I was looking at your necklace. It's beautiful."

Nika frowned and focused on her resumé. "I only have ten minutes, so let's get started." She placed a checkmark on a line. "Says you have five years of experience crewing on yachts. Why?"

Palmer gulped. That wasn't a question she expected. She had prepared for typical questions such as "What are your skills?" "Where are you from?" and "What is your experience? She had not anticipated "Why."

"I don't understand the question."

Nika peered at Palmer. "It's a simple question."

"Umm, I like the ocean. Uhh, I'm a hard worker." Palmer knew she was blowing the interview. "I'm sorry. I'm a little nervous."

"Why are you nervous? You have more experience than anyone

on our service staff."

"Because I want this job."

Nika scanned her resumé again. "Why did you leave your last job?"

"My mother was sick and needed someone to care for her until she recovered."

Nika tapped her pen rapidly on the paper. "I don't recognize any of the yachts you've listed on your resumé. We get a lot of chicks like you that fabricate shit on their resumés to fake their way onto our ship." Nika paused. "You don't look that stupid. Are you?"

Palmer's purse slipped off her lap and half the contents spilled out. "I'm sorry." She leaned over to pick up her things.

Nika rolled her eyes. "Do that later. This won't take long."

Palmer panicked. She had to do something quickly, so she straightened in her chair. "I've worked hard for an opportunity to work with the best people on the most luxurious yachts in the world. I grew up around boats and have a passion to travel the world. I love this business. Yes, I'm overqualified to clean cabins and just about anything else you might have me do, but I'm reliable, a hard worker and I get along well with everyone. Call my references."

"Do you understand the job description? You'll spend your days cleaning cabins and everything else on the boat. At night, you fill in as needed for our twenty-four-hour concierge service. Which means you'll have no time to spend fucking other crew members." Nika stopped and waited for Palmer to respond.

Palmer simply stared back at Nika.

"Look, let's cut through the bullshit. You're a cute, thirty-two-year-old, single woman who wants to crew on yachts? Give me a break." She pointed her pen at Palmer. "If you're looking for a sugar-daddy on this yacht, I'll personally throw you overboard the minute you wink at anyone on this ship. Fess up, why are you here?"

Palmer knew her next answer was crucial. "I'm guessing that we're about the same age, and here we are," she waved her arm in a circle, "sitting on one of the most expensive yachts in the world. Maybe for slightly different reasons." She glanced at Nika's empty ring finger. "But we may have some things in common that brought us here."

Nika caught the direction of Palmer's gaze and covered her left hand. "I highly doubt we have anything in common," she snapped back, placing Palmer's resumé back into the folio as she stood. "Wait here."

Palmer attempted to smile. "Nice to meet you."

Nika didn't respond. She walked quickly into the lounge area and disappeared.

This was a disaster, Palmer thought.

* * *

Nika knocked once and opened the door to Gunner's office.

"What's up?" Gunner said.

She slumped into a leather chair. "I'm filling the last of the crew we need for our trip back to St. Thomas. Rizzo's insisted that I vet all thirty of our current staff. He's paranoid, but he's especially agitated given the guestlist for our upcoming trip. We lost two crew members after your last voyage. You've filled one, but we need one more for the cleaning staff. I've interviewed and rejected several candidates. Just did another."

"Does she speak Spanish? Castillo's from Columbia."

"Her resumé says she speaks fluent Spanish and Italian."

"Perfect. So what's the problem?"

"I don't like her."

"Why not?"

"She's perky and experienced, but there's something not right." Nika paused. "Can you get by without her?"

Gunner frowned. "We're short five people, not one. I can't run this ship at the level of service Rizzo wants without a full staff."

"I know, but it's difficult to find reliable people to work on yachts, and you don't make it any easier."

"What do you mean by that?" Gunner said.

"You expect too much, especially of the men. How many people have you fired this year?"

94

Gunner brushed off the question. "All those guys wanted to do was chase girls and drink beer."

Nika laughed. "Sounds familiar. And you were a Boy Scout at their age?" She waited for a response, but Gunner shrugged. Frustrated, Nika said, "The woman is waiting on deck three. Would you give her a look?"

"Is this the girl Bonita recommended from my yacht club?"

Nika nodded and handed Gunner the folio with Palmer's resumé. Gunner waved her away. "I don't need a resumé."

Nika bristled. "I think you should at least know something about her before you interview her."

"What do you care? I'm the one responsible for everything on this ship. You can boss people around when you're onshore—but not here."

Nika glared at Gunner. "I know our trip isn't for a while, but I want everything set now. This is the first time Rizzo, Castillo and Bykov will meet in one place to finalize the agreement. Rizzo and I believe we can resolve the last remaining issues on the trip to Aruba."

"Look, Nika, we've had this conversation before. I control my ship and the security, not you."

Nika twisted her necklace as if she were about to say something but then changed her mind. "I'll wait for you in the lounge on level two. I need to grab some breakfast."

* * *

Gunner walked out on the deck and looked down at Palmer at the table one deck below. Over years of hiring and firing, he had developed a sixth sense about judging people. He believed that he could learn more about people by watching them than by talking to them. He noticed that Palmer couldn't sit still for more than a minute or two. He was like that too. He was impressed at the way she greeted staff as they passed by her. He watched Palmer twirling her sunglasses when suddenly she stood and walked over to the railing to watch the activity below. She reminded him of a woman who had crewed with him two years ago. He liked the way she carried herself with a sense of confidence. He guessed that she was more mature than most of the crew.

Gunner grabbed a cup of coffee and walked down to the deck where Palmer was waiting. She stood as he approached, extending her hand.

"Hi, my name is Palmer. It's a pleasure to meet you."

Her hand was soft but slightly damp. Gunner held her hand for a second longer and studied her face. Another thing he'd learned about people—eyes don't lie, and a hand can be a doorway into a person's soul. Her large, black eyes had unusual depth for someone so young, and her grip was firm but without an agenda. Gunner felt good karma with her and only needed a few more questions to confirm his instincts. Once again, it seemed, Bonita had found a winner.

Gunner never rushed an interview with cut-to-the-chase questions. He preferred to wait a minute and watch how Palmer responded to the silence. Most people in these situations had a compulsive need to fill the space. Palmer didn't say anything. She just smiled and waited for Gunner. *Well, she's passed the first test*, he thought.

Gunner noticed her eyes were distracted by a stunning 120-foot schooner in the distance. The crew had just set the sails and turned the ship into the sun to catch the wind.

"The old ships are treasures, aren't they?" Gunner said.

"Yes." Palmer smiled. "Just think, if those sails could talk—you wonder what amazing stories and adventures they would share."

They watched the ship sailing toward the horizon for a minute.

Gunner finally spoke, "Bonita called me a couple of days ago about your availability and sent your resumé. She said I was a fool if I don't hire you on the spot. You made quite an impression on her."

"The feeling was mutual. You're lucky to have her running your yacht club."

"You have quite the resumé. Which do you like better, crewing on motor yachts or sailboats?"

"I'm agnostic. I pick depending on the itinerary. Which do you prefer, sailing or steering huge motor yachts like the Destiny?"

"Hmmm, do I detect a little bias in that loaded question."

Palmer turned her head back to Gunner. "Maybe…"

Gunner sighed. "Your first sailboat is like your first love. You're never the same again."

"What was her name?"

"Rainbow. I built her with my own hands," he said shyly. "She's a beautiful forty-nine-foot sloop that I keep at my yacht club."

"I love the name." Palmer leaned closer to Gunner. "Rainbow. My grandmother told me something I'll never forget about rainbows. I lost a very close friend in college, and while I cried in her arms over her death, she whispered, *'Remember, rainbows are not possible without tears from the sun.'*" Palmer turned her gaze to the ocean again and then back to Gunner. "I didn't understand what she meant at the time. Maybe that's why I love the water so much."

Gunner stared at her for several seconds, but Palmer didn't look away. He glanced at her resumé again and noticed the tension in her shoulders. "Relax. I don't bite."

Palmer blushed. "Is it that obvious? Nika kind of... set me on edge."

Gunner chuckled. "Sorry, she can be aggressive. That's her shtick. I can only imagine how your interview went with her."

Gunner looked up at a white seagull hovering above them. It was a good sign. "What do you think of the Destiny?"

"It's amazing. I'd love to take a tour if I get the job."

Gunner nodded and patted her arm. "Sit tight. I need to talk to Nika. This won't take long."

* * *

Gunner found Nika reading the *Wall Street Journal* and eating off a plate of fresh fruit. A cup of espresso sat near her left hand.

She looked up from the paper. "Did you let her off nicely?"

"No, I like her."

Nika frowned. "I don't misjudge people very often."

"Neither do I. What're you so worried about? She's only cleaning cabins."

"Didn't you sense anything odd about her?"

"No, I checked her out. She couldn't fake the kind of questions

I asked."

Nika rolled her eyes. "I bet you spent more time looking at her boobs than vetting her background."

"Well, I already offered her the job."

Nika pushed her plate away and stood. "Fuck you."

Gunner's cell phone buzzed. "I have to take this."

Nika flipped him the middle finger and walked away.

Gunner shook his head as he reached for his phone. Suddenly, he stiffened at the number on the display. He knew what this call meant.

* * *

Palmer had no idea if she had won the job. It had been thirty minutes since her interview, and she worried that she'd blown it. If it were up to Nika, she didn't stand a chance.

Palmer was surprised by how different Gunner was from her expectations. He was shorter than she'd imagined, yet compact. Strong without an ounce of extra fat on his body, which Palmer assumed was a carryover from the military. Although he was from Maine, he had the classic, chiseled features of someone born in the western US.

During the interview, she had studied his tanned but smooth face, which belied his real age. Nothing in the dossier had prepared her for the magnetic presence he had exhibited when they talked. It had taken everything she could muster to keep her mind clear and focused on the interview. Every time she looked into his eyes, she lost her train of thought. She'd never met anyone like Gunner. Careful not to betray her emotions, she smiled and thought to herself, *This is one dangerous man.*

Palmer nervously walked over the edge of the deck and gazed into the distance, knowing that her career was in jeopardy if she failed to get this job. A tap on her shoulder startled her.

"How do you like my ship?" Rizzo asked, holding a tall drink.

Flustered, Palmer replied, "She's beautiful."

"Are you joining our crew?"

"I hope so, but after my interview with Nika, I'm not very confident."

He laughed. "Don't worry about her. She takes pleasure in making other women uncomfortable."

"She's very good at it!"

"Where are you from?"

"Miami."

"I love that town." He switched to Spanish. "*Tu salsa?* Do you salsa?"

"*Si, pero no muy bien.* Yes, but not very well."

"We must have a dance on our trip to St. Thomas. We always spend at least one night salsa dancing."

Palmer raised her eyebrows, "I'd love that, but I need to get hired first."

He put his oiled hand on her arm. "Let me worry about that."

Fifteen minutes later, Palmer heard a voice call out from the interior lounge.

"Congratulations!" Marco said, walking toward her with his hands in the air. "We have some paperwork for you to fill out."

Palmer spontaneously hugged Marco. "Thank you."

Marco blushed. "Don't thank me. You made quite an impression on the captain." He pointed to the stairs. "Follow me. We'll head to the crew lounge and finish gathering information."

As they walked down three flights of stairs, Palmer asked Marco, "How long have you worked on the Destiny?"

"Three years, but I've sailed with the captain for the last ten." He laughed. "He'll never admit it, but he can't run a ship without me."

"Is he a good captain?"

Marco paused at the bottom of the last stairs and looked at Palmer. "He's the best captain on the water, and I've worked for some of the top sailors in the world. He expects a lot from his crew, but he's fair, and he respects us. He's a man of integrity and never waivers from doing the right thing. I guess you could say he has a strong compass."

A man of integrity? Interesting description for a man working for a notorious criminal, she thought.

Marco's description of Gunner wasn't what she expected. Part of her assignment was to find out how deeply Gunner was involved in

Rizzo's drug activities.

"Marco, you hesitated when I asked about Mr. Rizzo. Am I missing something?"

"The atmosphere is different when Mr. Rizzo's on board. And well..." he shook his head, "...you've met Nika." Marco saw the look on Palmer's face. "Don't worry. Fortunately, the big kahunas don't pay much attention to us."

* * *

The crew lounge was luxurious. A large sectional centered the room in front of a big-screen television that covered one wall. Various pinball machines and other games filled another corner, along with a popcorn machine and an espresso bar. A kitchenette counter was filled with baskets of fresh fruits, nuts and various chips.

Marco waved at a half dozen young men and women scattered around the room. "Hey, everyone." He pointed. "Meet Palmer, our new crew member. She'll help us in housekeeping." Most smiled and waved except a young woman sitting alone across the room who barely looked up from her book.

Marco noticed and leaned over to Palmer and whispered, "Don't pay any attention to Zoie. You'll get used to her."

Palmer walked to the far end of the room and stood in front of a ten-foot aquarium. Mesmerized by the beauty of the fish, she said, "This is amazing. I love it."

"That's Skipper's idea. The ocean is his happy place. During our first week on this yacht, Gunner insisted on installing different aquariums throughout the ship. Our captain is an interesting man— tough as nails when he needs to be—but a soft heart."

Marco led her to his small office just off the lounge. He closed the door and pointed to a chair in front of his desk.

"This won't take long. I need to make a copy of your passport and have you sign a few employment documents."

Palmer handed her passport to Marco.

"Nice picture," Marco said as he made a copy.

Palmer blushed. "Looks more like a mug shot."

Marco handed her a pen and several documents.

The first one surprised her. "This is an NDA. Why do you need a non-disclosure agreement?"

"We have high-profile guests from around the world. What you see here stays here." Marco leaned forward. "This is taken very seriously. The rest of the docs are basic employment information. Is there a problem?"

Palmer smiled and signed. "I wouldn't know who to disclose information to anyway."

Marco looked at his watch and handed back her passport. "After you sign these papers, we'll do a quick tour."

* * *

Two days later, Palmer rose from her chair and carefully surveyed the flat to make sure there were no traces of her occupancy. Bob Davis, her boss, insisted for her safety that she keep a low profile, so she found a small place near the harbor. Palmer rose early to pack her bags. One small suitcase contained her toiletries, laptop and enough clothes for three months. The other carbon steel case contained her spare clothes, personal items, a metal briefcase and other intelligence documents that would be retrieved by a DEA agent after she vacated the room.

She checked her travel bag once more to make sure there wasn't any reference to her real name. Satisfied that her baggage and the room were clean, she left for the yacht.

Marco was on the docking platform when Palmer arrived. "Welcome aboard, Miss Palmer," he said. "We are so excited to have you start." He waved to one of the dockhands to pick up her luggage.

Palmer objected, "I can carry my luggage."

"I know, but I'm the first officer, and it's my prerogative." He laughed. "Think of it as my last grand gesture of chivalry before tomorrow, and I become a tough taskmaster." He pointed to Palmer as she stepped off the shuttle boat. "Once you crossed over, you are now mine. No more mister nice guy."

As they walked from deck to deck, Palmer couldn't believe the level of luxury. She'd been on other large yachts, but nothing compared to this ship. Marco showed her the housekeeping area and reviewed her daily routine.

"You'll clean every cabin every day even if we don't have guests," Marco explained. "The captain is very particular about making sure everything is perfect for Mr. Rizzo."

"Does the owner use the yacht very often?"

"Not until recently. He has come more often in the last month than in the last three years combined."

"What's he like?"

"Who? Gunner or Rizzo?"

"Both."

"I'll let you find out for yourself about the captain. But I'll give you a few tips regarding Rizzo. You're not allowed to speak to him or any guests unless they speak to you first. Rizzo demands high service but wants you to be invisible while providing it. Don't get me wrong. He's nice to the staff. He likes to joke around and have fun, but he does have a quick temper if something doesn't meet his expectations."

They reached the lower deck, which housed the crew's quarters. "I have you sharing a cabin with Zoie. She'll train you in your job responsibilities. She's nice but quiet. Nika brought her from Ukraine when she started to work for Rizzo."

He walked to the end of the hall and knocked.

A soft voice said, "Come in."

Marco opened the door. "Hi, Zoie, I want to introduce you to your new roommate."

Zoie stood and walked over to Palmer. "Welcome to your new home."

A twin bunk occupied the far wall. A small round table with two chairs occupied most of the open room. A small bathroom had two small closets. All the walls were covered with underwater photographs of fish and coral.

Palmer stared at the photos. "These are beautiful. Did you take them?"

"Zoie is our unofficial photographer. She takes amazing pictures."

Zoie blushed. "They're not that great. I just love the images I see underwater."

Marco turned to leave. "I'll let you get to know each other."

As Marco was walking out, the deckhand brought in Palmer's luggage and then left.

Zoie pointed to the upper bed. "I have the lower bunk."

They sat around the table and chatted for a half-hour. Zoie asked so many questions that Palmer felt like she was being interviewed all over again.

"What about you?" Palmer asked.

"Not much to tell."

Palmer waited for Zoie to continue, but she simply smiled. Finally, Palmer asked again, "How long have you been working as a crew member here?"

"Only several months."

Palmer waited again, confused as to Zoie's reluctance to talk about herself. "What yacht were you on before you came here?"

"Never worked on a boat before."

"Never? How did you get hired? They ran the most thorough background check and interview process I've ever experienced."

Before Zoie could answer, Nika walked into their cabin and smiled at Palmer.

"How is everything? I just wanted to make sure you were settled."

"Great," Palmer replied. "Marco and Zoie have been generous with their time."

"Wonderful. Make sure you let Zoie know if you have questions." Then she started a conversation in Russian with Zoie. Palmer immediately realized how Zoie got hired. Fortunately, Nika and Zoie had no idea Palmer spoke fluent Russian.

"What did you find out?" Nika asked Zoie in Russian.

"Nothing we don't already know. Her background story seems legit."

Nika smiled at Palmer as they continued their conversation in Russian.

"Well, let me know if you see anything suspicious."

"What's bothering you? She seems nice."

"I can't put my finger on it, but I'm never wrong."

They both glanced at Palmer, who returned their look with a big smile.

Nika squeezed Zoie's shoulder. "We have to be very careful until Bykov gets here."

Palmer had to use all of her training not to react when Nika said Bykov's name.

Nika turned to leave and switched back to English, "You're in good hands with Zoie."

After Nika left, Zoie looked at her watch. "We have an hour before dinner, so I'll show you what you need to know when we start tomorrow."

* * *

After a frantic call from Bonita regarding Cody, Gunner knew he had to schedule a quick trip to his marina. He reviewed his calendar and circled a date. An hour later, Gunner stopped by Marco's office to drop off a folder that contained his orders for the day. He opened the door and realized Marco was in a meeting.

"Sorry, I should've knocked," Gunner said when he saw the back of a woman at Marco's desk.

Marco smiled, and the woman turned around. "You remember Palmer," Marco said. "This is her first week, and we were doing a crew member orientation."

Gunner nodded. "Welcome. Sorry for the interview confusion with Bonita. We had to make a slight accommodation for Nika. Normally, we don't put you through an additional interview because I trust Bonita."

"No worries. I enjoyed meeting Bonita."

Gunner handed Marco the folder. "Make sure these things get done this week. And have the engineers check the port engine. It sounded funny during our last trip."

"I did that already. They didn't find anything."

"Check it again. Something isn't right—I can feel it when we turn into the wind."

Marco looked at Palmer and shook his head. "He's a ship

whisperer. I don't know how he can sense these things, but he's always right."

Gunner put his hand on Palmer's shoulder. "Marco likes to exaggerate. Plus, I don't want to lose an engine in the middle of the Atlantic in a storm. We're taking the southern route to St. Thomas during hurricane season."

"Following the same trade winds as Columbus?" Palmer asked.

"Something like that." Gunner smiled and looked at his watch. "I have to go ashore. Palmer, welcome to our team."

Marco put the folder in his top drawer. "Where are you going?"

"Some boring business."

"Anything I can help with?" Marco asked, concerned.

"Take care of our girl while I'm gone."

Marco looked at Palmer and smiled. "He means the ship, not you." He turned back to Gunner and said, "How long will you be gone?"

"Not sure. I'll call."

A few minutes later, Nika walked in without knocking and ignoring Palmer.

"I need an update on the supplies I ordered."

Marco pointed to Palmer. "We're almost finished. Can I call you when we're done?"

"No, I have a meeting with Rizzo in ten minutes, and I need that information now."

Marco squinted. "Why does everything have to be a crisis?"

Nika leaned toward Marco menacingly. "Do you want me to tell Rizzo that you're too busy to get him the information he wants?"

Palmer rose from her chair. "I can come back another time."

Marco waved his hand for her to sit back down. "I don't have the report. I gave it to Gunner to review, and he hasn't given it back to me."

"Where's Gunner now?"

"He just left for a meeting ashore."

Nika looked surprised. "I just talked to him this morning, and he didn't say anything about leaving." Then she remembered the cell phone call that Gunner didn't take while she was in his office. "Where is he going?"

"He didn't say. Just some business, he said."

"What kind of business? Does Rizzo know?"

"I have no idea. I just found out a few minutes ago. You might still catch him before he goes ashore."

Nika left the room and walked quickly toward the departure platform. As she reached the railing, she could see the shuttle boat was halfway across the bay with Gunner on the stern. She pulled out her cell and dialed the number for Gunner. He didn't respond to her multiple calls, so she left a stinging message to call her back.

After she had stormed out of his office, Marco apologized to Palmer. "Welcome to my world. Gunner and I have worked together for years. We run an efficient, smooth operation—and without a lot of drama. This is the first time I've seen Nika on board since Gunner and I took this job. We'd heard stories about, her but I just recently met her. Not sure what's up, but she disrupts everything she touches."

Palmer smiled. "Maybe that's why Gunner left."

Marco shook his head. "He knows how to manage people worse than her. I'm positive he left for another reason."

Marco picked up a pen and scribbled some notes on a tablet. "We should finish our orientation. You'll need to follow these instructions exactly as I tell you for all the cabins every day. Rizzo is very fussy and a hypochondriac to boot."

* * *

Nika was late for her meeting with Rizzo. He was stretched out in a lounge chair next to his private pool on the fourth floor. A half-eaten breakfast was still on the round table in the shade. Nika stopped at the table and poured herself a glass of orange juice.

"Sorry, I'm late. I was trying to get some information from Gunner to review with you." Nika pulled up a chair next to Rizzo and pulled out a thick notebook. "Did you know that Gunner left on your jet this morning?"

Rizzo continued to look toward the sun and didn't turn his head.

"No, but why do you care?"

"He's supposed to plan the logistics for our first shipment. I made a list of things that need to be completed before we leave Monaco."

"Do you know why they call Gunner the captain?"

Nika squirmed in her chair.

"Don't fucking forget it," Rizzo growled. "You're here for other reasons, so stick to what we discussed earlier."

"Sorry, I was just trying to help." Nika opened her notebook and took out a pen. "I've analyzed the first shipment. I think we can net this number after expenses." She hesitated for a moment and glanced at the young woman in the lounge chair close to Rizzo's chair.

Rizzo called over to the woman, "Baby, take a hike. We have some work to do."

The woman gathered her things and left.

Nika wrote the number on a blank page and showed it to Rizzo.

He sat up. "Wow. I was figuring half that amount. Are you sure?"

"I had to make several assumptions about what terms we can negotiate with Bykov for contributing most of the heroin from his sources. Also, I've been using my contacts to figure out the wholesale market for Columbian cocaine as well as the retail value I believe we can achieve when we sell to Europe. I've prepared a spreadsheet."

"Fuck the spreadsheet. That's your business. I only care about the final number."

Nika looked disappointed. "Are you sure? I spent a lot of time analyzing this. Here is the proof."

Rizzo waved his hand. "What about the agreements we discussed? We need one with Bykov and the other with Castillo to form the new cartel."

"I have a rough draft for you to review when you're ready."

Rizzo sat up and turned toward an attendant standing inside his suite. "Marie, bring me a bottle of water." He laid back down on the lounge chair. "I want you to go over the terms with Gunner when he gets back."

Nika stiffened. "I can negotiate with Bykov and Castillo. I already scheduled a conference call with Bykov tomorrow."

"Reschedule it for when Gunner returns."

"Why do you want me to meet with Gunner before we meet with Bykov?"

Rizzo took his sunglasses off. "Because I told you to. He knows the Columbians better than either of us. Do I need to explain that to you?"

"No, I just wondered…"

Rizzo snapped, "Are you fucking deaf? Now get out of here."

Chapter Six

Gunner was tired and swamped with a dozen issues that needed his attention after returning from his "business" trip. He was also filled with regret that he hadn't had more time to spend with Jett and Addie the last time he was in Virgin Gorda. They were the perfect example of the adage "good friends are food for the soul." One night had not been enough to recharge his batteries.

Gunner's desk was covered with maps of the Mediterranean and the Caribbean Antilles. He pulled out the nautical map of the Mediterranean and started to plot the trip from Monaco to St. Thomas. Even though the ship's computers could calculate the entire trip, Gunner was old school. He didn't trust computers and always plotted by hand their preferred route and devised backup plans in case of bad weather or other problems.

His insistence on creating a hand-drawn plan had come from his training as a sniper in Vietnam. In the jungle, he was on his own. He learned to anticipate and plan for every possible scenario. On the ocean, he had experienced too many bad storms in which the computers had gone down, and he was forced to navigate manually.

Gunner tried to ignore his buzzing cell phone. He needed to focus on planning this trip. After the third call, however, he scowled and answered.

"Yes."

"Gunner. It's me."

"Tom?" Gunner had stopped calling him Dad years ago. "What's wrong?"

"I know it's been a long time, but I want you to know that Kate died yesterday."

The phone went silent.

"Gunner, are you still there?'

"I'm sorry. What happened?"

"Mom fell and broke her hip a couple of months ago. The recovery didn't go well, and she was in constant pain."

Gunner could hear Tom sniffling. "Two weeks ago, she caught pneumonia and went into the hospital. The doctors said the bacteria from pneumonia infected her heart and caused a heart attack."

"I'm sorry, Tom."

"I set the funeral for this Saturday. It'll be a small affair, but that's what she'd want." He started to choke up again. "I can't believe she's gone."

"How are they treating you at the nursing home?"

"Most of the nurses are nice, but the men are rough. They moved me to the memory care area. That's what they call it. Nice description for a jail."

"How long have you been in there?"

"Are you kidding?" He chuckled. "Could be a day or months for all I know. It's a good thing I can't remember much these days. They say things are getting worse, but how would I know—I can't remember what I ate for breakfast!"

"Good thing you haven't lost your sense of humor."

The phone went silent again.

"How's my girl?"

"You mean the Rainbow? She's well. I refitted her last year with new sails. She's so fast now. I have a framed picture of you and me standing in front of her the day we launched her." Gunner paused and then continued in a sentimental voice. "That was a good day. Maybe I should sail the Rainbow up the coast to Maine this summer, and we can get you out of jail and take a cruise." They both knew that was a lie, but it fit the conversation.

"When will you be home for dinner?" Tom asked.

"What are you talking about?"

"Are you staying late after school?"

"Tom, are you okay? Remember, I'm at work in Monaco."

"What? Who is this?"

Gunner could hear Tom talking to a woman, and then one of them disconnected the call. He set the phone down, leaned back in his chair and looked out the window over the bow of the ship. A splash in the distance caught his eye. A large pod of dolphins was moving quickly across the bay. He wished he was as free as those dolphins. Free from regrets. Free from doubt and anger. Free from the past and things you can't fix. He picked up the phone and dialed a number he knew by heart.

"Hello?"

"Hey, Jett, how are you?"

"I'm glad you called. I just got off the phone with my parents, and they told me the news about Kate. How are you feeling?"

"I'm not sure. Mixed memories, you know…"

"When was the last time you talked to Tom?"

"Until a few minutes ago, it's been a while."

"Mom said the funeral is this weekend." Jett asked, "Are you going?"

"Yes. Tom sounded good on the phone. Had a rare lucid moment. It didn't last long before he relapsed, and a nurse hung up for him. He's lost in another world most of the time. I doubt that he would even know he was at Kate's funeral. Miss you, buddy. I'll call you when I get back and schedule another time to see you."

"Perfect. You'll be pleased with the progress I've made in our development here."

"Great. Talk soon."

Gunner returned to his maps and calculated the distance between Monaco and the Canary Islands. He knew they would need to refuel once before they crossed the Atlantic. As he was finishing the review, he was interrupted by a knock.

Nika poked her head around the door. "Are you busy?"

Gunner scowled. His day was always filled with interruptions. Before he could respond, she walked in and sat across from him.

Nika rubbed the leather on her armrest. "I need one of these in my office."

"Why? You don't meet with people."

"Very funny."

Nika leaned forward and put her elbows on his desk. "I need some help."

Gunner frowned and pulled several maps out from beneath her elbows. "What can I do for you?"

"I need help verifying the first shipment out of Ukraine. Rizzo's nervous about Bykov."

"Should he be?"

"Yes and no. I worked for Bykov before Rizzo hired me. He's a dangerous guy but greedy. As long as he thinks we are living up to our part of the deal, he'll be fine. Bykov will deliver the heroin, which will be transferred onto our container ship at the Odesa seaport."

"When are we starting the first shipment? It's June, and we have to be careful about hurricane season."

"I'm not sure yet. Let me get back to you with a departure date from Odesa. We still have negotiations to complete with Castillo. They're pretty proud of their Columbian cartel, and pricing has become a major sticking point. My best guess is around August."

Gunner rolled his eyes. "That puts us in the middle of hurricane season."

"I read that these ships can go anywhere in any weather."

"Where did you read that? In the comics? These are large, top-heavy ships, and they don't like Mother Nature."

"You'll figure it out. All I know is that once the deal is cut with Castillo, Rizzo wants the shipment to happen immediately."

"Anything else?"

"Nope."

Gunner's cell phone buzzed with an incoming call. The phone was on the desk halfway between them, and they both looked down at the number. Gunner quickly turned the phone face down.

"Go ahead. Take it," Nika said.

Gunner shook his head and let it ring.

"I can wait. Must be important if someone is calling you from Miami."

Gunner looked up in surprise. "How do you know where the call's coming from?"

"The prefix. I have friends who opened a club in Miami. It's one of the hottest spots in Florida. Who do you know there?"

"Never mind," Gunner said. "It's just a business call."

"Does it have anything to do with the Destiny?" Nika stared at Gunner's tapping index finger. "If you ever need something, my friends know a lot of people in Miami that could help."

"I'm fine." Gunner looked at his watch. "Hate to cut this short, but I have a meeting to prepare for."

"See, this wasn't so bad."

"What do you mean?"

Nika smiled, pointing her finger back and forth between them. "We talked and didn't yell at each other once."

After Nika left, Gunner hit the return number on his phone. A man answered.

"I'm returning her call," Gunner said.

The phone went silent. Gunner strained to hear the muffled conversation on the other end. Finally, the man said, "Hang on. She'll be with you in a minute."

Gunner wiped his sweaty palms on his knees. After a couple of minutes, he stood and paced around his cabin. Suddenly a woman's voice spoke to him.

"Sorry to make you wait."

"Who answered the phone?" Gunner asked. "I didn't recognize the voice."

"It doesn't matter. Are you alone?"

"Yes, in my cabin."

"Write this down. Are you ready?"

Gunner returned to his desk, pushed aside his maps, and pulled out a blank sheet of paper. "Ready."

The woman talked for several minutes without interruption. Finally, she paused. "Do you have any questions? Do you understand what you need to do?"

"Are you sure about this?"

"Yes, it's the only way."

Gunner stared at paper filled with scribbled notes.

"Are you still there?" the woman asked.

"Yes. I have to make some excuses, but I can be in Miami by the end of the week."

Gunner ended the call, walked to the credenza and stared at a photo of him with Jett and Cody on the deck of the Rainbow. Jett was holding up a large grouper, and Cody held a speargun. The framed picture released a flood of memories from his childhood. He replayed his conversation with Tom and dreaded returning to Maine for Kate's funeral.

* * *

Gunner tried to sleep on the flight to Maine, but he couldn't relax. He worried about seeing Tom. The last time they were together hadn't ended well. In addition, thoughts of his dear friends in trouble swirled in his head. Gunner was funding the carry costs of two spec houses Jett was developing in Virgin Gorda. They were not selling.

Then there was Cody—even though Bonita hadn't told him anything specific during that previous call, he could sense in her voice that something was wrong. She had dodged his questions about revenues over the last several months.

Rizzo and his expectations were his last concern. *Why me? Why does everyone look to me to solve their problems? I just want to be a captain and nothing more,* he thought.

Gunner was the only passenger on Rizzo's private jet. It was luxurious, with the capacity to seat ten. He sighed and drifted off to sleep, wondering what to expect when he saw Tom. Gunner didn't wake up until the wheels hit the runway. His view out the window showed a grey, rainy day. The jet taxied to the staging area of a local fixed-base operations (FBO) terminal for private jets.

After stopping at his hotel to freshen up, he headed for the nursing home to see Tom. Along the way, he checked for calls and had several from Nika, one from Marco and another from Miami.

At the nursing home, Gunner hesitated outside Tom's door. The hallway smelled of stale food and antiseptic cleaning solution. Someone had taped a picture of Tom standing next to the Rainbow to the door.

Gunner took a deep breath, gently knocked and slowly opened the door. Tom was sitting in his bed eating lunch off a tray. Gunner was shocked at how Tom had aged. He looked small, like a child, only with thin, pale hair that hung uncombed over his forehead. His thin body, dressed in a white hospital gown, accentuated his gaunt face.

"Hi, Tom. Can I come in?"

Tom dropped his fork in surprise. His eyes widened, and then he squinted to make sure he was seeing Gunner and not one of his hallucinations. "Yes, yes," Tom said, then pushed his tray away and waved for Gunner to come closer. Gunner leaned over the bed and gave him an awkward hug.

"What are you doing here?"

"I came back for..." Sadly, he realized Tom probably didn't remember Kate's funeral. "I came back to see you."

"How nice." Tom smiled. "You have to stay until Kate comes back. She's running some errands."

Gunner grimaced and pulled up a chair.

"You look good," Tom said.

Neither of them knew what to say.

"How are they treating you here?" Gunner asked.

"Fine, although the food is lousy." Then he smiled. "But some of the nurses are cute. I'm only staying here until tomorrow."

Gunner knew this was a fantasy. Tom had been living in a nursing home for over a year.

"That's good news."

Suddenly, Tom moved to the edge of the bed as if preparing to stand up. Gunner grabbed his arm, which was just skin and bones. "Here, let me help you."

Tom pointed to a round table in the corner. "I want to sit at the table and talk."

Tom was very weak but, with Gunner's support, slowly shuffled to a chair. As Gunner sat down, he noticed that the cloudiness in his expression, so evident a few minutes ago, was gone. Tom was back.

"I'm so glad you came. I have something to tell you," Tom said. "Kate died. I wanted a funeral, but the doctor said I was too sick to leave here. Almost all our friends are gone. A ceremony didn't make sense, so I had Kate cremated." He pointed to a box on the counter along the far wall. "I want to ask you a favor. Would you take her ashes back with you and spread them in the ocean the next time you're sailing on the Rainbow?"

Gunner reached over and grabbed Tom's hand. "Of course."

"Thank you. How's work now that you are a famous captain on a big yacht?"

"Work's fine. I'm not famous, but the ship is one of the largest private yachts on the water. She's slightly over three hundred feet."

Tom whistled. "Imagine what it took to build a yacht that big. More than a father and son."

They sat in silence for a long moment, each searching for the unspoken words and feelings that they had carried in their hearts since Gunner had left for Vietnam.

Finally, Gunner cleared his throat. "I have to ask you something. Why did you adopt me?"

Tom's lower lip quivered. "It's a long story." He hung his head for a moment. "We struggled to be the parents you always wanted, and I'm sorry for that. But we do love you—with all our heart."

"I know that." Gunner grabbed both of Tom's shaking hands. "There's no need to apologize."

"We tried to be good parents," Tom said. "You have to admit—you weren't the easiest boy to raise."

Gunner smiled and nodded as he leaned back in his chair. "I need to know something important. What can you tell me about my biological parents?"

Tom squirmed in his chair. "We don't have any information about your parents. Back in those days, the adoption agency was adamant

116

that we never try to contact them. They believed it would be harmful and confusing for you."

Gunner's shoulders slumped. "I was hoping to find out a little about them—who they were, where did they live?" Gunner looked up at Tom. "Something about who I am."

"I'm sorry. They didn't give us any facts. Frankly, we were so excited to have you that we didn't care." Tom tried to stand but fell back into his chair.

"What do you need? I'll get it for you."

Tom pointed to the counter. "Can you hand me that book next to the photo of you?"

Gunner walked over and picked up a thick, leather-bound book and placed it in front of Tom.

"What is it?" Gunner asked.

"A photo album."

Gunner looked confused.

Tom patted the cover of the book. "This is for you. Even though Kate became too sick to fulfill our dream of retiring on the Rainbow, I decided to keep a scrapbook about you and your adventures." He opened the first page, which contained a picture of Kate holding baby Gunner waist-deep in the water in front of their house.

Gunner was stunned. "I had no idea you had these. Why didn't you tell me?"

Tom shrugged. They both knew why, and it didn't matter anymore.

Gunner slid his chair around to sit close to Tom. The book was filled with photos, newspaper and magazine clippings of Gunner's achievements in the yachting world, with hundreds of pages of Tom's handwritten notes accompanying each section. They spent the next few hours going over each page. Some provoked laughter and others tears. Tom paused at a photo of him and Gunner standing next to the Rainbow the day they had finished building her. It was the same photo Gunner had in his cabin on the Destiny.

"Building that sailboat was the best thing," Tom said. "I was so excited to launch the Rainbow and see how she would ride in the water, but I didn't want the building of her it to end because this was the one thing we did together."

Gunner leaned over and gave Tom a long, hard hug.

Tom wiped the tears from his eyes with the back of his hand. "I want you to have it."

"Thank you, I love you—Dad."

Gunner helped him back in bed and gave him some water. Tom closed his eyes for a few minutes, then suddenly sat up. "Who are you!" he yelled at the top of his lungs. "What are you doing in my room? Nurse!"

Gunner tried to calm him down, but it only made him more agitated. A nurse came in and looked at Gunner. "You're lucky you had a nice visit. He hasn't been lucid for weeks." She leaned over and said to Tom, "You're fine. That nice man over there is your son. Come on now, I'll get your medicine."

Tom shook his head and said in an angry voice. "I don't have a son."

The nurse looked at Gunner. "I think you'd better leave. Don't worry about what he said. He gets these hallucinations. He's such a sweet man."

Gunner picked up the photo album and the wooden box containing Kate's ashes. At the door, he looked back, knowing this was probably the last time they would see each other.

* * *

Gunner headed back to the airport. After the jet took off for Monaco, Gunner walked up to the cockpit and told the pilots, "Change in plans. I need to go to Miami."

"No problem. How long will you plan on staying there?"

"A few hours. Just stay onsite and be ready to take off when I get back."

Gunner handed a hundred-dollar bill to each of the pilots. "Let's keep our stop in Miami between us boys, okay? When I get back, we need to make a quick trip to Bimini."

"Yes, sir."

Gunner returned to his seat and looked at the photo album Tom had given him. He thought about how parents have such an influence on their children's lives. Jett had been given the best childhood with loving parents, yet his dad's obsessive insistence on Jett taking over his firm drove his son away. Cody's abusive childhood had damaged his ability to trust anyone.

Gunner stared at the photo of him and Tom standing next to the Rainbow. *Why is life so complicated?*

He tried to envision what his biological parents might have looked like. Which parent gave him blue eyes? Where did they live? Did he have brothers and sisters? Growing up with Kate and Tom, he had always felt he was a guest. Maybe that's why working on ships made sense—he was never in a port long enough to call it home. Never on one yacht or in one place long enough to have a relationship.

A black sedan was waiting for Gunner when they landed at the Miami FBO. A young man dressed in a black suit held open the rear door and nodded to Gunner as he approached the sedan. Gunner paused and looked in the back seat. A woman with silver hair and sunglasses patted the seat next to her.

"It's good to see you. How was your flight?" Before he could answer, she barked at the young man. "Let's go. We need to hurry."

* * *

Three hours later, Gunner walked up the short steps to enter Rizzo's jet. He nodded to the pilots. "Let's get going."

"Good meeting?"

Gunner shrugged and asked, "How long is the flight to Bimini?"

The pilot replied, "You have time for one drink."

After takeoff, he stared out the window. This trip was not what he expected. He recalled the last time he had sailed from Miami to Bimini. The gulf stream was quiet on a moonless night. There was something magical about sailing in the middle of the night. Sailing was freedom—freedom from everything. Gunner had never felt that he belonged around people. He always felt like an outsider, always alone, as if a part of him was missing. On the water was the only place he ever felt at home.

Gunner worried about the safety of Vin, another friend. The news he'd just heard that the Columbians had tried to kill Vin at his beach restaurant on St. Vincent was a surprise. Gunner knew that he didn't have much time to protect his friend.

He was amazed at how fast the landscape and pace of the drug business had changed. For years, the Caribbean, starting from the Bahamas to the Exuma Islands over to the Virgin Islands and then turning south to Venezuela—enjoyed an odd form of equilibrium. Most islanders lived modest but happy lives. They depended on tourists for most of their income, but some needed to supplement that by dabbling in the local drug trade—just weed and a little cocaine to locals and tourists. That had all changed several months ago when the Columbians showed up on the islands.

Vin had grown up in Miami. His parents were originally from St. Vincent, but they had moved to the States shortly before he was born and named him after St. Vincent. Gunner had met him in Vietnam, and they'd become brothers while serving their tour together. After returning from Vietnam, Vin spent a year in Miami, floating from job to job. Nothing was keeping him in Miami, so he decided to move to St. Vincent to be around his extended family. Vin was a tall, lanky man with skin as black as a cave. With a wide smile and infectious laugh, he made everyone around him happy. Vin ran the best beach bar in the Caribbean on the leeward side of St. Vincent. Whenever Gunner was passing through on a trip, he made a point to schedule an anchorage in the bay in front of Vin's beach bar.

Gunner had spent many long nights with Vin drinking local dark rum from a wooden keg behind the bar. Vin knew all about the small marijuana and cocaine trade so prevalent in the islands. The local government officials and police looked the other way as long as they received a small cut and no harm came to the tourists.

Now Vin was in big trouble. Everyone was required to pay a "tax" to the Columbians, or their businesses were shut down, or worse, they were killed. Vin was too stubborn to pay and was forced to run. Gunner knew that hiding in Bimini would only protect him for a short time. The islands have ears, and secrets never last long. Gunner had to devise a quick plan to save him.

It was late morning when Gunner's plane touched down on the

small airstrip on Bimini. He hurried to a bar called the End of The World for a late breakfast. The building is just a large hut with a bar running the length of one wall. The rest of the room was filled with mismatched chairs and tables. Bleached conch shells, lobster traps and old buoys hung from walls. Gunner loved this place.

He sat on a stool at the bar and yelled, "Jimmy, are you still seeing the schoolteacher you met the last night we partied together?"

Jimmy rushed out and gave Gunner a bear hug. He was a large man who embraced Gunner like a grandmother. "Where have you been? It's been months since I saw your ugly face."

"Spending most of my in the Mediterranean sailing Rizzo's yacht back and forth between Sicily and Monaco. You didn't answer my question. What about the girl?"

Jimmy shook his head. "Ah, mon, she left me for a rich businessman passing through on one of your fancy yachts."

"Too bad. I bet she'll be back once she finds that fucking for money isn't the same as fucking for love."

"The usual for breakfast?"

Gunner nodded and looked around. There were only a few locals in the bar at this time of the morning. "How's business?"

Jimmy turned his head as he scrambled a batch of eggs. "Not bad for this time of year. As you know, it slows down during hurricane season."

"Any trouble lately?"

"No, as long as I pay."

"How much?"

"Now it's $1,500 per month."

"Goddamn it. Somebody has to stop this. Where's the police?"

Jimmy laughed. "Who do you think collects the payments?"

A few minutes later, Jimmy set down a plate of soft scrambled eggs and a pile of lobster mixed with fresh goat cheese. He leaned on the bar in front of Gunner and waited.

Gunner took three bites in a row before he declared, "I've traveled all over the world, and you make the best lobster scrambled eggs I've ever had."

Jimmy smiled but then leaned closer and whispered. "Bad guys were here two weeks ago asking about you."

"Who was it?"

"Columbian punks." Jimmy pretended to spit on the ground. "They're such arrogant assholes with their cheap beach shirts open to show off the five-pound gold package hanging around their filthy necks."

Gunner chuckled. "Ah, come on. Tell me how you really feel."

Jimmy pointed his finger at Gunner. "Someday, I'm going to kill one of them, and it's all your fault."

Gunner finished his eggs and pushed the plate across the bar. "What about our mutual friend?"

Jimmy looked around the bar. "Tucked away on the other side of the island. You know the hut."

"How's he doing?"

"Scared shitless. But that hasn't affected his appetite, especially for my good rum."

"Sounds like the Vin I know." Gunner said. "Anyone ask about him yet."

"No, not yet. But it's only a matter of time. Half the island knows he's here because he plays Bob Marley tunes late into the night and annoys the neighbors." Jimmy crossed his arms. "What are you going to do?"

"I don't know yet. It's complicated." Gunner laid a twenty on the bar. "Thanks, Jimmy. I'll see you later."

"Here, take this." Jimmy handed Gunner a bottle of rum. "It'll save me a trip taking it over to him. Also, use my scooter behind the hut. Just don't wreck it."

Gunner rode the scooter to the other side of the island, covered mostly by scrub brush, sand, coral and a few palm trees closer to the water. Young barefoot children played soccer along the roadside while small groups of men sat on metal chairs in the shade, smoking and drinking beer.

He pulled up to the last hut at the end of the road. The door was slightly ajar, so he pushed it open and walked in. The room was thick with a haze of ganja, the local term for marijuana. A large window faced the ocean. He turned quickly to his left when he heard loud groaning in the bedroom. He slowly parted a curtain of beads and tensed for the worst until he saw the naked back of a woman riding Vin like a horse as he sat in a chair.

Tapping the young woman on the shoulder, Gunner said, "I don't believe we've met."

The woman shrieked, jumped off Vin and frantically looked around the room for her clothes.

"Relax," Vin said as he grabbed her arm and pulled her back onto his lap, "He's an old friend—and harmless." He laughed. "At least he used to be."

Gunner set the bottle of rum on the table next to the bed. "A gift from Jimmy."

"Love that man."

Gunner glanced at the women. "We need to talk."

Vin sent her off with a pat on the butt. "I'll see you tomorrow."

Vin grabbed the bottle and pulled the cork. He took a long pull and handed it to Gunner.

"We didn't have a chance to talk when you called me," Gunner said. "So fill me in."

"Fuckin' Columbian mafia is screwing up everything for us. They come around every month with their hand out. At first, I thought this was just a one-time thing—some rogue tough guys from Columbia trying to take advantage. But then we started hearing of people washing up on beaches because they didn't pay up. I told them to fuck off, and then one night, they came for me. I heard them enter the restaurant, so I ran out the back door. I found out later that they burned the place down. That's when I called you."

Vin stood up, pulled on his shorts and walked to a window. "Remember that night in 'Nam when we thought we wouldn't make it?"

"Which one?"

"Fuckin' Viet Cong. At least they had a reason to fight, but these assholes are just greedy punks." Vin sighed. "We survived so much shit. I'm not going to let these idiots ruin my life or my friends back home." Vin picked up the rum. "Come on. Let's go outside and catch up."

They pulled up two chairs outside.

"Do you ever think about that night we were hunting on the Ho Chi Minh trail and got trapped?"

"I try not to."

Vin and Gunner were part of an elite squad that operated off the grid. They'd go into the jungle for up to three weeks at a time, usually deep into Cambodia or North Vietnam. Their orders were to kill people who used the various trails leading into South Vietnam. They operated in sniper teams of two. They'd "hunt" only at night and hide during the day.

Gunner was an outstanding shot. He could knock a guy's glasses off at three hundred yards. They'd set up on a trail, and Vin, as the spotter, would dial in the information that Gunner needed to make adjustments for distance, wind and other variables. Each night they'd find a different trail with some open space. They'd wait until a column walked past them carrying supplies and weapons. Gunner would aim his silenced rifle and start with the last person on the trail. He was like a machine, quickly pulling off numerous shots within seconds. Sometimes he could shoot several combatants, working his way up the column, before someone would cry out or make enough noise to alert the others.

"When was the last time you saw Jett?" Vin asked.

"Six months ago, in Haiti."

"Haiti? What the fuck were you doing with him there?"

Gunner smiled and took another drink. "He bailed me out of jail."

Vin laughed. "How many times has he saved your ass?"

"Who's counting."

"So, how is Jett?"

"Good. I talked to him on the twenty-first."

"Shit." Vin sighed. "You're so good at always remembering stuff like the date Stevie died. Is Jett still married to Sky?"

"No, That's over. I don't think their relationship was never the same after Stevie died."

"Damn, that was horrible." Vin frowned. "Love Jett. My favorite bookworm. I'm glad he eventually switched from law to developing real estate and didn't go back to run his dad's firm."

The hot sun was making Gunner sweat. It reminded him of arriving in Vietnam back in 1970. He had enlisted in the army two days after finishing the Rainbow with his dad. He was shipped to Vietnam and wounded on one of his first patrols. After he recovered, he volunteered to become part of the special sniper unit where he met Vin. Extended time in the jungle had quickly reverted his senses to their primal nature. His hearing became more acute. Night vision returned. His sense of smell increased so dramatically he could smell the Viet Cong soldiers long before he could see them.

A natural leader and killer, Gunner was in his true element when in the jungle. The only times he felt that same self-awareness was when sailing deep into the ocean during a howling storm. Gripping the helm of a sailboat that was heeling close to the water had that same intensity.

But all that was long ago. In his lounge chair, Gunner stretched and scuffed his bare feet in the soft white sand. "I never get tired of this view. The water over this reef has one of the prettiest range of blues and greens."

"Gunner, are you having problems?"

"Why do you ask?"

Vin lowered his sunglasses. "Because you look like shit."

"I'm fine." Gunner frowned. "Don't worry about me. It's you we have to deal with right now."

Vin leaned forward in his chair. "It's a fucking cluster."

Gunner moved his chair closer to Vin. "I have to fly back to the Dominican Republic and check on Cody and Bonita. I'll be back in Monaco in two days. Just stay quiet here." He looked out over the ocean. "I can help you, but you need to do exactly what I say."

Then he leaned forward and started to explain his plan.

* * *

Gunner left Vin more worried than ever. He was confident that Vin was safe in Bimini for now, but for how long, he didn't know. His phone showed that Nika had been trying to reach him. On the way back to the airstrip, Gunner finally returned her calls.

"Where the hell have you been? I've been trying to reach you since you left."

"Been busy."

"Where are you?"

"At my marina," he lied.

"What are you doing there? I thought you were flying back from Maine."

"I needed to pick up some things."

"When will you be back? Rizzo wants you to review the terms of the deal with Bykov."

"I have no interest in the terms. Whatever you've drafted is fine with me. I just run the ship."

"Rizzo insists."

Gunner sighed. "Fine, leave it on my desk, and I'll look at it. I should be back the day after tomorrow."

Gunner had planned his visit to be a surprise to Cody. On her last call to Gunner, Bonita hadn't sounded sound like herself. Something was wrong. He had recently injected more cash into the marina because Cody had insisted the marina needed some repairs and upgrades. Gunner was angry with the lack of communication and feared the worst.

Gunner understood Cody's insecurities and his need to be a big shot. He also knew Cody was capable of lying to him about the marina operations. It didn't matter because Bonita would tell him the truth. But he was anxious to review the financial status of the marina because it was bleeding money.

* * *

After the pilots landed in the Dominican Republic and parked the jet at the local FBO, Gunner handed them a card with the name of a hotel and restaurant. "Best in the city," he said. "Use my name when you check in. Everything for the hotel and dinner is already taken care of. See you tomorrow morning around nine."

Gunner smiled as he stepped out of the taxi at the marina. He was only several feet from the entrance when a string of firecrackers exploded in the vacant lot next to the marina. A group of teenagers cheered and gathered to light another string. Gunner flinched and hunched over, while grabbing his head and leaned against the wall. He tried to fight the panic of another PTSD episode. All he could hear was the chatter of AK47s shredding thick jungle foliage and Viet Cong yelling as they scoured the area trying to find him and Vin.

Gunner held his head with both hands and fought the urge to vomit. Over time, he'd learned these violent bouts of PTSD would pass—he just had to hang on long enough. Gradually the panic and nausea subsided. His breathing slowed, and his vision returned. He was relieved that no one saw him.

He wiped the sweat off his face and took a couple of deep breaths before he walked away from the yacht club. He needed time to recover, so he took a walk along a boardwalk overlooking the marina.

Gunner remembered how difficult it had been for Cody to return to normal life after their tour. Cody and Gunner had taken jobs in Miami while Jett went to law school. They had seen each other regularly, but Miami was not a healthy place for Cody. He had spent too much time and money in clubs with people of dubious backgrounds from all over Latin America. Cody had struggled with PTSD and turned, unfortunately, to alcohol and drugs. Gunner understood his pain.

After a fifteen-minute walk along the harbor, Gunner's headache had subsided, so he walked back to the marina. The open layout of their small office was designed for boat sales and administrative activities for the various businesses. Gunner had insisted that Cody keep his expenses low, so Cody was allowed just one employee—Bonita—who squealed when she saw Gunner walk in. She jumped from her seat and wrapped her arms around him.

"I'm so glad you could come."

"This worked out perfect."

Bonita kissed him on the cheek. "Did you go home? I'm sorry about Kate."

"She's in a better place."

"Did you see Tom?"

Gunner sadly nodded.

She hugged harder than he expected and then whispered, "I've missed you."

Gunner pulled her away just enough so he could see her eyes. "Are you okay?"

She looked away. Before Gunner could ask another question, Cody banged on the glass window of his office to get Gunner's attention. Cody, on a call, waved and pointed to his phone.

Gunner turned back to Bonita. "How's my favorite girl?"

"Lonely without you."

"I bet you say that to all the captains that walk through this door."

"Only to old bachelors like you."

"Don't start on me again."

"You're so pathetic. You should've married a sweet girl like me long ago."

Gunner glanced over to see if Cody was still on the phone. "Why does Cody always have the drapes partially closed every time I stop by?"

"You know why."

"Is he taking his medicine?"

She shrugged. "Most of the time."

Gunner shook his head. "He's been like this his entire life. Everything's dark in his world." He smiled and grabbed Bonita around the waist again. "That is—everything except you!"

Bonita was a godsend to Cody, and Gunner loved her like a sister. Even though Cody acted like he was the boss, Bonita ran the business. Cody could be as charming as he could be mean. Like a light switch, you never knew what would set him off. Nevertheless, Bonita and

Gunner both had a soft spot for him.

Gunner glanced at Cody and pointed to his watch, then turned back to Bonita. "He's not working, is he?"

"Probably on the phone with one of his bookies."

Gunner frowned. "The building looks good with new white paint, but what about all the other renovations I ordered? I don't see anything done on the marina."

She looked at the floor. "I wanted to call you, but…"

Gunner lifted her chin and looked into her face. "Don't worry. I'll talk with him. We're going to Billy's Beach House for lunch."

"Oh, God, get off my side. The last time you went to lunch with Cody, I didn't see either of you for three days."

Cody finished his call and came out to see Gunner, who was still holding onto Bonita. "Hey, can you take your grimy hands off my girl?"

"Why should I? She needs better lovin' than you give her."

Bonita squeezed Gunner's neck again and kissed him on the cheek. Then she pointed her index finger at Cody's nose. "I know where you're going for lunch. If you're not back in two hours, I'm coming to look for both with a baseball bat."

* * *

It was a typical day on the island—blue skies and seventy-five degrees. They found a table on the deck of the restaurant and ordered gin and tonics and lunch to come.

"Great to see you again," Cody said. "I didn't expect you."

Gunner watched Cody's right knee bouncing rapidly under the table. "Just wanted to check on a few things. I'm still short one crew member and hired the woman that Bonita sent over. But I need Bonita to find one more."

"It's not the people. The problem is with the captain they report to."

Gunner laughed.

"No, I'm serious. You have a reputation." Cody shook his head. "I have to beg people to work for you."

"That's not true. I haven't lost a female crew member in over six months." He smiled. "They love me."

"But you treat the men like shit. It's a fucking revolving door on your yachts."

"I have high expectations, but I run a good ship. You know that. These guys aren't men. They act like teenage boys who don't have their frontal lobes developed yet. I can put up with it on some yachts, but not with this new owner. This guy, Rizzo, is one serious dude."

The waiter came with their food. They ate in silence for a minute.

"You look different," Gunner said.

"What do you mean?"

"I don't know—nervous maybe. Anything you want to tell me?"

"I have an important phone call this afternoon with a woman who's representing a buyer for a boat."

"I'm not talking about that." Gunner waited for Cody to fess up.

The server interrupted them with two fresh drinks. "Compliments of the owner," she explained.

They waved their thanks at the man behind the bar.

"Let's get this over with—why hasn't the marina been renovated the way we discussed? The only thing that's been done is a new coat of paint." Gunner waited for an answer.

"No worries. Just waiting for materials."

Gunner glared at Cody. "Cut the bullshit. What's going on?"

Cody fiddled with his glass. "Things have been slow lately, but I have a great opportunity to change that."

"Enlighten me."

"I have an order for three go-fast boats at one million a pop."

Gunner leaned forward and glared. "We've talked about this before. No drug money boats."

"Why not? We can make up all the money we lost last year with one order."

"Who wants to order the boats, your Russian friends?"

Cody avoided looking at Gunner.

"I thought so." Gunner pointed his finger. "Cancel the order. We don't need that kind of trouble."

"But they want two more as soon as possible. Anyway, I'm not breaking the law—just selling some boats."

Gunner sat back in his chair. He placed his sunglasses on the table. "Look at me. You don't want to get involved with these people. It's a very slippery slope."

"What do you mean by that?"

Gunner sighed and took another drink of his gin and tonic. "Just do what I said."

They sat in silence for a minute, looking out over the water, until Gunner asked, "How are you feeling these days? Taking your medicine?"

Cody didn't answer.

"For Christ's sake, if you don't take your meds, the nightmares and migraines will take over again."

"I'm fine. Bonita's my warden. She makes sure that I don't go off the rails."

"Will you call me if you need anything or just need to talk?" Gunner stared at Cody until he nodded.

"How do you like Rizzo's yacht?" Cody asked.

Gunner frowned. "I hate these stinkpots. I'd much rather be on the Rainbow. I'm the babysitter of thirty immature crew members that you provide for me. My biggest problem is keeping them in their berths at night." Gunner shook his head.

They both laughed.

"How's Bonita?" Gunner asked.

He took another bite of the calamari. "Great. But she misses her family. I send her back to Miami every other month for a visit."

"You should marry that girl before I do or someone else."

Cody scowled. "Don't start that again."

"Well, what's holding you back?"

"I don't want to be tied down." Cody pointed at Gunner. "What's your excuse?"

"Just think about it. Other than Jett and me, who the hell would put up with you."

Cody shook his head. "I know."

Gunner checked his watch. "I need to get back to Monaco."

Chapter Seven

The flight from the Dominican Republic back to Monaco was uneventful. Gunner was glad to be back on the yacht and focused on the upcoming trip to St. Thomas. After a long status meeting with Marco, he was confident the ship was ready. Gunner arrived on the bridge and took the captain's chair. "Marco, are we ready to shove off?"

"Yes, Captain."

"Navigation, do you have us dialed into the Canary Islands? We'll need to refuel there before we cross the Atlantic."

"Yes, Captain," the young man answered.

"Where's my coffee?"

A young sailor rushed to pour Gunner a cup from the coffee pot on the counter.

"Marco, start the engines. Are the tenders ready to escort us out of the harbor?"

"They're in position waiting for your order."

Gunner pointed to the open water. "Let's go."

* * *

Later that evening, Rizzo was busy entertaining twenty guests. As required, Gunner mixed with the guests during happy hour and dinner. He hated wearing his all-white captain uniform. It was so ostentatious. He mingled just long enough to keep Rizzo happy and then stepped out onto a large deck where Nika was standing against the rail under a night sky.

"Counting shooting stars?"

"It's so beautiful," Nika said without changing her gaze toward the horizon.

"I never get tired of it. Why aren't you dancing with the others?"

"I needed some fresh air." She lit a Dunhill cigarette. "I hate these parties. Such boring people."

"Look." He pointed. "We have company." A dozen dolphins surfaced just off the bow. They leaped and chased each other, leaving blue, fluorescent streaks.

She leaned closer to the rail. "What's causing the water to glow?"

The dolphins frolicked in the large wave created by the bow.

"The dolphins' movement in the concentrations of algae or plankton triggers a bioluminescent reaction, and they glow in the dark. Some call plankton the fireflies of the sea."

"Amazing."

"Must be your lucky night," Gunner said.

Nika turned and looked at Gunner. "Why do you say that?"

"Because dolphins are considered a sign of good fortune for sailors. They're a gift from the sea and bring good luck, especially to young, beautiful women."

Nika laughed. "How many women have you used that line of bullshit on?"

Gunner feigned a look of shock. "None. You don't believe me?"

"Hardly."

Gunner smiled. "You may not by the first, but you are the prettiest."

Nika shook her head. "I'll give you credit—that was the most original line I've heard."

"Captains learn in sailing school how to charm beautiful women. Part of our job description."

"Let me guess." She laughed again. "You got an A in that class."

Gunner smiled as she turned back to find more dolphins. After a minute or two, she turned around to face him, leaning back against the railing. "We haven't talked like this since the night we met at Rizzo's pool."

"I know."

"So, I have to be nice to you?"

"Up to you." Gunner stepped closer to her along the railing. "Remind me—how long have you worked for Rizzo?"

She smiled and threw her cigarette into the water. "It's a boring story, but if you recall, I met Rizzo while I was working for Bykov.

"And you met Bykov how?"

"I was working in Kyiv for another client. There was a misunderstanding of sorts."

"And Bykov helped you out?"

"With a great favor."

"Is it uncomfortable to be working for Rizzo when you used to work for Bykov?"

"Do all captains ask so many questions or just you?"

"I ask questions because your story is far from boring. What made you come to work for Rizzo?"

She didn't answer but turned her face to the moon. She licked her dark red lips and brushed the hair away from her face.

"What're you doing?" Gunner asked.

"Drinking the moon. You should try it sometime," she said. "It's good for the soul."

"Ahh, so you have a soul. I wasn't sure."

"I was speaking of your soul." She smiled coyly.

"Enjoy the evening," he said. "We arrive in the Canary Islands tomorrow night." Gunner looked at his watch. "I have to check on our course."

* * *

Later that night, Gunner carried a small pillow and a rolled-up mat onto the observation deck, the highest point of the yacht just above the bridge. He stretched out and wished his mind were as calm as the sea. The deserted decks below glowed softly from the halo of various night lights. As he stared at the Milky Way, he wished he were on the Rainbow.

"Sorry, I didn't know anyone was out here," Palmer said from behind him.

Gunner sat up and turned his head. "What are you doing?"

Palmer sat down next to him and crossed her legs. "The same thing as you."

Gunner frowned.

"I can leave if you want. Just give me an order."

Gunner laid back on his pillow.

Taking this as a dismissal, Palmer started to get up when Gunner said, "You can stay."

Palmer set down her book on the deck and stretched out on her back with her hands behind her head. "Amazing. You can almost touch the stars from here."

"What are you reading?"

"*The Runaway Jury* by John Grisham. It's one of the hottest bestselling books of the summer. It just came out."

Neither spoke for a long time until Gunner asked, "How's the job so far?"

"Fine. I enjoy the intellectual stimulation of cleaning bathrooms and making beds."

"I knew you'd be perfect for the job."

"Thanks for the opportunity," she said sarcastically. "I'm forever grateful."

Gunner smiled, and then they fell quiet again.

Finally, Gunner asked, "Why are you up? Can't you sleep?"

Palmer paused. "Not tonight."

"Happen often?"

Palmer didn't answer right away, but then asked Gunner, "What keeps you up at night?"

"Making sure the crew stays in their cabin."

Palmer laughed. "How's that working?"

Gunner chuckled. "Maybe I should start midnight bed checks."

"Have you seen *Mutiny on the Bounty*?"

"Okay, bad idea." After a few moments, Gunner turned his head toward Palmer. "Why?"

"Why what?"

"Why are you on the Destiny? You're too smart to be cleaning cabins."

"I don't know." She hesitated. "I can't explain it, but I love water, and I've always wanted to crew on one of these mega yachts. Just to see what it's like."

Gunner pointed toward the ship below. "Is it what you expected?"

"Yes and no."

Gunner waited. Palmer didn't explain, so he added, "Funny, isn't it? We think we know what we want, but so often when we get it, we realize it's not what we've been searching for." He sighed. "It's as if the universe is playing a joke on us because we have to start all over without a clue."

Palmer nodded. "T. S. Eliot said something like that."

"Who?"

"A famous poet. My college professor asked only one question for our final in a philosophy class. He quoted Eliot, 'We shall not cease from exploration, and the end of all our exploring will be to arrive where we started—and know the place for the first time.' Then the asshole gave us three hours to write what it meant."

"A cruel sense of humor." Gunner turned his head toward Palmer. "What did you write?"

"At first, I wrote, 'Fuck You! This is bullshit.'"

Gunner chuckled. "Really?"

Palmer sighed. "I scratched it out because I needed this class to graduate. I was angry because I paid good money for that course, and it ended with a question rather than any answers. I'll never arrive where I started. My parents are dead, and I never knew them."

Gunner grunted and said, "I understand."

Palmer looked skeptical. "I doubt it. How could you understand what it feels like to be alone?"

Gunner sat up and stared at her for a few seconds. "I'm not sure you understood what your professor was asking."

"I should've had you write the essay for me."

"Sorry, but you won't find any revelations here either. This ship is a temporary waystation for people. Everyone's looking for something, and for some crazy reason they believe they might find it on this yacht." He shook his head. "They all move on at some point."

"Have you found what you're looking for?"

"We were talking about you, not me. Do you have a boyfriend back home?"

Palmer shook her head.

"Why not? You're smart and pretty."

She shot back, "I don't see a wedding ring on your finger."

"You said your parents died when you were young," Gunner said. "Where did you grow up?"

"What are you doing?"

"Nothing. Just getting to know you better."

"Why? You're the captain, and I'm a lowly cabin cleaner."

Gunner didn't respond at first but then added, "I'm sorry. I didn't mean to be rude. It may be hard to believe, but it gets a little lonely on the bridge."

"My parents were killed in a car accident when I was very young. I'm an only child without any relatives. I was raised in the foster care system and can't count the number of different places I lived in."

"Must've been rough."

"What about you?"

"Grew up in Maine." Gunner glanced at Palmer. "It sounds as if we have the same love for the water. It's in my DNA."

"What about your parents?"

"They are…" Gunner hesitated, "…nice."

"Nice?" Palmer said. "That's how you describe a park, not your parents."

"My parents are very different than me."

"Why did you decide to become a captain?" Palmer asked.

Gunner's eyes tightened. "Divine intervention. In 1970, I found myself lying in a Vietnam rice paddy. Half of my squad had been killed in the first few seconds of an ambush. The Viet Cong were slaughtering us from a tree line fifty yards away. It was raining so hard we couldn't pinpoint where the fire was coming from. I was hit in the left shoulder and knew it would be only a few minutes before I'd be killed. In those few seconds, I could see my dad standing next to the sailboat we built together in our backyard. He was smiling with his hand on the side of the boat. I prayed for the first time in my life, 'Please God, let me live.' At that moment, the rain stopped, and a huge rainbow appeared, and the Cobra gunships circling above us to clear the area of the Viet Cong suddenly had visibility. That rainbow was the most beautiful thing I'd ever seen. I knew then that if I survived my tour, I'd always live and work near the water." Gunner stopped speaking and stared at a full moon reflecting off the calm sea below them.

"Is that why you can't sleep?"

Gunner didn't respond. *How can I tell her my nightmares are filled with the faces of the Viet Cong I saw through my scope as I killed them?* he thought.

"Do you have PTSD?" Palmer asked.

Gunner changed the subject. "What about you? Why can't you sleep?"

"I have bad dreams too." Palmer couldn't be honest and describe the night she almost had been killed by the Russian mafia in Ukraine.

Gunner asked, "What do you want to do with your life? You can't work as a crew member forever."

"I don't know."

"Paint me your perfect job."

She shook her head and looked away.

"What's wrong?"

"You'd make fun of me."

"I'd never do that."

"It doesn't matter because women aren't allowed in your exclusive boys' club."

"From what I heard about you from other crew members, you don't seem the type to let anyone stop you from doing what you want."

Palmer grimaced. "So, it's that bad?"

"No, it's that good. Come on, tell me your dream."

She hesitated for a second. "I'd like to become a sea captain like you."

Gunner laughed. "Careful what you wish for." Gunner pointed to the ocean. "My love for water is the only constant in my life. Maybe I can help you."

"What's the point. I'd never get hired. I'm not aware of one female captain of a yacht over 150 feet." She sighed. "Plus, I don't have the money for the certification courses to get a license, so cleaning the toilets on big yachts was the next best thing." She laid back down. "It's so hard."

"What's so hard?"

"Everything."

"Remember, you're not alone as long as you're on my ship."

After a few minutes, Palmer turned her head to Gunner. "Thank you."

"For what?"

"You're the first person I've had a real conversation with since I lost my best friend in college."

"Friendship cuts both ways," Gunner paused and then added. "It's been a long time for me too."

"I don't want any charity," Palmer said.

"Do you know the difference between charity and grace?"

Palmer scrunched her face in confusion. "No."

"Love."

Palmer stared at Gunner for several seconds before she finally confessed, "I don't get it."

"Grace is a gift that's unearned." Gunner smiled. "If you want, I can teach you the basics of running a ship while you're working here. I know the director of one of the best schools for yacht certification, and they offer scholarships. I'll contact him and have him ship the textbooks you'll need for the initial captain certifications. The academics will not be hard, but it'll be difficult to accumulate the hours you need on the water to be certified for larger yachts. But I can help you with that. I have great connections with other captains."

"Why would you do that for me?"

He smiled. "Because we're friends."

* * *

It was dawn when Palmer left Gunner, but the ocean horizon glowed as she finally walked back to her cabin. She should feel tired after talking all night, but oddly, she was energized. This was not what she expected. She hadn't engaged anyone in a conversation like that since having all-nighters with her college roommate.

Palmer slipped into her cabin, careful not to wake Zoie. As she lay in bed, she had to remind herself that Gunner was one of the bad guys. Her job was to put Rizzo in prison along with anyone else involved with the new cartel. The DEA was convinced Nika was part of Rizzo's criminal organization, but they didn't have any hard evidence on Gunner yet. She closed her eyes. Maybe today, she would find some information of value from the other crew members or from snooping around the ship while housekeeping.

Later that morning, Palmer walked into the crew galley for breakfast and sat down next to Zoie with a plate of fruit and a coffee.

Zoie looked at Palmer's plate. "Watching your calories this morning?"

Palmer pushed blueberries around her plate. "No, just not hungry."

"Short night?"

Palmer glanced at Zoie out of the corner of her eye. "What do you mean?"

Zoie laughed. "Come on. We're not in high school, and I'm not your mom busting you for sneaking out. Who's the lucky guy?"

Palmer didn't look up. "I couldn't sleep, so I took a walk around the ship."

Zoie shook her head. "No reason to be shy." She waved her arm around the room. "Half the ship plays musical beds every night." Zoie pointed to the clock. "I'm so glad we're finally underway."

"Do you know the itinerary yet?"

"Nika told me St. Thomas and then Aruba."

Palmer changed the subject. "Hey, can we switch up the room schedule today? I need some variety. I'm tired of cleaning the same cabins every day."

Zoie frowned. "I don't think so. Nika's very particular about her cabin. And Gunner likes certain things done his way."

"Oh, come on. No one will know except you and me."

Zoie shook her head again and walked away.

* * *

The next day, Zoie sprained her ankle and was put on crutches giving Palmer the opportunity she was looking for. Finally, she would have access to the cabins of Rizzo, Gunner and Nika. She was sure that she'd find some incriminating information.

Palmer knocked on Nika's door three times and waited. She glanced down the hall in both directions before she slowly opened the door and yelled out "Housekeeping" to make sure Nika wasn't in. The cabin had a large, multi-purpose room that opened into a large bedroom and private bath. A large desk was filled with maps and various papers. Behind the desk was a long credenza under a series of small windows.

Palmer thought it odd that the room had no framed photos or any other personal items in it. She quickly shuffled through the documents on the desk for any information about the cartel, careful to make sure the papers were replaced in the same order.

On the bottom of one pile, she found a fax in Russian. She quickly read the note. Bingo! The fax described how a shipment had arrived at the Odesa seaport and had been transported to a warehouse awaiting further instructions. Palmer cross-referenced the information with the map of Odesa lying next to the stack of papers, then took out a miniature camera and snapped several photos, which were immediately encrypted.

Palmer froze when she heard a loud noise in the hallway. She glanced at the bucket and mop she had left next to the door, calculating how long it would take to sprint across the room and pretend to be cleaning. *Stupid mistake*, she thought. Fortunately, after a few moments, the chatter moved down the hall.

Palmer breathed a sigh of relief, moved the cleaning equipment close to her and went back to investigate. The desk drawers were all locked. There was nothing unusual in the bedroom except a half-empty bottle of Russian vodka and a carton of Dunhill cigarettes. She entered the bathroom and searched the medicine cabinet behind the bathroom mirror. Palmer felt sorry for Nika when she saw it contained several bottles of Prozac and Valium. She shook her head and closed the cabinet door.

During a quick search of the closets, she found a small safe. Palmer took pictures of the locking mechanism, and the safe serial number hoping her team at the DEA would know how to unlock it. She jumped when she heard someone enter the cabin. She closed the closet door and started to dust around the bedstand between the bed and the closet.

Zoie popped her head into the bedroom. "Happy?"

Palmer turned and feigned surprise. She placed her hand on her heart. "You scared me. What are you doing here?"

"Just checking on you."

Palmer froze for a second when she realized that she had set her camera on the bedstand next to the closet. She said a prayer and tried to casually step between Zoie and the bedstand.

Zoie moved into the room on her crutches and looked around. "Make sure the toilet and bathtub are spotless, otherwise she'll know I didn't clean it."

"No problem," Palmer said. "How are you feeling?"

"Bored. I'm sick of sitting in our cabin." Zoie adjusted the crutches under her arms. "When are you done?"

"I have Gunner's cabin next and then four more after that."

Zoie cocked her head. "You okay?"

"Why?"

"You're sweating, and your face is red."

Palmer wiped the sweat off her forehead. "Don't you think it's hot in here?"

Zoie glanced at her watch. "I have to go. Meet you for lunch at noon."

Zoie left, and Palmer sat down on the bed to let her heartbeat return to normal. Even though she'd been undercover for a long time, she still became nervous when searching someone's home—or in this case, cabin.

Palmer moved on to Gunner's cabin. She laughed as she closed the door and compared the two cabins. Gunner's main room was a mess. Piles of old yachting magazines covered half of his credenza, along with dozens of picture frames of Gunner with various celebrities and friends in locations around the world. A large map on the desk had a line drawn from Monaco to the Canary Islands, where Gunner had scribbled in terrible handwriting "Refuel." Next to Santa Cruz de Tenerife, the main port in the Canary Islands, was a handwritten note indicating the estimated fuel amount and cost, along with a list of supplies he needed before sailing to St. Thomas.

She quickly searched the rest of the cabin but didn't find anything to link Gunner directly to the cartel or other criminal activities tied to Rizzo. Before Palmer had been hired, she had assumed Gunner was an active part of the Rizzo's organization. *One couldn't be a captain on the Destiny and work closely with Rizzo and be an innocent bystander,* Palmer had thought.

She was confused. She liked Gunner. Despite their age difference, to her surprise, they have a lot in common. She was enchanted by their unexpectedly intimate conversion. Even though the story about her dream job as a captain wasn't true, she was surprised by his offer to help her. He seemed like such a nice man, although she knew from experience that her heart was a bad judge of character. It was only a matter of time before she'd find the evidence the DEA believed would make him an accomplice. *This is my last assignment,* she thought. *Once this is over, I'm out of the spy business.*

***

Two days later, the crew refueled and restocked supplies in the Canary Islands and resumed their trip across the Atlantic. As they left port, Marco printed off the latest weather report. Marco frowned and handed the report to Palmer while pointing to the headlines in red capital letters. Although Palmer was hired in housekeeping, this was the first time that Gunner had invited her to observe the operations on the bridge.

Palmer quickly read the weather report and handed it back to Marco. "What does this mean?"

"Not good," Marco said as he studied the data again. Without looking up, he shouted across the room to Gunner. "Cap, a low pressure is forming downstream, right in the middle of our usual route to St. Thomas."

Gunner nodded but didn't take his eyes off the deep blue horizon.

Marco added, "The winds are picking up, and this system could turn into a hurricane before we can reach the islands." He paused, waiting for Gunner to respond.

Gunner motioned to Palmer to join him outside the bridge. The air was heavy with heat and humidity. Palmer watched Gunner close his eyes and take a deep breath.

"Can you feel it?" Gunner asked.

"Feel what?"

Gunner opened his eyes and turned to Palmer. "This is going to be a big one."

"How can you tell?" she asked. "It's a postcard day."

Gunner frowned and rubbed his chin. "The pressure has dropped rapidly since breakfast. Don't you feel it?"

"Are you kidding?" Palmer said, astonished. "I'm not a human barometer."

"Marco can teach you how to read the ship's gauges, the computers and the navigation charts, but I want to teach you how to trust your instincts. Someday, if you're lucky, you may become a captain, and you'll have to make difficult decisions. The ship and people's lives are your responsibility. You won't find the answer to your options in a book. You have to trust your judgment, and that comes from experience and respect for the sea. The weather can change within an hour, and you have to be prepared to change course quickly."

"Story of my life."

"Close your eyes."

Palmer reached for the railing, but Gunner gently touched her hand. "Don't hold onto the railing. Feel the ocean beneath us."

After a minute, he asked. "What do you feel?"

"Small swells followed by a large wave."

"Don't open your eyes until I tell you." After another five

minutes, Gunner tapped Palmer on the shoulder. "What do you feel? Any change?"

"I'm not sure, but I think the swells are getting bigger and coming just a little faster."

Gunner squeezed her hand. "Now look to the south."

In the distance, small clouds had appeared just above the horizon where moments before, the sky had been clear.

Palmer frowned. "I'll never be captain. I can't feel what you do."

"Sailing is about a personal relationship with the sea. Not about the boat. Not about the technology we use to run it. The sea is fickle. She can be as kind and gentle as your best friend or as violent as anything on earth. But it's never cruel. Never making excuses. That's something only we do to each other. The sea's exactly who she needs to be as she dances with the southern hemisphere jet streams."

Gunner stopped when he realized that Palmer was staring at him. He shrugged. "Don't pay any attention to what I said. I'm just an old sea dog."

"That was beautiful," Palmer said as she placed her hand on his bare forearm.

Gunner flinched.

She noticed a small rainbow tattoo on his arm. She leaned closer and touched the tattoo with her index finger.

Gunner shifted uncomfortably and pulled his arm away. "We need to prepare the ship." Avoiding eye contact, he asked her, "Can you work with Marco to inform the crew to start locking everything down below?"

"Aye aye, Captain." She smiled and left him at the railing.

Gunner checked his watch. It would be dark soon, and he needed to make some decisions. Before he could walk back inside, Nika stepped out from the bridge and walked to the railing beside him.

"Private lessons?"

Gunner sighed but didn't answer.

"She's a little young for you, don't you think?"

"Fuck you."

"I don't get it," she said, shaking her head. "Girls always fall for the white uniform, especially the young ones."

"What do you want?"

"Does it ever get tiring?"

"What?"

"This." Nika waved her arms. "Everyone expects you to take care of them. To advance their careers. To give them advice. To solve their problems. Bail them out of trouble. Your buddies, Cody and Jett, call when they need help. And then your little pet, Palmer—"

"That's enough," Gunner growled.

"My, aren't we sensitive today?" Nika lit a cigarette and took a long drag. "I'm curious, who do you go to when you have a problem? It must get lonely, living all by yourself in a cabin at the top of this ship."

Gunner gripped the steel railing. "What do you want, Nika?"

"Rizzo is nervous about the Columbians. He's worried that they'll double-cross him. Castillo is extremely ambitious."

Gunner scoffed, "Like someone else we know."

Nika shrugged slightly. "You have connections throughout the Caribbean. Can you find out if Castillo is planning anything nefarious for when we get to Aruba?"

Gunner laughed.

"He doesn't trust Castillo," Nika added.

"Does he trust anyone?"

Nika shook her head. "I don't understand why, but for some reason, he trusts you."

"Aah! So, I have that going for me," Gunner said. "Careful, trust can be a fickle friend. Like the difference between blame and forgiveness. It can depend on your point of view." He stopped and turned to Nika. "The only thing you can trust about me is that I have a lot of experience at both."

The sound of laughter from Rizzo's guests floated to them from a pool three floors below.

Gunner leaned closer. "So, Nika, what's in this for you?"

Nika flicked her cigarette over the railing without responding. Then she crossed her arms, leaned with her back against the rail and turned to face him. "Money. What else is there? What about you? You can't be a captain forever."

Gunner shook his head. "I wish I had a nickel for every unhappy, wealthy person I've met over the years."

Marco poked his head out from the bridge and yelled, "Captain, we need you."

"Nika, sorry. I'm busy right now. We have a major storm approaching. I'll let you know if I find out anything about Castillo."

* * *

Palmer left Gunner on the bridge and returned to the crew lounge. Marco arrived shortly after and began giving instructions to the crew. Palmer slid into a booth next to Zoie.

"Where have you been?" Zoie whispered.

"On the bridge with Gunner."

"What for?"

Marco stopped speaking and pointed at Zoie. "This is important, pay attention." He handed out a list of tasks assigned to each crew member. "I want these done within two hours. No excuses. We have diverted our route to avoid the worst of the storm, but this system is so large we'll have to sail through part of it. Tell the guests they have to stay in their cabins until further notice."

Palmer looked at her action list—secure the supply rooms, provide bottled water and snacks to each of the guest cabins and then report to the bridge. Palmer was surprised at the last item. *Why was she was called to the bridge?* she wondered.

Palmer asked Zoie, "Where are you off to?"

"Galley, kitchen supply room and then the boat bay to secure all the tender boats and other equipment." Zoie frowned as she reviewed her list. "This is going to take more than two hours."

"I'll come to the boat bay to help you after I get my list done. I've never been close to a hurricane. This is going to be fun."

"I doubt it. I guarantee half the guests will be barfing in their cabins, and we'll be the ones cleaning it up." Zoie leaned closer to Palmer. "What did Gunner want with you on the bridge?"

Palmer shrugged. "Just chit-chat."

"Come on, fess up. Gunner does not 'chit-chat.'"

They started to walk when Palmer turned to Zoie and asked, "What do you think about Gunner?"

"What do you mean?"

"I don't know—just curious." Palmer shuffled her feet. "I'm still trying to get to know everyone on board. We better hurry, or Marco will have a fit. Meet you in the boat bay in an hour."

* * *

After checking with the bridge one more time, Gunner tried to get some sleep. A rush of wind through the open portal window woke him up. He had given strict orders for Marco to wake him if the winds reached over thirty miles per hour. The earlier stars were gone, and the ship was rolling significantly in heavier seas.

He checked his watch—two o'clock. Earlier that afternoon, he had adjusted the navigation setting to avoid the hurricane, but the direction of a storm this strong could change quickly. Even though he wasn't due on the bridge for another four hours, he knew the storm would make this a long night.

He drifted off for a time but woke up from a dream. Why, of all times, did the ghost of a father he'd never met interrupt his sleep? His dreams were usually about an imaginary mother, but the main character in this one was an apparition that called his name as if searching for a child who had been lost in the woods. The ghost lurked just outside of Gunner's vision, never showing its face, but somehow Gunner knew it was his real father. In desperation, he shouted to the ghost a question that had haunted him since childhood—"Who am I?"

The imaginary father never answered. Maybe his real father couldn't answer because he didn't have any history with Gunner after he was born. Even though they shared the same blood and the same genes, they shared nothing else. They had no memories of each other because Gunner's biological father was absent when he was born and never came to the hospital.

No one believed Gunner, but he remembered things before he was born. He recalled his mother singing soft lullabies while cradling him in her womb. While the rest of the world was born into soft hands and loving eyes, Gunner was born upside down and backward with his eyes away from his mother and loud cursing in his ears. He had been violently yanked out of his mother like a baby calf. A breech delivery, they would later call it, usually with a shrug and a sad shake of the head. What kind of God would drag a baby into the world upside down and then take his parents away?

Gunner was born prematurely. At thirty-four weeks, Gunner was not ready to be born, and her parents weren't home. Once the contractions began in earnest, his mother had waddled to her next-door neighbor's house, desperate for a ride to the hospital. The baby was born on the floor of the neighbor's living room, where his mother had collapsed after her water had broken and the bleeding had begun. Gunner's first physical contact with the world was in the rough, calloused hands of the neighbor, a retired rancher, who wrapped the infant in a scratchy wool barn blanket that smelled of dust and horses.

Instead of smiles and shouts of joy, the first sounds Gunner heard were of his mother crying and the neighbor frantically telling the police to hurry, followed by a string of curses about how a winter storm would delay their arrival. The touch of wool and the sound of a siren still made Gunner cringe.

Gunner's father never held him at birth because the ambulance had taken Gunner away before he arrived at the neighbor's house. People say it's not possible but during Gunner's stay in the hospital, he remembered the nurses feeding him and rocking him to sleep in the nursery as he waited each day for his father and mother to take him home. But they never came.

Two months later, he was taken away by his new parents, Tom and Kate.

When Gunner reached his thirteenth birthday, his parents shared that he was adopted. He wasn't surprised. In some ways, he had always known. He didn't look or act like them. He was stocky but athletic, while his parents were physically small and slight in stature. Always impatient and impulsive, he wore his emotions on his sleeve, loved the outdoors and water, and hated structure and school. In contrast, his parents were intellectuals, sedentary by nature, quiet, stoic and preferred music and literature to nature.

The only thing Gunner had in common with Tom was their mutual love of sailing. Other than building a sailboat with his father, Gunner was left on his own for most of his youth. He spent most of his time alone and outdoors, swimming, sailing and exploring the woods near their home.

As he grew older, rather than believe that he was unloved and abandoned by a mother that never wanted him, Gunner had made up a story that his biological parents were young—too young to keep him when he was born. Maybe that's why his father and mother had refused to see him at the hospital.

Gunner knew that experts insisted people couldn't remember their births because babies don't have memories. He'd been told he must have imagined what had happened. But he also knew the experts were wrong. Gunner remembered. He remembered everything.

It was always in the dark, late at night, when he would let the anger creep into his heart. He hated his biological parents for abandoning him. *Who gives up their flesh and blood?* Gunner blamed them for never contacting him and leaving him alone, never knowing who his real parents were.

Now, as an adult, he shook his fist at the ghosts that haunted his nights. He often wondered what happened to his parents. Did they marry? Did he have siblings? Did they go separate ways? Did they ever think about him? How do you forgive parents you never met?

In the end, he always blamed himself because he was the cause of their distress, the evidence of a sin that could not be forgiven. If only he could meet his real parents, maybe then he could forgive them—and perhaps they could forgive him.

A loud knock woke Gunner. From outside the cabin door, Marco said, "Captain, sorry, but the winds are gusting over thirty miles an hour, and the swells are reaching twenty feet." He paused. "You told me to wake you."

Gunner sighed and rolled out of bed. "I'll meet you on the bridge in fifteen minutes."

He flicked on the light and looked at his watch. It would be dawn in an hour, and then the fun would begin.

On the bridge, the windshield wipers were on full speed, but it was impossible to see much due to the wind and rain.

Gunner glanced at Marco. "Status report."

"Weather report has gotten worse. The winds could reach a category four, between 113 and 156 miles per hour near the center of the hurricane. We're getting gusts over forty already, and we're only on the fringe."

Gunner walked over to the radar. "Any signs of ships in our area?"

"No, we're fifty miles south of the normal shipping lanes."

"I don't care. I want someone watching the radar continuously until I give the order to stop. I'm convinced this storm has scattered ships all over the place. Any water damage?"

"No water breeches. Watertight so far."

"Good. What about the guests? Anyone checked on them?"

"Only two guests have complained. The usual seasickness. I sent the ship's medical officer to handle the house calls."

* * *

As dawn arrived, the winds were increasing. In the early light, the crew cringed at the wild, angry seas surrounding the ship. Marco suddenly yelled out, "Brace yourself."

Everyone gripped something as a huge wave burst over the bow of the ship, flooding everything on the first level. The crew looked worried as the bow of the ship climbed the next thirty-foot wave before plunging into the steep trough of the next swell.

Gunner stood next to the young man steering the ship and gave him some reassurance, "Steady now. You're doing great. Just make sure we stay perpendicular to the waves as best you can. We'll be in some trouble if the ship gets sideways to a large wave."

The young man's hands trembled as he held a coffee cup.

Gunner walked around the bridge and put his arm around some of the younger crew. He laughed, "Everyone, relax! We're driving a three-hundred-foot yacht. She can take much worse than this. We'll have an adventure for a couple of hours, and then everything will be back to normal."

He walked to the radar and studied the weather report. After a minute, he ordered the ship's navigator to turn south another twenty degrees and hold that track. Then he yelled over his shoulder, "Somebody, get me a hot coffee."

Gunner continued to scan the weather report when suddenly he looked up. "What was that?"

The crew looked confused. No one answered.

"Did anyone feel that?" Gunner scanned the room. "Marco?"

"I didn't feel anything."

Gunner rushed to the ship's phone. "Jacob, this is the captain. Is something wrong in the engine room? Did we hit anything? Something is wrong!"

He nodded a few times, while listening to the response. "Yeah, I remember," he said, then laughed. "Crossing Cape Horn was far worse," he said before hanging up.

He walked to the window and scanned the chaos outside. The yacht rolled through the next trough but was slow to recover. Gunner turned and yelled at Marco, "I knew it! We must be taking in water. Check the boat bay. Get a crew down there ASAP and call me."

Ten minutes later, the phone rang on the bridge. Gunner grabbed the handle. "Marco, what do you have?" Gunner listened for a minute, then said, "Good. Glad the damage is only at the waterline. Yeah, I'll send a crew to help."

Suddenly, he pointed at a huge wave. "Brace yourselves!" Another rogue wave hit the ship, at least fifty feet high. Papers, coffee cups, pens and maps flew into the air as the ship crested the wave and dropped into the trough. The ship shuddered but held its tack into the next swell.

"Marco, you'll have to do the best you can to make the patch while we're bouncing around." Gunner said. "Glad the crack is not severe. Must've been something drifting in the ocean. I want a report every fifteen minutes to make sure the pumps are keeping up."

Gunner sat in the captain's chair and assessed the crew on the bridge. No one was talking as they shared nervous looks. Trying to reassure everyone, he shouted, "This is fun!" above the noise of wind and rain pounding the window. After a few minutes, he picked up the phone and dialed. "Palmer, Gunner here. Come to the bridge. I want to show you something."

A few minutes later, Palmer stepped onto the bridge. Gunner pointed at the waves battering the bow of the ship. "What do you think?"

"Terrifying, but—" she stopped speaking as a wave covered the deck of the first floor with white foam. "But beautiful."

Gunner smiled. "Exactly."

"Are we safe?" Palmer asked.

"Absolutely." Gunner added, "There is only one scenario that would cause a serious problem in a storm like this."

"What's that?"

"If we lost power." Gunner smiled. "However, no worries. We have twin engines and redundancy for all critical systems."

Palmer cringed as they began to climb the next wave. "Isn't that what they said on the Titanic?"

Gunner laughed. "Oh, ye of little faith," he crooned. But then he stood up from his chair, "Shit!" An instant later, multiple alarm bells rang, and the engines stopped.

Palmer asked. "How did you know something was wrong?"

Gunner ignored her, walked to the control panel and put his hand on the shoulder of the sailor. "Try to keep her into the wind as best you can." Gunner picked up the phone again. "Jacob, talk to me . . . I understand. Call me as soon as you find out what caused the shutdown. Do you think it's mechanical or the computers? We should never lose power to both engines at the same time."

The ship started drifting with waves pushing the bow more parallel to the waves. Each swell caused the ship to roll more violently. After ten minutes, the phone rang, and Gunner picked up. "Jacob, we need power now." He listened for a few seconds. "What about the backup power generator?" Gunner frowned. "Fuck the computers. We have to bypass the computer and manually reboot the primary engine. We only need one engine for now. We can work on the second one later. I'll be right down to show you how."

Gunner glanced at Palmer and shook his head. "I'll be right back. This is a good lesson for you if you're going to be a captain. You can't rely on computers or other people for every problem or you are fucked. You have to *own* everything about the ship."

Twenty minutes later, the right engine started, and they slowly resumed the trip. By the time Gunner returned to the bridge, the rain had stopped, and the waves were less severe. He sat in his chair and sipped his coffee.

"Palmer, is this your first hurricane on the water?" Gunner asked. "You looked scared."

Palmer blushed. "Never felt so helpless. So humbled at the sheer power of the sea."

"Good, that's what I wanted you to learn today. You have to respect the sea." Gunner looked at Palmer. "The minute you take her for granted, she'll turn on you." He paused. "Do you understand what I'm trying to tell you?"

"Not a clue," Palmer said.

"Ah—people have a choice to forgive mistakes, but with the sea, you may never get a second chance."

Six hours later, they broke through the last of the storm into calm seas. Rizzo called Gunner for a meeting on the patio of deck level four. A table was set for three with fresh juices, fruit and various baked goods. Rizzo was already seated when Gunner arrived.

Rizzo smiled as he sipped a cappuccino and waved for Gunner to have a seat. Rizzo was dressed in a colorful Hawaiian shirt and white shorts. He always wore dark designer sunglasses so people couldn't read his eyes. "Do you want to order something from the chef?"

Gunner waved him off. "No, I already ate."

"Quite the storm."

Gunner nodded. "Sorry, it got a little exciting for a while when we lost power. I'll have the entire engine overhauled when we get to St. Thomas. This will not happen again."

"Good, but that's not why I wanted to see you." Rizzo lit a cigar. "What do you know about this guy, Carlos Castillo, the head of the Columbian cartel?"

Gunner shrugged. "Just the generic profile of a Columbian boss. Ambitious, ruthless, cruel."

Rizzo waited. "And...?"

"He's different than the 'B' players. More dangerous."

"What do you mean?"

Gunner raised his finger at the waiter standing a dozen feet away. "One Bloody, please." He played with his fork. "Castillo is not motivated by making more money, just by accumulating power. Guys like that will do anything to achieve more power." Gunner smiled. "You know the kind."

Rizzo burst into laughter. "God bless you. You're the only one with the balls to talk to me this way." He pulled his chair closer to Gunner. "Seriously, I've never met Castillo. Our arrangement was negotiated through Nika and Bykov." He looked around the table to make sure no one was within earshot. "I'm nervous when I'm not in complete control. And I'm dangerous when I'm nervous."

"I understand. So, how can I help you?"

"Can you use your contacts to find out more information about Castillo?"

"Why don't you ask Nika and Bykov?"

"Because I don't trust them."

Gunner nodded. "I'll check around and see what I can find out."

The waiter approached the table carrying Gunner's Bloody Mary. After he left, Gunner asked. "Are you having second thoughts?"

Rizzo took his sunglasses off. "What are you, some kind of a savant?"

"Something like that."

Rizzo looked out over the railing. "Beautiful morning, isn't it? Reminds me of the ocean below my seaside home in Sicily. I'm glad you had a chance to see my country by helicopter—so you can understand why I'm doing this."

Gunner waited.

Finally, Rizzo turned back to Gunner. "You saw the poverty of my people in Sicily. I can't continue to provide the money needed to operate the schools, hospitals and everything else without a larger source of revenue. If I don't do this deal, hundreds of businesses will fail because my organization is the only one that provides the capital they need to run their businesses. As you know, the Italian government is corrupt and doesn't give a shit about Sicily. We are on our own—and have been for a long time."

"Set aside Castillo for the moment. What about your side of the deal with Bykov? How sure are you that he'll deliver the goods?"

"I have good sources in Ukraine that will verify the shipment before it leaves the dock."

"Who is your source?"

Rizzo didn't answer.

"Not Nika."

Rizzo nodded. "She has the relationship with Bykov."

"I thought you said you didn't trust her."

"I know."

"Then what are you worried about?"

"Everything else."

"Rizzo, why don't you shut this down and figure out another way to expand your cash flow that doesn't involve heroin, Bykov or Castillo?"

Rizzo sucked on his cigar. "I'm stuck."

Gunner nodded.

"I never asked for this," Rizzo said angrily. "I was born into the responsibility passed on to me by my father, his father, and his father."

"How much time do you have before the shipment leaves Odesa?"

Rizzo tilted his head toward the lounge doorway. "Let's ask her?"

Nika pulled out her chair and set her wide-brimmed hat on the seat between her and Gunner. "Good morning, gentlemen. How long have you been here? Did I make a mistake on the time?"

"No, no," Rizzo reassured her. "We were just catching up on the ship's status after the storm." Rizzo passed a plate of food toward Nika.

She waved him off, lit a Dunhill and opened her notebook. "I have a long list of issues to discuss."

Rizzo laughed. "Can't you relax for once? Look around. It's a beautiful morning, and we're having a nice breakfast."

Nika frowned and gave Gunner a dirty look before turning to Rizzo. "Sorry, I thought you wanted an update."

Rizzo waved his cigar at her. "Fire away."

Nika hesitated, glancing between Rizzo and Gunner.

"For Christ's sake, Gunner can stay and hear anything you have to say."

Palmer appeared from the lounge area with a bucket and started to mop the outside deck. She stopped when she saw Gunner at the table with Nika and Rizzo. Gunner waved, but Palmer just smiled back.

Nika saw the exchange. "Before we begin, I've been getting complaints about Palmer."

Gunner frowned. "Bullshit, I've heard nothing but good things about her from the staff, and the guests love her.'

"I told you that I didn't trust her, but you hired her over my objections. There's something wrong about her."

Rizzo grew angry. "I don't give a shit about staff issues. You two figure it out. I want to talk about the shipment of heroin from Odesa."

Nika began her update. After a few minutes, Gunner stood up. "You don't need me. I have to get to the bridge."

On the other side of the deck, Palmer was pretending to clean up debris from the storm. She had been disappointed when she saw Gunner having breakfast with Nika and Rizzo. She tried to mop close enough to overhear their conversation, but all she could pick up was a word here and there. She had heard "Odesa" and something about a shipment.

"Hey, Palmer," the bartender said as he was busy clearing glasses off nearby tables, "You look as though you are going to barf or something."

Palmer shrugged. "I'm fine. I must've eaten something bad at breakfast."

Sadly, Nika had confirmed what Palmer had hoped wasn't true—that Gunner was part of the Rizzo criminal organization. She picked up her equipment and left the deck, returning to her cabin and trying to fight back tears. She cursed herself for becoming so friendly—emotionally connected, even—with Gunner. Stupid mistake. At the Academy, they taught that one should never get involved emotionally with targets.

That afternoon, Zoie flew into the cabin and flopped onto her bunk without looking at Palmer. "I'm exhausted. I just finished cleaning the puke off the bathroom floor from the last guest cabin. God, I hate this job!" She rolled over and leaned on one elbow. "What's the matter with you? Are you crying?"

"I need to get some air." Palmer turned her face away from Zoie and walked toward the door. "I'll talk to you later."

Once outside, she walked to the bow of the ship and watched the flying fish skitter and skim the waves as they tried to avoid the larger fish from below. After several minutes, she noticed a dozen crew members gathered at the railing on the third level. They shouted and waved at her to join them.

As she approached, she heard a loud pop and then another. She realized they were shooting clay pigeons off the boat with shotguns. Gunner was supervising the event. He had put up a prize of a hundred dollars for anyone who could beat him over twenty-five shots. He bragged that so far, he'd never lost a match.

The shotgun shoot was a tradition they had done every time they achieved the halfway mark crossing the Atlantic. One of the new crew members was a cowboy from Texas who grew up shooting shotguns. The crew went wild after he hit twenty-four out of twenty-five. They were already counting their prize money when Gunner looked at Palmer with a grin and loaded the shotgun. "Any side bets?"

Palmer shook her head. "I don't like to gamble."

Gunner snapped off twenty-four hits in a row. The crew groaned as he loaded the last shell into the chamber. He laughed and then yelled, "Pull."

He let the clay drift way out from the boat. Just before it hit the water, he pulled the trigger and shattered the clay. He turned and held out the shotgun to Palmer. "Wanna try?"

Palmer shook her head. "No, thanks. I don't know anything about guns."

"Come on, it's fun," Gunner insisted while the rest of the crew egged her. "Here, let me show you." Gunner loaded the shotgun and pointed at the trigger. Then he showed her how to position the stock tightly against her shoulder with her cheek resting lightly against the smooth wood stock. "Once you yell, 'Pull,' we'll release two clays. Just lead the clays slightly and pull the trigger."

Palmer pretended she didn't know what she was doing and let Gunner help.

"Just relax," Gunner said and then backed away and nodded to the man on the clay machine. "Say 'Pull' whenever you're ready."

Gunner's eyes narrowed as he noticed that Palmer didn't quiz him regarding how the safety works on the shotgun gun. Just before she said "Pull" she snapped off the safety without looking.

She missed the first two targets. She held the gun to Gunner. "Sorry, I guess I'm not cut out for this sport."

Gunner leaned close to Palmer as she handed him the gun and whispered in her ear, "I'm always amazed at how some things aren't always what they seem."

Palmer froze and didn't move for a second. "I have to meet Zoie. Thanks for the lesson."

* * *

Gunner returned to his cabin and looked at his calendar. Time was running out. His next call was to Bonita.

"Hi, how are you?"

"Are you in town?"

"No, we'll land in St. Thomas tomorrow. I'll fly over once I get everything settled. How's Cody?"

The phone went silent.

"Shit, is he using again?"

"We can talk when you get here," Changing the subject, she added, "How did Palmer work out for you?"

"Good so far. She's a hard worker and full of surprises."

"What surprises?"

"I have a feeling there is more to Palmer than she wants us to believe." Gunner looked at his watch. He needed to catch Jett before dinner. "See you in a couple of days."

He leaned back in his chair and stared out the window as he dialed Jett in Virgin Gorda.

"Where are you?" Jett yelled on the phone.

"A day out. How's the project going?"

"Great," Jett yelled at someone to turn off the bulldozer. "Hey, sorry, I couldn't hear you. We're framing two homes now and starting the site work on the third lot."

"Any luck on the sales? I have another payment to make to the bank next month, and we've burned through my initial construction loan. I'll have to fund the rest using cash."

"We've had a few prospects tour the site, but nobody is serious yet. I've tried to avoid cost overruns, but we've had trouble with material cost increases and labor problems after the hurricane flattened the island last year."

"I know. You're doing the best you can. I'm just getting squeezed right now by my lenders for your project and the marina."

"More problems with Cody?"

"He likes to spend my money. Bonita's worried about him."

"I don't know why you put up with him.'

"Bonita alluded that he's using again."

"Gunner, you've taken care of him since our childhood. He's not your responsibility forever. You set him up in the marina so he could have a job and a future. And this is how he repays you. He shits on you and poor Bonita."

Gunner didn't respond.

"How many times has he been in treatment? Why don't you let him go?"

"You know why."

Jett sighed on the phone. "I understand, but it's not fair to you."

Changing the subject. "How's Addie?"

"Amazing. As much as try to avoid talking about you, she can't wait to see your eyes."

"You sound jealous."

"Of course," Jett said. "She's the nicest woman I've ever met."

"I knew you'd enjoy her. I plan on stopping by next week."

"Great. I'll let Addie know. See you soon. Oh, did you hear anything from Vin? He sounded upset the last time we talked. I can't believe the fucking Columbians burned his restaurant down."

"I sent him to Bimini. Jimmy is hiding him for now."

"Gunner, what's happening? The buzz throughout the Caribbean is that the Columbian cartel and their thugs are taking over. Somebody has to stop them."

"I have to go. We can catch up over dinner. Give Addie a smooch from me."

* * *

The rest of the trip was uneventful. Once the ship was secure in the main harbor on St. Thomas, Palmer called Bob, her boss, on her cell phone to arrange a time for an update. He had flown in from Washington the previous day to meet with her in person. Later that afternoon, Palmer looked at her outfit in the mirror and picked up her purse.

"Look at you!" Zoie said. "Where are you going dressed like that?"

"I wanted to do some sightseeing while we are here."

"I'd go with you, but I have to work."

"Next time. See you later."

Palmer stepped onto the dock and fished her sunglasses out of her purse. She walked quickly to the end of the pier and checked her cellphone for service. "Hi, I'm getting into a taxi and will meet you in fifteen minutes."

Palmer walked into the restaurant and waited for her eyes to adjust to the indoor light. She walked to the rear of the restaurant and spotted her boss at the last table.

He didn't bother to stand but grumbled, "What happened? I expected you yesterday. I've wasted another day here."

She pulled out a chair and sat down. "And hello to you too."

"What have you learned so far?"

"Well, I have confirmed that once the heroin is secured in Odesa, it will take two to three weeks to arrive in Aruba. Rizzo wants Bykov to join him in St. Thomas and sail with him to Aruba for the first shipment. Rizzo has an assistant named Nika. She's a piece of work, but she's smart and seems to be the one coordinating the deal with Bykov."

"When do you think the shipment will leave Odesa?"

"Not sure. It may take another month or so. Rizzo is waiting on Bykov."

"What have you learned about Castillo and the Columbian cartel?"

"Nothing new. Just that this guy is a monster and will do anything to gain more power."

"What about the captain? Is he part of Rizzo's gang?"

"I can't tell yet. He's…"

"What?"

"I don't know. I've observed him meeting with Nika and Rizzo and overheard them talking about Aruba."

Bob shook his head. "Well, what more evidence do you need? It's obvious that he's involved."

Palmer nodded. "You're probably right."

Bob leaned closer to Palmer. "I need you to be extra careful until you get to Aruba."

"Why?"

"We're pulling you out after the shipment arrives in Aruba. We have intel that your cover might be compromised."

"Not again. How? By whom?" Palmer fidgeted with her fork. "Can you find out if that's true before we leave for Aruba?"

"I'll try, but I can't make any promises. Just be very careful." Bob checked his watch. "I have to go but contact me before you sail to Aruba."

Palmer waited for five minutes until she was sure Bob was gone and then walked out of the restaurant and returned to the ship.

* * *

The following weeks were slow, with plenty of downtime for the crew. Palmer was sunning on the back of the boat when Marco tapped her on the shoulder. "Sorry to bother you, but Gunner wants to see you."

A few minutes later, Palmer knocked on Gunner's cabin door and poked her head in.

Gunner pointed to the chair in front of his desk.

"I noticed that you haven't left the ship all week. What do you have planned while we are docked here?"

"Nothing. I'll sightsee a little but mostly hang around here and work."

"I was talking to Bonita because I need to make a short visit to my marina. I have to check on our business and Cody."

Palmer smiled. "She's sweet. Say hi from me."

"I'll be back in a few days. When I'm back, I need to run over to Virgin Gorda to see Jett and check on our housing project." Gunner hesitated. "I had my sailboat brought over from my marina and planned on sailing her over to see my friends. Since you're alone, do you have any interest in tagging along?"

Palmer hesitated. This could be a mistake, given the tip that her cover might be compromised, but it was a great opportunity to learn more about Rizzo and the shipment details. Besides, she knew how to take care of herself.

"Don't worry," Gunner said. "The house has five bedrooms, and you'll love Jett and Addie. They are my best friends." Gunner quickly added, "I thought it would be a good time to teach you a few things about sailing a larger boat."

"Sounds fun. What do I need to bring?'

"Not much—a swimsuit and casual clothes. Addie is an amazing cook, so we won't go to any restaurants."

"Thank you. It will be nice to get off the yacht for a few days. Let me know where and what time I need to meet you."

Chapter Eight

Palmer finished packing for her trip with Gunner when Zoie walked in and noticed Palmer's carry-on next to her bunk. "Going somewhere?"

"I have three days off, so I'm getting off this ship and going to the beach."

"Where?"

"Not sure yet."

Zoie looked skeptical. "You're packed but don't know where you are going?"

Palmer avoided eye contact, grabbed the handle of her case and started toward the door. "See you in three days."

Palmer met Gunner at a small marina on the side of the island opposite the Destiny. He grabbed her bag and headed down the pier. When they reached the Rainbow, he said, "Welcome to my girlfriend," then swung his leg into the cockpit. After setting Palmer's bag on the floor, he reached for her hand to help her into the boat.

"Thank you," she said, looking around the yacht. "She's beautiful."

"Forty-nine feet of waterline. Large enough for deep water but small enough for me to handle if I'm sailing alone."

Gunner stowed her bag and showed her around the galley. "We're almost ready to set sail. Why don't you change? You might be more comfortable in a swimsuit. The waves are a little rough today, and you might get wet from the spray."

Several minutes later, Palmer stepped into the open cockpit

wearing a bright blue bikini.

Gunner tried hard not to stare. "Are you ready? Unhook the bowline while l I grab the stern line, and we'll be off."

Palmer saluted. "Aye aye, Captain."

They motored out of the harbor. Once they cleared the last reef, Gunner shut the engine off. "Take the helm while I set the sails."

Palmer watched Gunner take off his shirt and begin winching the mainsail. His back glistened with sweat as he cranked up the mainsail, and she felt a flutter in her stomach. She also noticed several scars on his back and a few on his legs that only bullets could have caused.

Gunner glanced back to Palmer and smiled after hoisting the sail. As he tied off the rope onto the cleat, the sail caught the wind and started to heel over. "Turn her into the wind a little. I need to set the jib before we're ready to get fully underway."

Palmer loved the feel of the smooth teak helm and the yacht rolling through the waves. A fine mist of water sprayed over the cockpit from a large wave, and Palmer licked the saltwater off her lips. Gunner jumped into the cockpit and stood behind Palmer. "Let her drift downwind slightly." The yacht heeled as the wind filled the sails. "Now turn her into the wind a little while I take the luff out of the mainsail." Gunner cranked the mainsail in until the sail was tight. The yacht picked up speed.

After they set the sails, Gunner ducked into the galley and reappeared carrying two rum and limes. "Now we can relax."

The wind blew strands of hair across Palmer's face. She took a sip of her drink and faced the sun. "It feels so good. What a perfect day."

Later that afternoon, Palmer said, "Tell me about you."

"Like what?'

"How did you learn to sail?"

Gunner watched a seagull dive for some baitfish on the surface. "Let's talk about you instead."

"Nice try."

"Remember, I grew up in Maine. I think we discussed how my father taught me how to sail, and we built this boat together."

166

"Must be quite the father. You're lucky to have a dad willing to spend that much time together. What about your mother? Do you stay in close contact with them?"

"My mother died recently."

"I'm sorry. Losing a parent is hard."

"We loved each other but weren't close."

Gunner shrugged and stared out in the distance, just letting the waves rock them in silence. Finally, he asked, "What about you?"

Palmer looked at two sailboats on the horizon. "What time will we get to Virgin Gorda?"

"Don't change the subject. Tell me about your parents."

"Remember, I told you my parents died when I was young."

"Sorry, I forgot.

"Can you remind me what happened?"

"It was all my fault."

"What do you mean, your fault?"

"I was taking dance lessons. My mother wanted to cancel because the weather report warned about an approaching ice storm. Stupid me. I had a fit and insisted on going anyway." Palmer wiped a tear from under her sunglasses. "They slid off the icy road and hit a tree on the way to pick me up after my class."

"You can't blame yourself for an accident."

"But if I hadn't insisted..."

"Stop it," Gunner said. "Life is full of those situations. Do I go left or right?" Gunner thought of the decisions he had made every day in Vietnam that sometimes resulted in soldiers getting killed. "What happened to you after that?"

"I was punished for my sin over the next twelve years. My parents didn't have any relatives, so I was raised by several families through the state's foster care program until I turned eighteen."

"That must've been difficult."

Palmer nodded and looked up at a snow-white seagull circling above the mast. "Wouldn't it be nice to spend your days floating in the air? Free to choose where you go without a care in the world."

Gunner nodded. "We need to tack. Loosen the left line and get ready to crank the right once the mainsail swings through. We'll adjust the jib after we set the mainsail."

As the yacht heeled to the opposite side, Palmer began to crank hard to tighten the loose line until the sail caught the wind. Gunner let the yacht settle on the new tack before he told Palmer to take the helm. He pointed to the luff in the top part of the mainsail that was flapping in the wind. "Slowly point the bow into the wind."

As the bow gently turned, he said, "See how the wind fills the rest of the sail? It's the opposite of what you think one should do. Instead of turning away from the wind, you need to turn into the wind to make better headway. You have to work harder, but you control the yacht. You dictate where you are going. In contrast, going downwind seems as though it would be easier, but you end up with far less control."

Palmer rubbed her hands along the smooth wheel of the helm and kept her eyes on the mainsail. "Are you talking about sailing or life?"

Gunner laughed. "A little bit about both."

Palmer asked, "We talked about your parents, but what about siblings?"

"I was their only child." He grunted. "I was something they ordered from a catalog. Male baby, Caucasian, and less than two-months-old.

"What do you mean by that?"

"I'm adopted."

Palmer turned to face Gunner.

Gunner added, "I tried to love my parents, but there is something different about being adopted versus birth parents. I never knew why they decided to adopt me. Growing up, I watched other parents love their children in ways that my parents never did. They were kind and gave me everything I wanted except the one thing I needed the most." He paused, not finishing his thought. "I wasn't like them, and nothing could change that. I felt more like a guest than living in my own home. I realized later that it wasn't their fault. They had good intentions and gave me what they could."

"That sucks," Palmer said. "I read somewhere that indifference is far worse than rejection. Unfortunately, we've experienced both."

"That's why I enlisted in the army after graduating from high school and went to Vietnam. I didn't fit in at school or home. I didn't know who I was then—and still don't. At least you remember your parents. You know where you came from. I don't know how to explain the hole in my soul—not knowing my past. Not knowing why I am the way I am. I have so many questions that will never be answered."

Palmer pointed to his scars. "Did you get those fighting in Vietnam?"

Gunner looked embarrassed and put his shirt back on. "The Viet Cong gave me a few souvenirs."

"Have you made any contact with your birth parents?"

"Never heard from them. I doubt they ever searched for me. Why would they? They would've kept me if they had wanted me."

"You don't know that. Have you tried to find them?"

"No. I'm not sure I want to know the truth. What if my mother is a drug addict? What if my father is in prison? What if—"

Palmer interrupted. "What if they are wonderful and they've been looking for you all your life."

"I don't believe that. Mothers don't just give their babies up for adoption because everything is great."

"Did you fill out the paperwork to allow the agencies to grant birth parents the right to contact you?"

"No."

"Then how do you know they aren't looking for you right now? Unless you file the paperwork, the agencies can't provide any information about how to contact you." Palmer paused. "Wouldn't it be nice to know, once and for all, who you are? I understand it might end up as a big disappointment, but at least you'd know. I'd do anything to have the possibility of finding somebody from my family.

Gunner frowned.

Palmer took a step closer to Gunner. "As someone very wise once said to me, 'Sometimes you have to make hard decisions. Sometimes you have to point into the wind to get to where you want to go.'"

Gunner smiled. "Don't believe everything you hear."

"I'm serious. If you'd let me, I'll help you fill out the paperwork. I did this for a friend of mine in college. Once you submit the documents, then it's up to the parents to contact you."

"But what if they didn't fill out the request on their end?"

"Then we've only wasted a few hours, and you can let it go."

"I'll think about it."

Palmer took her sunglasses off and looked at Gunner. "I understand what it feels like to be alone. I've searched my entire life to find somewhere to belong."

Palmer stiffened thinking about the sexual abuse she had endured in foster care, the boys she met in college who only wanted sex, and the male bosses who treated her without respect at the Academy even though she was better at their job than them. She thought about barely surviving two assassination attempts caused by the betrayal of men she had trusted with her life while working undercover.

She shook off the bad feelings and thought about her roommate. Finally, she said, "The only person that truly loved me was a friend in college."

"Do you keep in touch with him?"

"No, *she* died of an overdose of heroin."

Gunner stared at her. "What are you doing on the Destiny?"

Palmer flinched. "I know who Rizzo is. I wanted to gain some experience working on a mega-yacht. And I realize that I'm speaking out of both sides of my mouth."

"So, you sold your soul."

"Something like that." Palmer added, "What about you? What's your story? What did you have to give up to be a captain on the Destiny?"

"Hah!" Gunner wagged his index finger, "Very funny. Not falling for that."

"If I were a priest, I'd love to hear your confession."

"That would mean ten years of Hail Marys." Gunner rubbed his face. "Everyone has a story. Have you considered that sometimes people are forced to make decisions they don't want to make? How some people can be good and bad at the same time?"

Palmer's eyes lit up. "Are you suggesting that Rizzo is not an evil person? Are you condoning his organization, which is responsible for killing hundreds of thousands of people by distributing heroin all over the world?"

"No," Gunner shrugged. "I don't condone Rizzo or his drugs. I'm only saying that life is complicated. Things aren't always what they seem on the surface." He smiled. "For example, some people are good at handling shotguns, and some say they are not."

Palmer flared. "And sometimes people have good reasons for not sharing everything." They stared at each other for a long moment. Gunner nodded, and then Palmer sighed. "Promise me one thing before we get back to the ship," Palmer said.

Gunner stared at her. "What's that?"

"You'll let me help you fill out the paperwork to find your parents."

"I'll think about it." Gunner pointed to islands off in the distance. "Good timing. We should be at the beach in time for dinner. You'll love Jett and Addie."

"I owe you an apology."

"For what?"

"For insinuating that all men are bad. And for sticking my nose into your business about finding your parents. That's your choice." She waved her hand over the sailboat. "And thank you for this… and for helping me start the certification classes for becoming a captain someday."

Gunner shrugged. "It's no big deal, and I'm glad to help."

* * *

Jett and Addie were waiting on the shore when Gunner motored onto the beach in a dingy. Jett helped Palmer out of the little boat and grabbed her carry-on while Gunner leaped out and picked up Addie, twirling her in the air.

"How's my favorite girl?"

She hugged him and kissed him on the cheek. "You have a girl in every port, but I don't care as long as I'm the favorite." She waved at Palmer. "Put me down. I need to meet this friend of yours." She winked at Palmer and reached out for a hug. "We've heard a lot about you."

Gunner shook his head. "Don't believe a word she says. You should never trust older women—they have no filters and bad memories."

Jett stepped close to Palmer and extended his hand. "I'm Jett—so glad to meet you. Don't pay any attention to either one of them, otherwise, we'll be here for an hour."

"Jett, it's nice to meet you," Palmer said. "Gunner mentioned that you grew up together. I'd love to hear some stories tonight about little Gunner terrorizing the neighborhood."

"That depends on how much time you have."

Palmer checked her watch. "I have all night."

Jett looked at Gunner. "Do I tell the truth or continue to lie about you?"

"Your choice." Gunner dragged the dingy to the edge of the palm tree line. "Just remember, I have a few of my own stories about you."

Addie nodded to Palmer. "This ought to be fun."

Palmer looked back to the Rainbow floating in the azure blue water fifty yards away and then down the empty beach covered in powdered sugar sand. "This is probably the most beautiful beach I've ever seen."

Gunner yelled while unloading the dingy. "Wait until you see the view from Addie's patio. She has the best sunset view on the island."

"Come on, Palmer." Addie hooked her arm into Palmer's and started to walk off the beach. "We're going up to the house while the boys fight over who's doing the cooking tonight."

Addie took Palmer up a small trail through heavy tropical foliage and palm trees, then up a hill to a sprawling beach house perched on the edge of a cliff overlooking the ocean.

Palmer gasped as Addie led her onto the west-facing patio. "The views are fantastic! The sunsets must be breathtaking from here."

Addie smiled. "Jack insisted that we build on this exact spot."

Palmer looked confused. "You mean Jett?"

Addie sighed. "Sorry, I assumed Gunner explained everything.

Jack was my husband. He died several years ago. Jett is Gunner's best friend and now my good friend. He came several months ago to develop the excess land I owned into six luxury properties. Gets lonely here by myself. Gunner thought I could use the money and gain a few nice neighbors."

"I'm sorry about your husband. Gunner didn't explain much other than I'd love both of you."

"Typical Gunner." She put her arm around Palmer as they enjoyed the view. "Love the guy, but he's not the best communicator."

"How long have you known each other?"

"Twenty years. He was a young sailor trying to work his way as a captain up the ranks to larger and larger yachts. He always anchored his client's yachts off our beach because it was calm, west-facing and a long stretch of beautiful sand. Gunner never liked Jack, but he and I became wonderful friends. Funny how you meet some people in your life, and you know in minutes that they'll be lifelong friends of the heart. Over the years, we've had countless dinners on this patio with Paz, the governor of Virgin Gorda, and a few other close friends that live here."

"You're lucky to have such wonderful memories."

Addie nodded and changed the subject. "I can't wait to see what Gunner is cooking for us tonight."

"I didn't know he could cook. He doesn't look like the type."

"That's my Gunner. Probably the most complex man I've ever met. He's always full of surprises." She turned to Palmer. "Take you, for instance. You are a huge surprise."

"What do you mean by that?"

"You're the first woman he's ever brought to our little place in paradise. In fact, you are the first woman I've seen or heard him talk about in years."

"It's not like that. I work for him in housekeeping on the yacht."

"I know who you are."

Palmer stammered, "He only brought me here because he felt sorry for me all alone in St. Thomas while other crew members went on vacation. We'll be docked in St. Thomas for the next three weeks."

"Gunner never has ulterior motives. If he brought you here, you're a lucky girl. He's very loyal and protective of his friends. Once he accepts you as a friend, he will guard that friendship with his life."

"I don't know what to say."

Addie smiled as they listened to Gunner and Jett laughing their way up to the house. She pointed toward the path from the beach. "That laughter is music to my ears. Come now, I'll show you to your room. Gunner insisted you stay in the casita next to the pool."

Addie watched for Palmer's reaction out of the corner of her eye. When Palmer flinched, she added, "Gunner's staying in his usual room above yours with a private patio overlooking the cliff. He doesn't like to sleep indoors, and I have a cot set up on his deck." Addie grinned at Palmer's look of relief as she led Palmer to her room. "Now I know why Gunner likes you so much."

Palmer looked confused. "What do you mean. We hardly know each other. It's only been a few months since I started work on the yacht."

"Whatever you say, dear." Addie pointed to the table next to her bed. "There's extra bottled water in the fridge. I picked the fruit this morning. The mangos are perfect right now. Let me know if there is anything else you need."

"This is heaven." Palmer sat on the bedspread designed with a rainbow arching over dozens of colorful ocean fish and dolphins. "Love the rainbow. Same name as Gunner's yacht."

"This is Gunner's favorite room." .

"Addie, thank you for having me."

"Don't thank me, thank Gunner." Addie stood in the doorway. "The boys haven't seen each other for months. Tonight should be legendary."

"Legendary?"

"You'll see what I mean. Why don't you relax and freshen up? We typically meet for a cocktail on the patio at sunset."

* * *

Palmer lay on the bed and watched the wooden fan circle above her until she heard a knock on her door. She realized she had fallen asleep and rubbed her eyes as she yelled, "Be right there."

"It's me!" Gunner poked his head in and said, "Addie wanted to know if you were joining us for a drink and the sunset?"

Palmer yawned. "What time is it?"

"Almost four-thirty." Gunner smiled. "Jett dropped off your luggage, but you were out cold."

"I can't believe I fell asleep."

"I can," Gunner said. "This place has a wonderful effect on people. What do you think of Addie's home?"

"Amazing. Kind of like a treehouse in a tropical jungle."

"Other than floating on the water, this is the only other place where I can relax."

"Do I have time for a shower?"

"Sure, we'll have a cocktail waiting for you on the patio."

Thirty minutes later, Palmer walked on the patio where Jett, Addie and Gunner were seated with cocktails in lounge chairs facing the sunset. Addie pointed for Palmer to take the empty chair next to her. The patio was an extension of the main living room overlooking the ocean.

"I'm sorry that I'm late. I don't know what happened to me." She was barefoot and wearing a light blue summer dress with a purple flower behind her left ear. "I didn't know what to wear. Is this appropriate?"

"You look beautiful," Jett said. "What do you think, Gunner?"

He only grunted until Addie slapped him gently on the side of his head.

"Yes, I agree with Jett."

"Men," Addie rolled her eyes. "These two knuckleheads are the most unromantic men I've ever known."

Jett sat up and jerked his thumb toward Gunner. "Hey, don't lump me in with him."

Gunner handed Palmer a glass of pineapple, lime juice and rum. "There goes the sun."

The sun turned into a blazing ball of orange, red and yellows as it gradually sank into the horizon. No one spoke a word, mesmerized by the display.

Jett spoke first. "I never get tired of watching these sunsets."

Palmer sighed. "It's so peaceful."

Everyone stood and nodded as the sun was just a sliver of red, shimmering over the horizon. As it disappeared, they cheered and clinked their glasses together.

Addie pointed to her glass. "I could use a refill." She winked at Palmer. "You boys start dinner while Palmer and I finish setting the table."

Jett motioned to Gunner, and they disappeared into the house. In the kitchen, Jett poked Gunner in the arm. "She seems like a nice girl."

Gunner nodded but didn't look at Jett as he pulled three live conch shells and five large lobsters out of a cooler.

"Well…" Jett waited.

Gunner picked up a small hatchet. "She's a nice girl. She was all alone on the yacht while we are docked in St. Thomas, and I thought she would enjoy your company. Let me rephrase that, I mean Addie's company."

Jett slapped him on the back. "I'm giving you shit, but I liked Palmer as soon as we met her."

Gunner chopped a hole in the top of the conch shell and then inserted a knife to cut the snail attached to the top spiral. Then he pulled out the large snail and cut the foot off. Placing it on a wooden board, he began to pound it until it was flat and tenderized.

"What are you making?"

"Conch cakes."

"Perfect! Chef, what can I do?"

"Make me a drink."

Jett came back with a tall glass of rum with lime on ice. "What else is on the menu?"

"Second course, Thai soup with minced conch and lobster. The third course, stuffed lobster grilled over the open fire pit served with coconut lemon rice." Gunner pointed to the BBQ grill on the patio.

"Can you start the fire?"

Jett returned a few minutes later, holding two empty glasses. "The girls are talking as if they'd known each other forever." He started to refill the glasses. "How are you doing these days?"

"What do you mean?"

"How are your migraines? Are you sleeping at all?"

Gunner shrugged. "It comes and goes—you know the drill."

"Still having that dream?"

Gunner tapped a chef's knife on the cutting board, started to mumble something, but then stopped and concentrated on chopping the conch into small pieces.

"What about you?" Gunner asked without looking up from his work.

"Funny, once I got here, my nightmares stopped. I haven't had one dream about Vietnam."

Gunner made seven round cakes, set them on a baking pan and topped each with a large tab of butter.

Jett leaned against the counter, watching Gunner cook. "Tell me about Palmer," he said. "Why is she different. You haven't talked about a woman since—well, you know."

"She signed up as crew in Monaco. Bonita sent her over because she thought Palmer would be a solid worker instead of the flaky kids we usually end up hiring.

"She appears older than most of your crew. What's her story?"

Gunner retrieved the seafood cakes from the oven and placed them in a warmer.

"I'm not sure. Like most young people working off the grid on yachts, she's looking for something. The crew typically stays for six months to a year. When they realize they can't find what they are looking for on the yacht, they move on. My bet is Palmer will do the same as all the others."

"Sounds familiar."

"Don't start on me."

"Why do you like her?"

"I know this sounds weird, but I like her because we have some things in common. I admire how she's had to make her way in a tough life."

Jett grinned. "So, what made the connection between you guys?"

"I found out that her dream was to become a captain someday. I've tried to talk her out of it, but she seemed so serious that I started to help her prepare for the certification classes. I have all the old textbooks."

Gunner filled a pot with fresh clams and steamed them in white wine until they opened. He added coconut milk, lobster, conch, butter, cilantro, sliced jalapeños, bok choy, scallions and red curry paste. "This needs to boil for ten minutes. How is the grill looking?"

Jett checked the coals. "Ready when you are."

Gunner looked around to make sure the girls were still on the patio. "We need to talk later."

Jett picked up two live lobsters and pretended they are fighting. "What about Rizzo?"

"What about Rizzo?" Gunner said as he cracked the lobster tails in half and soaked them in browned butter.

"You knew who he was before you took the job. Do you ever worry about his involvement in the mafia?"

Gunner set his knife on the counter and stared at Jett. "What are you saying?"

"Nothing," Jett said while avoiding eye contact. "I was just wondering if you ever hear anything about his drug operations."

"No, I mind my own business and just drive the boat."

Addie walked through the open patio doors into the kitchen. "How's dinner coming?" She leaned over the boiling pot of soup on the burner and sighed. "This smells so good!" She rubbed Gunner's arm. "We have missed you."

Gunner blushed. "I miss you too. I need to make a better effort to get back here more often. But it's been busy the last six months."

"Palmer is delightful. I'm so glad you brought her. She has an old soul and is so easy to talk to."

"I haven't noticed," Gunner said.

Addie laughed. "You are such a liar." She put her hand on her hips. "I know why, but you can't be afraid to let Palmer get to know you as we do. You can't live your life alone."

"I'm not alone." Gunner picked her up in the air. "I have you…"

Jett threw his hands in the air. "Hey, put my sweetie down."

"…and I have Jett," Gunner finished.

Addie winked. "Gunner, don't let Jett near anything sharp. I don't want to spend the night in the emergency room stitching up his hand."

A loud knock interrupted them and Paz, the governor of Virgin Gorda, walked in. They all cheered and rushed over to greet him.

Gunner hugged Paz. "Addie didn't tell me you were coming."

"I wanted it to be a surprise," Addie said.

Addie led Paz to the patio while Gunner finished stuffing five whole lobster tails with a mixture of herbs and shellfish.

The outdoor patio was lined with tiki torches. As they sat down under the stars for the first course, Paz stood up to make a toast. "To my dear friends—old," he pointed his glass toward Jett, Gunner and Addie, then swung his glass toward Palmer, "and to the new. You are a man of few words, Gunner, but food is your language of love." He waved his hand over the table filled with seafood. "And tonight, we are blessed with an abundance of your love."

They all raised their glass as Paz exclaimed, "Salute. Here's to us!"

Halfway through the meal, Jett asked Palmer to tell them about herself.

Palmer played with her napkin. "Oh, there isn't much to tell. I was looking for a change and always loved the water. I answered an ad looking for crew members, and here I am."

"Where did you grow up?"

Gunner raised his hand. "Let's not ruin a nice dinner with your fifty questions."

"I agree," Addie chimed in. "Jett, tell Paz how the development is going and your new idea."

"We have two homes done, but nothing sold yet. The other four lots are ready to break ground." Jett leaned toward Paz. "I know that many people lost their homes in the last hurricane. Since I have the crews on-site and some extra time, Gunner and I were wondering if we could set up a fund to begin rebuilding those homes. I can provide the labor and expertise at cost if the government can subsidize the hard construction costs and provide low-interest loans. I have a friend in the States that has developed an inexpensive way to build housing in half the time it usually takes."

Paz smiled and looked at Palmer. "See why I love these guys?"

Gunner tapped the table with his hand. "Let's not get mushy."

"It's a great idea. Let me check with the treasury department and see what we can do." Then Paz frowned. "There is something else I want to discuss. The Columbian cartel is gaining more control in dozens of island nations throughout the Caribbean." He paused. "At first, we all thought they were just making noise by increasing their presence in Aruba. But now, we Caribbean leaders agree we have a serious problem. Our way of life is threatened by a small group of ruthless criminals who bully, threaten and kill to get what they want. Individually, small island nations don't have the resources to combat the cartel." He shook his head and looked at Gunner. "But somebody has to do something to stop this."

"Why look at me?"

"I was hoping you could tell me if there's any truth to the rumors going around about a new cartel being formed between the Columbians and the Italian mafia."

"Who told you that rumor?"

"Our mutual friend, Rayaan." Paz waited for Gunner to respond.

"What did he say?"

"He said the port improvements and a new private airstrip under construction are part of a plot to bring in larger amounts of drugs." Paz took a sip of his drink. "Is it a coincidence that you are sailing to Aruba on a yacht that just happens to be owned by Rizzo?"

The table was silent for a long minute. Everyone stared at Gunner.

"I honestly don't know, Paz. I'm just the captain. I have no interest in sticking my nose into Rizzo's business. People who do that end up as fish food."

"What if Rizzo is involved? Isn't there a Russian coming to sail to Aruba with Ruzzo next month?" said Palmer.

Gunner's eyes narrowed. "How would you know that?"

"I, umm," She gulped her drink and played with her fork and asked, "Marco told me to prepare the largest guest cabin for a man named Bykov."

Everyone turned back to Gunner.

Addie jumped up. "Palmer and I need another cocktail. Which one of you is going to take care of us?"

Jett clapped his hands. "Wait. We have a surprise for you. Everyone should follow us down to the beach."

Addie grabbed Palmer's hand. "I love surprises."

They walked single file down a path through tropical foliage to the beach. Five chairs were set in a semi-circle facing the ocean. A beach fire burned with small orange cinders shooting into the air. A cooler with cold beer, rum and ice offered libations. The torches cast a flickering, yellow glow over the group as they reverently stared at the stars for a few minutes and listened to the waves gently washing ashore.

Palmer was the first to speak. "I could die right here and never regret a thing." She wiped a tear from her face. "Sorry, I don't know what's wrong with me. It's just that…" She took a deep breath. "I have never experienced anything like this. I watched tonight how much you love each other. You have created an amazing family."

Addie turned to Palmer. "What about your family? Tell us about them."

Palmer looked at Gunner in awkward silence. "Who needs another drink?" Gunner asked, trying to change the subject.

Paz raised his hand and added, "Palmer, I agree. This place is paradise, and old friends are good for the soul." Paz looked at Gunner. "Isn't that right?"

"Absolutely."

A few hours later, they began to pack things up to bring back to the house. Jett and Palmer were still lounging in their sand chairs when Addie yelled, "You guys stay and enjoy. We've got everything handled here."

Jett looked at Palmer. "I'm not quite ready to end this beautiful night. Are you?"

Palmer shook her head.

After everyone left, Jett turned to Palmer. "So, what do you think about Virgin Gorda so far?"

"The most beautiful place I've ever been. How did you end up here?"

Jett smiled. "As you know, Gunner is my best friend. I was developing luxury single-family homes in Telluride, Colorado. My marriage was disintegrating, my spec homes were not selling and I was broke." Jett paused and stared out over the calm water. "Gunner did what he always does for all of us when we're in trouble. He swoops in and saves us."

"How did he do that for you?"

Jett nodded toward the house. "He convinced Addie that I could develop the extra land she owned. It provided her with needed cash and some neighbors. Plus, it gave me a job and a new start."

"There is one thing that I don't understand," Palmer said. "Why doesn't Gunner have a girlfriend?"

"You'll have to ask him."

"Has he ever been married?"

"No."

"Why not?"

Jett turned the question around. "What about you?"

"It's complicated.'

"Isn't it always?"

Palmer nodded.

"I can see why you and Gunner like each other. I don't mean to pry, did something happen to make you afraid to hurt or be hurt."

"Is that what happened to Gunner?"

Jett took a deep breath and looked at his watch. "We should probably head back to the house."

* * *

The next morning, Palmer was up before sunrise. She made herself a cup of coffee and went to the beach for a walk as the sun was coming up. Addie was already on the beach, sitting in a sand chair and drinking her coffee. She looked up when she heard Palmer.

"I love this time of the morning," Addie said. "It's so peaceful. I never get tired of watching the sandpipers running between the waves as they search for the little crabs." She set her coffee cup in the sand. "Let's go for a walk."

As they strolled down the empty beach, Palmer said, "Again, thank you for having me."

Addie replied, "You're welcome. Although, for some reason, it feels like you've always been with us."

"I had a nice talk with Jett last night after you left."

Addie smiled, "Jett has been a blessing. Gunner knew what we each needed, and he made it happen."

"Jett told me a little about his situation in Telluride," Palmer said. "It sounded terrible."

"He was taken advantage of by a heartless woman that never loved him. She was a ladder climber and used him. I don't know if Jett told you about Stevie, his son who died when he was young—the love of his life. The marriage fell apart after his death. Jett confided to Gunner that he could never trust a woman again. And he would never want to risk having another child."

"What about you?" Palmer asked. "What do you want?"

"Same thing we all want. To love and be loved." Addie stopped walking and turned to Palmer. "My life with Jack was a mistake. He was handsome and wealthy, and we had this beautiful home here. Things were fine until I had a miscarriage that ended badly. My uterus was damaged by the doctor's mistake. Then I found out that I had uterine cancer, which meant I could never have children again. Jack was an alcoholic and began to abuse me because I couldn't bear his children. Frankly, it was a relief when he died. I never remarried because who would want to marry an infertile woman." Addie resumed walking again. "I was resigned to live my life through my dear friends— Gunner, Paz and a few others. I believed that was my destiny until…"

"Until you met Jett?"

Addie blushed. "Funny how life works. I thought happiness was only for others, not me. All I wanted in life was to have a family. To have children and a husband that loved me." She paused. "But I lost the dream—do you understand what I'm trying to say?"

Palmer turned and hugged Addie again. "I do."

"Jett gave me my dream back. Although we'll never have children, we learned that love isn't about sex, it's more about intimacy and respect. Jett is the first man in a relationship that I ever felt truly respected me for who I am. Nothing more, nothing less. He understood that intimacy is not limited to physical sex. More importantly, it's about caring for each other."

"Where are those people?" Palmer asked. "I've been looking for them my entire life without success." She choked up. "I'll never have a place to call home."

"Is that why you work on yachts and live out of a suitcase—moving from yacht to yacht around the world?"

"It's complicated." Palmer struggled to explain. "Every time I try to trust a man, I end up disappointed or angry. I've given up on finding that special person to share my life with."

"Honey, I know this is an overused cliché, but home is where your heart is, not a physical place. It resides with someone you love."

"That's part of the problem. I loved my parents and lost them. I finally found a person to love in college and lost her to a heroin overdose." Palmer tried to hold back the tears and her voice quivered. "Every time I find love, I lose it." They continued to walk along the beach, watching the seagulls soar above them. "I've been alone so long that I'm not sure I can be with another person."

"What about Gunner? Isn't he worth it?"

"We are just friends—barely know each other. And he's my boss. He has his life, and I have mine. He's been very generous with his time, but there's nothing there between us. He can be so charming but always seems to hold back, like there's an invisible wall between us." She stared down the beach. "Besides, we have no future."

"You are not only smart but very perceptive. True, he rarely lets people behind his wall, but when he does, they are friends forever. Part of his problem is the trauma from Vietnam. Something happened that he's unwilling to discuss. Jett knows, but he won't say what happened. He only told me that Gunner has recurring nightmares that still haunt him." Addie sighed. "Gunner once shared how hard it was not to know where he came from or why he's the way he is. He describes it as having a hole in his heart."

"I know what he's missing. I was nothing more than a monthly income check to my foster parents."

"Maybe that's why you have an unexpected friendship with Gunner. He wants to find his past, to find his real biological parents, but he's afraid of what he might learn. And you want to find a home but are afraid to take the risk." Addie turned and cupped Palmer's face in her hands. "Listen to me. We can't change the past. We all have ghosts. But we also have each other. Time and distance don't matter when it comes to love. You have found a family with us if you want it. You may continue to travel the world, but from now on, your place with Jett, Gunner, and me will always be your home."

Addie wiped the tears from Palmer's face. "Sounds corny, I know, but I believe you were meant to be here."

"I don't know what to say." Palmer hugged Addie. "Thank you."

They wandered back to the house to meet the boys. They spent the rest of the day sailing around the island, snorkeling at various reefs and enjoying the sun. Later that evening, Addie and Palmer made dinner. Another beautiful meal, another beautiful day. They lingered around the pool after dinner for a short time, but everyone was tired and went to bed early.

* * *

A few hours later, Palmer woke to the gentle whirring sound of the ceiling fan. For a second, she couldn't decide if this was a dream or not. She had slept in so many different hotel rooms over the last two years that she was always disoriented at first. A full moon shone through the open windows. She stepped out of her casita to get some fresh air when she heard Gunner's voice on the deck above her. She cocked her head to listen and realized he was talking on his cell phone. She looked at her watch and wondered who he would be talking to at two o'clock in the morning. She stepped to the edge of the deck to listen better.

"I know. I know," Gunner said, irritated. "You don't have to yell. Everything will work out. Trust me."

Palmer heard his footsteps as Gunner paced around the deck above her.

"Yes, there is always a risk." Silence. "I know it's a big deal."

"What do you want to do about Bykov after this is over?" Silence again. "Are you sure?"

Palmer froze when she heard Gunner say Bykov's name.

"Don't worry. I'll handle this once I return to the yacht."

Dejected, she walked back into her room and cried herself to sleep.

* * *

Later the next morning, Gunner made brunch for everyone. Palmer was the last one up and greeted everyone already on the patio.

"Hello, sleepyhead," Addie said. "How did you sleep?"

"Fine, I think I was over-served last night."

Gunner pointed at Jett. "It's his fault."

Jett shook his head. "Sure, throw me under the bus."

Gunner handed her a tall glass of fresh orange juice. "This will help. Otherwise, Addie has some Advil around here somewhere."

Palmer sat in a chair and kept her sunglasses on to hide her puffy eyes.

As they ate breakfast, Addie leaned over to Palmer and whispered, "Is everything alright? You haven't spoken a word this morning."

Palmer tucked a strand of hair behind her ear. "I'm fine."

Gunner's phone buzzed. He frowned as he looked at the number on the display. "Excuse me. I have to take this call." He walked a short distance away, outside of earshot.

The male voice said, "Gunner, it's Jimmy."

"What's wrong? You sound out of breath?"

"I just left Vin's beach house." There was a long pause. "Gunner, they found Vin and killed him."

186

"How? God damn it!"

"I don't know how they found him. Someone had to betray us. The Columbians are using him as an example of what happens if you resist. Our dock boy saw a new boat anchored in the bay earlier. He said the men on the boat looked Latin American. I'm sure the killers were from the cartel."

"Jimmy, be careful."

"They won't hurt me. I pay them too much damn money."

"Can you handle the funeral arrangements? I'll pay for everything."

"Yes, but don't come. I don't want you anywhere near here. I've lost one buddy. I can't afford to lose you too."

Gunner hung up and walked back to the table.

"What's wrong?" Addie asked. "You look upset?"

"I'm sorry, but we'll have to cut our visit short," he lied. "They need me back on the ship."

"Who cares about you?" Jett teased. "Palmer can stay with us while you play captain." Jett nodded at Addie. "Right?"

"Sorry, we're a package deal," Gunner said.

"How soon do you have to leave?" Addie wondered.

"Within the hour. There's always some crisis."

* * *

As Gunner loaded their bags onto the dingy, Addie pulled Palmer aside. "Remember what I said. We're friends now no matter where you go in life."

"You have no idea what that means to me."

Addie smiled. "I think I know." She handed her a small glass rainbow wrapped in white tissue paper. "Promise me that you'll never stop reaching for that wish of yours at the end of the rainbow."

Palmer squeezed Addie's neck for a long time.

Gunner watched the exchange. "Am I missing something?"

Addie shook her head and kissed Palmer on both cheeks. "Lord, what would these boys do without us?" And then she whispered, "Take care of Gunner. He's under a lot of pressure."

* * *

Back on St. Thomas, Palmer looked at her watch. She was late for another meeting to update Bob regarding her trip with Gunner to Virgin Gorda. Palmer spotted Bob at an outside table as she stepped out of the taxi. The café patio was filled with the late afternoon crowd enjoying the warm sun and good food.

Palmer sat down. "I only have a few minutes. I have to report back for my shift."

"What do you have for me?"

"Your intel is correct. We're scheduled to sail to Aruba next month. Bykov is flying in to join Rizzo on the ride to Aruba. This will probably coincide with the arrival of the first shipment of heroin."

Bob grinned. "That's great. Good job."

Palmer scanned the nearby tables. "Any update about my cover being blown?"

"No, just be careful." He sipped on a cup of coffee. "What else do you have for me?"

"That's it."

"What about the captain?"

Palmer fidgeted with her sunglasses. "You were correct. He's involved with Rizzo and the shipment. I heard him talking on the phone about the cartel late at night while we were in Virgin Gorda."

"Stay close to him." He leaned forward. "You've done a great job gaining his trust. I'm putting you in for a promotion when this is over."

Palmer didn't react.

Chapter Nine

Gunner wrestled with how he felt about Palmer after their time together on Virgin Gorda. He's never let a friendship with a crew member grow into a relationship beyond work, but Palmer was different.

He looked at his watch and realized he had forgotten a meeting with Nika and Rizzo. He scrambled to the lounge on the third floor. Rizzo and Nika were seated at a round table overlooking the pool.

"Sorry, I'm late."

Rizzo waved his hand. "Nika has an update on the status of the shipment in Odesa."

Nika shuffled through several papers and pulled out a schedule. "I was told there's a delay in the heroin delivery. Some problems in Afghanistan. Bykov told me the product won't arrive for another month."

Rizzo groaned. "Fuck! Are you sure? Is there anything we can do?"

"No, but Bykov reassured me this will not happen again."

"Gunner, what do you think?"

"We don't have any choice, but you need to tell Castillo." Gunner glanced at Nika. "I need to know the minute that the shipment leaves Ukraine so I can prepare the Destiny for the trip."

Nika nodded. "I understand."

Rizzo stood. "Keep me informed. I have another meeting to attend."

* * *

Gunner saw Palmer cleaning tables on the deck below. He hurried down to catch her.

"Hi, Palmer."

Palmer smiled. "How are you?"

"Busy, but I was wondering if you wanted to have dinner tonight. I know a great place near the harbor."

"That would be nice. I'm off around four."

"Great. Meet me at the shuttle boat at five."

Gunner found himself thinking about Palmer all afternoon, which concerned him. He had plenty to focus on. He caught his breath when Palmer stepped through the door and waved at him from the stairs leading down to the shuttle. She smiled beneath a floppy straw hat and wore a red ankle-length summer dress. He helped her into the boat while the deckhands released the lines from the yacht.

"You look great," he said.

Palmer blushed. "Thanks."

When they were seated at the restaurant overlooking the harbor, Gunner said, "I'm sorry we haven't had a chance to get together after Virgin Gorda. I've been crazy busy."

"No worries. I loved your friends. Thank you for taking me."

"They loved you."

The waiter asked for their order and left to get their drinks.

"I've made a decision, and it's all your fault."

"Perfect," she said. "I've always wanted to be the cause of a man's downfall."

"I want you to help me with the paperwork to find my parents."

"Of course! I would be honored."

The waiter opened a bottle of wine and filled two glasses.

Gunner raised his glass. "What should we drink to?"

Palmer pointed to Rizzo's yacht Destiny.

Gunner followed her gaze. "To destiny. I like that."

"Do you know why Rizzo named the yacht Destiny?"

"We were having dinner one night. He told me that he built the yacht after his father died and named it Destiny. It was a critical time in his life. He was forced to decide whether to take up the mantle and continue the legacy of the family as the new patriarch or walk away from the support his family had provided to the people of Sicily for years. As we talked about his family, he mused over the concept of destiny. He asked me what I thought, 'Is our destiny preordained or do we have a choice?'"

"What did you tell him?"

"I said, 'I don't know. We all have crossroads in our lives. I found that it's only when we are on the precipice do we make real changes in our lives.'"

Palmer nodded and sighed without looking at Gunner.

"What's wrong?"

Palmer turned back to him. "Nothing." She smiled and raised her glass to Gunner's. "To our destiny."

They made eye contact and clinked glasses.

"I wanted to tell you we won't be sailing to Aruba for another month. Since we have some downtime, maybe you'd like to start studying for the yacht certification? We could meet a couple of times a week."

"I'd love that. Thank you."

Gunner smiled and reached for his wine. "Ok, then it's settled."

* * *

Two weeks later, Gunner sifted through the mail stacked on his desk. Most of the mail was junk, but he froze when he saw a manila envelope with a return address from an adoption agency in Montana. He stared at the envelope for a minute before opening it. Inside, he found a letter introducing him to his biological family along with photos and a letter from his dad inviting him to meet at their ranch in Bozeman. He couldn't stop the tears as he read and re-read the letter.

After composing himself, he called Palmer.

"I want to thank you."

"What for?"

"They found my parents in Montana."

"Gunner, that's awesome!"

191

"I can't believe it. My family sent a letter and photos." He shifted the phone from one ear to the other. "Palmer, I have four siblings."

Palmer didn't respond.

"Are you still there?"

"Yes, I'm so happy for you."

"I need to ask you a favor."

"Anything."

"They invited me to meet as soon as possible. I know this is unusual, but will you come with me?"

"I don't think that's a good idea. You need to spend time with them. I'd be a distraction."

"Please. I'd appreciate it."

"I understand, Gunner. I do. I'll come."

"Thank you!"

* * *

Two days later, Gunner raised his empty cup at the flight attendant as she walked by their seats in First Class.

She smiled. "Refill?"

"Yes, thank you." Gunner turned to Palmer. "Would you like another?"

"Sure, I've never flown in First Class before. This is awesome."

"Coffee, no cream. And champagne for my friend."

"Celebrating?" the attendant asked.

"Kind of," Gunner said, handing the cup to the attendant.

Gunner didn't take his eyes off the green farmland below as they crossed the heartland of the Midwest. "The world seems so different at 35,000 feet," he said to Palmer. "People going about their lives…" He retrieved a file and studied the photo of his new family.

Palmer's hand steadied his knee, which was bouncing up and down. "Nervous?"

He nodded.

"Don't worry. Your family will love you."

"I've imagined this moment all my life. It's such a paradox. I always wanted to find them, but at the same time, I didn't."

"What's the worst that can happen?"

She squeezed his hand. "Have you figured out what you want to say when you meet?"

"What would you do if you were me?"

Palmer closed her eyes, thinking about her parents. "I would hug them and never let go."

The attendant set their drinks down.

Palmer looked at the photo again and smiled. "Amazing how much your siblings look like you and your dad." She peered closer to the photo and then added. "Except the young woman on the left. She must take after her mother."

Gunner turned and stared out the window again.

"I'm sorry about your mother," Palmer said. "Such a shame that she died before you had a chance to meet."

"I should have done this sooner. I'm such a fool."

"There's no way you could've known she had cancer."

"But only three months ago…"

"Don't." Palmer set the photo back on his tray. "You can't change anything."

Gunner sighed. "I've decided the first thing I will do when we meet is to ask for their forgiveness."

Palmer turned her head. "Look at me." She touched his chin and made him look at her. "There's nothing to forgive."

Gunner shrugged. "I'm a coward. I should've signed the papers years ago."

"Why didn't you?"

"I was afraid."

"Of what?"

"Just about everything. What do I tell them when they ask about my life? I've just wasted the last twenty-some years sailing around the Caribbean and babysitting narcissistic rich people."

"Tell them everything."

"I can't do that."

"Why not?"

Gunner finished the last of his coffee.

"There are things—" He paused and looked out the window.

"Go on."

"I've hurt people."

Palmer rubbed his hand. "Oh, Gunner."

"I can't change some of the things I've done."

"Is that why you chose to become a captain, moving from ship to ship and port to port?"

"What do you mean?"

"No risk when there's no commitment to a relationship." Palmer sipped her champagne. "Trust me. I understand. We're not that different. We've been on our own forever. Ironic—I dream about a place to call home, and yet I've been burned so many times I prefer to stay alone."

"I've wondered why you moved so much."

"If we don't have a home and avoid the risk of relationships, then we…" She paused. "…can hide our past and control the future." Palmer was thinking about her last two years undercover. "Am I right?"

Gunner nodded.

"One thing I've learned from Addie is that we are not damaged goods. We deserve happiness."

"But it's easier if I just stick to myself and not get involved with anyone," Gunner whispered. "That way, I can't hurt anyone again."

"Nor can anyone hurt you," Palmer added. "What are you the most afraid of?"

"Betrayal. Seems like every time I've trusted someone, every time I've loved someone, I've been betrayed."

Palmer squirmed in her seat. "What happened to you?"

"I fell in love with a local woman while I was in Vietnam. We planned to be married after I finished my tour. She disappeared when the Tet offensive started. I found out later she was part of the Viet Cong and was just using me to gather information." Gunner turned to Palmer. "I trusted her, but I was conned. She never loved me—and she broke my heart. Trust can't be repaired like a flat tire. It's the bedrock of any relationship." He paused. "I don't think I can ever trust anyone like that again."

Palmer thought about betrayal. She knew how Gunner felt. Growing up, she prayed that each new foster family would be different. Prayed they would love her. Prayed she'd never have to fear that her bedroom door would open in the middle of the night. As for trust, after two years of working undercover and two assassination attempts, she had learned to not trust anyone.

Her stomach churned as she realized she would soon be added to Gunner's list of betrayers once she arranges for his arrest, along with Rizzo and Nika. She wished that she'd never accepted the undercover assignment to serve on Rizzo's yacht. She had seen many times when good people went to jail for committing bad crimes, but this was different.

"Your face is flushed," Gunner said. "Anything wrong?"

She struggled to take off a sweater. "It's hot in here."

"Sorry to bore you with my pity party."

"But Gunner, don't you see—you have Jett and Addie. They love you. Don't they count?"

Gunner smiled. "You're right. I have a lot to be thankful for. It's just…"

"What?"

"But what if I don't like my new family? What if they're losers? What does that make me?"

"Someone told me that doubt and fear are great deceivers. Don't project yourself into someone else's life choices. I'm a poster child for making excuses and blaming others for my life." She tilted her head. "Look at it in this way—what is there to lose? At least you will finally know. You can move on with your life."

The pilot announced they would be landing in twenty minutes.

"Thank you for coming," Gunner said. "I'm lucky to have you as a friend because you are the only person I can trust to understand what I'm talking about."

Suddenly, Palmer lurched forward in her seat and unbuckled the seatbelt. "I'll be right back." She rushed into the bathroom and threw up.

* * *

Palmer grabbed Gunner's hand as they walked through the airport exit. Dozens of people were waiting on the other side of the doors to greet family and friends.

"This will be a first," Gunner said.

They had walked just five paces when Gunner heard his name called out. A group of five people huddled outside the security door were waving at him. A tall man smiled and held up a sign with his name. Gunner immediately recognized the five of them from the photo.

The siblings backed away politely as Gunner faced Jeb, his father, for the first time. The man's face was creased and leathery from years in the sun. Jeb took off his cowboy hat, and the same wavy hair as Gunner's fell around his neck. He wore a blue, long-sleeved shirt with white pearl buttons and a leather vest.

Jeb was slightly taller than Gunner in cowboy boots, but they had the same wide shoulders. Gunner stepped toward his father and reached out his hand to shake, but Jeb stepped so close that it made Gunner backup. He studied Gunner's face and then turned his head slightly toward his kids and nodded.

"We have the same color eyes," he said. Then he grabbed Gunner's shoulders, leaned close to his ear, and whispered. "We never stopped looking for you."

That was all Gunner needed to hear. Slowly, Jeb wrapped his arms around him.

His brothers and sisters stood quietly while they embraced until one of the girls grabbed Palmer's hand.

"I'm Brandy, we're so glad you came," she said. "Gunner told us about you in the last letter."

So this is what it feels like to have family, Palmer thought.

After a minute, Jeb wiped away some tears and introduced the family, "This is Brandy. She's the oldest, married and works as a nurse at our local hospital. Next is Kyle, our only available bachelor, followed by his better-looking, younger brother, Buck. He's married with two kids who we love dearly but drive us crazy. And then Mary Beth—she works on the ranch with me.

Palmer marveled at how much three out of the four siblings

looked like Gunner and their father. All were dressed in jeans and cowboy hats except for Mary Beth. Jeb explained that she was named after her mother's middle name. She wore a pretty summer dress and sandals instead of cowboy boots. Her shoulder-length brown hair was tied back in a pony, which accentuated her deep brown eyes. She had a calm presence to match what Palmer sensed was a kind heart.

"We've waited a long time to meet you," Mary Beth said before smiling shyly.

"So have I," Gunner said.

Brandy stepped close to Gunner. "We have a present for you." She handed him a small box tied with a blue ribbon. "It's a gift mother had saved since you were born—but don't open it now. Wait until we get to the ranch."

Jeb stared at the hat in his hands. "I'm sorry about your mother. It was so hard, when we got the notice they found you, to realize she'd never see you."

Palmer grabbed Gunner's arm and squeezed it.

"I'm sorry, son," Jeb said.

* * *

The ranch was nestled at the end of a six-mile valley. A classic log ranch house sat next to two barns that overlooked large green pastures filled with the horses they raised as a business. The kitchen was the largest room in the house. The thick oak table was always set to accommodate a dozen people because the kitchen was constantly filled with friends, family, workers, veterinarians and neighbors. The walls were covered with photos, ribbons and medals from the numerous rodeo awards.

They quickly overcame the uncertainty of meeting each other. They laughed, talked and cried late into the night. At dawn, everyone else had gone to bed, but Jeb and Gunner were still talking. The kitchen table was littered with beer bottles, poker chips, playing cards and junk food. The sun was peeking over the horizon when Jeb said, "That was quite a night."

Gunner grinned. "I'll never forget it."

"I love this time of the morning." Jeb grabbed his cowboy hat.

"Let's take a walk."

The mountain air was cool and clean. A light fog floated above the winding stream flowing from the far end of the valley.

"I know you must have a lot of questions," Jeb said.

"I have to say something first." Gunner glanced at Jeb. "I'm sorry. Will you forgive me?"

Jeb looked surprised. "For what?"

"For never completing my side of the paperwork for us to meet."

"I don't blame you. After so many years, why would you want to find us? I'm sure you assumed that only terrible parents would give up their son." He paused and rubbed the stubble on his chin. "But the truth is I've been waiting my entire life to ask *you* for forgiveness. For living most of your life without us. I should've never let our parents bully us into giving you away for adoption. It was a cruel mistake that your mother and I have regretted every day of our lives."

Jeb pointed to a bench overlooking the creek. "Just before your mother died, we sat at that bench, and she made me promise that if I ever found you, I would tell you that you were not a mistake. Tell you how much we loved each other and loved you. Our parents insisted they knew what was best for us. I want you to know that we married as soon as we graduated from high school and immediately started to look for you. We filled out all the paperwork and waited. The agency would not give us any information. It was heartbreaking. Liz prayed every day that we'd find you. Now tell me about you?"

Gunner spent the next hour describing his life—how he had grown up in Maine, served in the Vietnam war and later became a captain in the yachting world.

Jeb asked about Vietnam. He disclosed to Gunner that he had been in the army during the Korean war.

"I was in a special sniper unit," Gunner said quietly. "I hated and loved it at the same time."

Jeb nodded and listened.

"It was so bizarre. But for the first time in my life, I found I was good at something."

"You don't have to say anymore. I understand. The doctors say

I have PTSD… PSTD… or whatever they call it. I think it's bullshit. It's our penance for the things we had to do. I don't sleep much and prefer the outdoors."

Gunner shook his head. "Me too. I dread the night because that's when the ghosts come."

"Tell me about Palmer. She seems like a sweet young woman. I didn't notice a ring."

Gunner blushed. "She's become a very good friend. Besides, she's too young for me."

"Age has nothing to do with love."

"I have issues, both physical and psychological. We don't have a future, and I don't want to hurt her."

Jeb nodded. "Issues from Vietnam?"

Gunner sighed. "It's complicated."

"Have you tried counseling?"

Gunner nodded. "Once. I was fucked up and living alone in Miami."

"Did it help?"

"No. I still have the same nightmare."

Jeb nodded. "Me too. I have one that never goes away. We have to live with what we've done."

They talked for two hours before they heard laughter coming out of the open kitchen window. "Sounds like the girls are up."

They walked into the kitchen and saw the women lounging in bathrobes, drinking coffee and chattering non-stop. Gunner patted Palmer's shoulder and sat in a chair next to her.

"Good morning. How did you sleep?"

"Like a log," Palmer said. "I didn't wake up once. Must be the mountain air."

Jeb started to make omelets and hash browns.

Palmer pointed at Jeb and yelled, "Like father, like son. Gunner is an excellent cook too." She walked to the counter where Jeb was busy shredding the potatoes. "Can I help?"

"Absolutely. Grab the apron on the hook, and you can start cracking the eggs."

Jeb paused and watched Gunner talk with his siblings. His voice quivered as he said, "Liz would've loved this."

Palmer touched Jeb's shoulder. "She's here. Can't you feel it?" At that moment, Gunner made eye contact with Palmer and smiled like there was nobody else in the room.

Brandy stood and picked up Gunner's gift off the counter. "Open your present."

Gunner waved her off, but Brandy insisted, "This was mother's last wish."

Gunner carefully removed the blue ribbon and opened the box. Inside was a copy of his birth certificate with Liz and Jeb's names circled, the hospital ID band from his tiny ankle, a picture of his pregnant mother just before she went into labor, and another picture of her and Jeb when they got married.

At the bottom of the box, Gunner found a letter. He carefully unfolded the paper and closed his eyes.

"What is it?" Mary Beth asked.

"A letter from our mother. Please excuse me." He took the letter and walked outside.

From the kitchen window, Palmer watched Gunner read the letter. Her heart ached when he finished the letter and knelt in the tall meadow grass looking into the sky. After a moment, he folded the letter, wiped his face with the back of his hand and walked slowly back to the kitchen. He smiled when he saw Palmer's face in the window.

Gunner pulled a chair out from the kitchen table while still holding the letter in his hand. No one spoke for a moment until Brandy cleared her throat and asked, "Can you read the letter to us?"

Jeb stopped cooking and leaned against the counter while Gunner unfolded the letter again.

"To my dear baby…" Gunner stopped to gather his emotions. "My dear baby…" Gunner hung his head. The letter shook in his trembling hands.

Palmer leaned over and whispered, "Do you want me to read it?"

Gunner nodded and handed her the letter.

Palmer scanned the first paragraph for a second. "Oh, Gunner."

He looked at Palmer with sad eyes. "I know," Gunner said softly.

Palmer started to read. "To my dear baby, I'm so sorry that I don't know your name. I'm so sorry that I don't know what you look like. I don't know your voice or your laugh. I wish that I could have been there when you took your first steps, when you skinned your knees and lost your first tooth. I regret not being there to hold you in my arms, wrapped in a soft blanket when you were sick with the flu. I wanted so much to be there when you attended your first dance, when you graduated from high school, when you got married…"

Palmer's voice cracked for a second.

"Even though I missed these important times in your life, you were with me every day. I looked for you in the tall grass of the meadows near our house. I searched for you in the pine forests of our green mountains. I looked for you in the stars every night before I went to bed. But I see you in my dreams. I know you, and if we ever meet, you will already know me."

Jeb wiped his eyes while the sisters wept softly.

Palmer took a deep breath and then continued to read.

"My dear, sweet boy, I woke up frantic in the middle of the night before you were born. I felt something was wrong. I don't know how it was possible, but I knew that you were trying to speak to me. I grabbed a pen and wrote this down as fast as I could because I didn't want to lose it. When I finished writing and read it for the first time, I felt an amazing calm come over me. The fear had disappeared. I didn't realize what a gift you were giving me until you were gone. For years, whenever I felt that same frantic fear, I would pull out this poem and hold it close to my heart."

The Awakening

Floating in darkness
a slow awakening begins.
Weightless in the warmth of my black universe,
something disrupts the silence.
A soft sound emanates from all directions at once.

Afraid at first, until the rhythm of the steady beat becomes
a soothing connection with something I don't understand.

Time is not a concept to me.
No days, no nights, no beginning, no end
as I drift and dream.

Out of the darkness, a new sound awakens me.
A voice sings softly,
teaching me love through a song.
Then another new sound…a laugh
I learn joy from a voice I cannot see.

Something pushes against me.
Frightened, I cross my arms and legs,
wrapping them tightly in a ball to protect myself.

New sounds.
Different voices,
loud and urgent.
Unknown forces press against my body
disrupting my world.
Squeezed into a tunnel by contracting movements
faster and faster.
I push against the walls to make them stop.

A moment comes when a muffled scream turns into a soft cry of joy
as I burst into blinding light.
I gasp at my first breath. Choking, spitting
and I wail at the unknown,
Finding solace only in the steady drumbeat
pulsating underneath the soft, warm skin against my naked body.
Trembling, until a familiar voice begins to sing.
I open my eyes to see the unseen…
And know who I am.

We love you and always loved you,
Liz and Jeb

No one spoke as Palmer carefully folded the letter and handed it back to Gunner. "That was beautiful."

The room was silent until Jeb stood and grabbed his cowboy hat off a hook. He didn't turn around, just said, "I'll be back later."

Palmer watched Gunner read and re-read the letter. The siblings quietly left the room to give Gunner some space.

"Are you all right?" Palmer asked.

Gunner could only nod his head up and down.

Palmer leaned close and whispered to Gunner, "No more chasing rainbows. You got your wish."

Chapter Ten

Marco greeted Gunner and Palmer when they returned from Montana. "How was your trip?"

Gunner grinned. "Amazing."

As Marco helped them off the shuttle, he said, "You didn't miss much while you were gone, but Rizzo and Nika want to see you as soon as you get settled. They're next to the pool on level three."

Before they walked into the ship, Gunner faced Palmer. "I don't know how to thank you."

Palmer blushed. "It was my pleasure. I better go."

Marco watched the look they gave each other. After Palmer left, he asked, "Was meeting your family what you expected?"

"I'm a lucky man."

* * *

Rizzo smiled when he saw Gunner approaching and waved.

Gunner pulled out a chair. "What's up? Marco said you wanted to see me?"

Nika checked her watch. "Bykov and his entourage are scheduled to land at the airport in two hours. Are we ready for them?"

"I have a staff meeting in a half-hour to confirm. Did you get a final number?"

"Yes, I gave Marco the information."

"What about the other guests?"

"Castillo and his group are arriving later this afternoon."

Nika flipped through several pages in her notebook. "Marco and I will meet each group and get them settled. We have a welcome reception scheduled for seven o'clock with dinner to follow. I have Ricco's helicopter scheduled to shuttle Castillo and his people back to St. Thomas late tomorrow after we finish negotiations."

Rizzo lit a new cigar and blew smoke into the air. "Gunner, do you have a suggestion for an itinerary?"

Gunner nodded. "I suggest we sail to Tortola today and then work our way down island to Aruba."

"Sounds great."

Gunner looked at his watch. "I need to leave. Lots to do before we depart. I checked the weather, and we should have a beautiful night for sailing."

* * *

Happy hour was scheduled early because the sun sets fast on the ocean. The seas were calm. The yacht was cruising at a smooth twelve knots, and the weather was perfect.

Everyone had gathered on the deck next to the main dining room for cocktails and to watch the sunset. Dozens of hors d'oeuvres covered two tables. Several couches, tables, propane firepits and various chairs created an outdoor patio lounge.

Gunner looked down at the party from the bridge. Rizzo used this yacht as a floating office and entertainment venue. Each couple had been assigned a personal host to cater to their needs. If they requested something that was not on board, the helicopter retrieved it from the nearest island.

Gunner hated attending the daily happy hour ritual but was required to mingle with the guests. Dressed in all-white, he surveyed the men in a group while a dozen women huddled near the bar on the open deck one level below. As the captain, he had access to all the passports of each passenger and used their identification to perform a brief background check. Sometimes he found extensive background information, but other guests were more mysterious. These were the guests that Gunner loved to approach because they made these boring parties and dinners interesting.

Gunner leaned on the railing. From above, he noticed Nika in a red dress waving at him on the lower deck. She looked stunning in a light red wrap with a red flower tucked above her left ear. He nodded, but she continued to wave at him to join the party. He mouthed back to her, "I'll be down in a minute."

As Gunner entered the open deck, the reaction was always the same. Every woman in the lounge turned her head and followed him as he approached Nika. He never understood why women loved men in a uniform.

Gunner mingled easily with everyone, and that's one of the reasons why Rizzo hired him as captain. He required Gunner's attendance for cocktails and dinner every night. Rizzo observed how Gunner could tell an ultra-rich Russian oligarch to fuck off or tell a stunning woman she was full of bullshit and yet make them laugh at the same time. But it was his eyes that freaked people out. The color of a blue iceberg, his eyes could charm a woman or terrify a man who made the foolish mistake of crossing. To the women, Gunner was a modern-day Zorba the Greek, but to men, he was Troy, The Warrior—just born in the wrong era.

Gunner approached Nika and looked around at the group.

"My my, don't we look handsome tonight," she told him.

"Works every time."

Nika laughed and turned toward the sun. "I love these sunsets." She held her empty drink in the air. "Can you get this poor, vulnerable girl a drink?"

When Gunner returned with their drinks, Nika was surrounded by Rizzo and four other men. She was telling a story that ended with a punch line that made them all laugh. He handed Nika her drink.

Rizzo put his arm around Gunner. "Gentlemen, meet Gunner, the best captain I've ever had. I should know because I've fired most of the top captains in the world over the last fifteen years."

The guests all chuckled on cue.

Rizzo turned to Gunner. "I'd like you to meet Carlos Castillo. His family keeps me supplied with Columbian coffee that tastes amazing, but he charges me a ransom for the privilege."

Castillo nodded.

"Next to Carlos is the mutt of the group, Miguel Perez. His Venezuela oil fuels my yacht, but I've never received a liter of free petrol. I hate his company but love his wife. She's the only reason I invite him on these trips."

Miguel extended his hand to Gunner, who shook it.

"Now, Diego Ortega. He's my charity case. The Ortega's are nothing but poor farmers from the Sonoma area of Mexico." Diego raised his glass to Gunner.

"And last but not least, meet Ivan Bykov." Rizzo gave no further explanation in his introduction.

Bykov gave Gunner a slight nod but didn't extend his hand.

"It's my pleasure to meet each of you," Gunner said.

Castillo asked, "Where are you from?"

"Maine."

"I recognize the east coast accent," Castillo said. "I'm in New York often."

"Business or pleasure?"

Castillo ignored the question and glanced at Nika. "Do you get to New York?"

"Not enough," Nika said.

"Let me know if you ever want to take a quick trip. I can send my jet to pick you up." Nika feigned shyness. "And of course, Rizzo, you're invited too."

Rizzo laughed and said, "Fuck you, Castillo. Stick to your own women." He turned to Gunner. "Make damn sure he doesn't sit next to Nika at dinner."

"Yes, sir," Gunner said.

Nika licked her lush lips and gave Castillo a pouty smile. "I love it when men fight over me."

Ortega asked Gunner, "How long have you been a captain?"

"I've been sailing since I was a boy."

Bykov interrupted, "Gunner, where did you get your education?"

Gunner's eyes narrowed for a second. "At a university a long way from here."

"Did you enjoy the experience?"

"Enjoy would not be a word to describe the program. It was an intense international curriculum crammed into two years, but I survived."

"When did you attend?"

"1970 to 1971."

Ortega sipped his scotch. "We're almost the same age. Where did you say you attended the university?"

"It's not in operation anymore."

"Why is that?"

Gunner's eyes clouded over for a second. "My education was probably very different than your college experiences. Lucky me, I was selected for a full immersion program that included two tours in Vietnam." Nobody spoke until Gunner quickly added, "Forgive me, but I must check with the bridge before we sit down to dinner."

After Gunner returned to the deck, the chef came outside and announced that dinner was ready.

Once everyone was seated, the staff handed each guest a glass of champagne and Rizzo made a toast, "To new and old friendships. The four of us have a unique opportunity in history to corner the market. Salute to our success!"

Everyone clinked glasses. Rizzo made eye contact with Gunner from across the table. Gunner smiled back and set his champagne down.

The dinner conversation floated across different topics from around the world. They spoke English so everyone could understand each other. Gunner asked Perez about the oil business and learned that the man's family had built most of the refineries in Venezuela. Once refined, large tankers moved the oil and gas to the Dominican Republic and distributed it throughout the eastern seaboard of the US.

"Why use the Dominican Republic?" Gunner asked.

"It has an ideal location and the best deepwater ports in the Caribbean."

"What else does your family invest in?"

Perez smiled and glanced at Castillo and Ortega. "We are expanding into a variety of businesses."

"Mr. Castillo—"

Castillo waved his hand. "Please call me Carlos. We are friends now."

Gunner nodded. "Carlos, how did you get into the coffee business?"

Carlos shrugged.

Rizzo added, "They are the largest exporter of coffee in the world."

"Gunner, don't listen to him," Castillo said. "He exaggerates all the time."

Palmer was one of the servers hovering around the dinner table. Gunner noticed how she moved from guest to guest, filling their glasses with wine or water before their glasses were half empty. He watched her focusing her attention on Bykov and Castillo. Halfway through dinner, he gestured for Palmer to come over.

"What are you doing?"

"Do you need something?"

"You're doing a great job, but give our guests some space. I'll let you know if we need anything."

Palmer's face turned red. "Of course, sorry."

After she left, Gunner asked Castillo, "How do you distribute your coffee?"

"Two primary paths. We work with Diego and use his network to move coffee through Mexico and into the west coast of the United States. The other distribution network goes through Aruba and the east coast of the US."

After dinner, the men decided to play poker. Gunner watched from the bar until Rizzo waved at Gunner to join them. Gunner shook his head but walked over to their table to say goodnight. Rizzo pulled out a chair next to him, across from Bykov and insisted that Gunner join them.

"Thanks for the offer, but I need to check the bridge before it gets too late."

"Nonsense. Sit down and get another drink," Rizzo said.

"I don't play poker with our guests."

"But as your guest," said Bykov. "How can you refuse?"

Gunner was trapped. "Because I play to win."

Bykov laughed. "Then sit. I always play to win, and I never lose."

Rizzo patted the empty chair next to him.

Gunner stared at Bykov. "Don't say I didn't warn you."

They played late into the night until only Gunner and Bykov were left. Gone were the jokes and casual banter. The pot was up to $1,500. No one was speaking as the two players looked at their hands and stared at each other. Rizzo sensed the game had evolved into something more than poker.

The dealer looked at Bykov to see if he wanted any cards, but the Russian kept the hand he'd been dealt. Gunner took two cards.

Bykov started the betting. Gunner raised, and then Bykov said he was "all in," raising the pot to $3,000. Gunner looked at his cards and then studied Bykov's face before throwing his cards face down and burying them in the deck. "Congratulations. You're too good for me tonight."

Bykov smiled as he scooped up the chips. "I'll let you try your luck again tomorrow night."

Gunner walked to the bar. The bartender handed him his usual. A minute later, Rizzo joined him for a drink.

"You are an interesting man."

"What do you mean?"

"Sitting next to you, I know you had the cards to beat him. Why did you let him win?"

Gunner swallowed the rest of his drink. "Consider it an investment for tomorrow night." He smiled and walked away.

* * *

Gunner was relieved when Castillo, Perez, Ortega and their entourages left the yacht by helicopter the next morning. Rizzo called twice, but Gunner didn't answer because he was too busy getting the ship ready for departure.

On the bridge, Gunner watched Marco run through the pre-departure checklist. He was an excellent first officer and friend. Marco handed Gunner the itinerary for approval.

"I want to make one change, Gunner said. "I want to anchor off the beach on the leeward side of the next island stop. The bay has crystal clear water, and it's out of the wind."

"No problem."

"Are we ready?"

"Yes, Captain."

"Let's go."

* * *

Later that afternoon, they dropped anchor for the night. Gunner made sure everything was secure before heading to the boat bay to meet Bykov.

The crew was busy preparing the scuba gear for their dive. Marco handed Gunner a black wetsuit. Gunner dunked it in the water and started to work the wetsuit up his legs. The peculiar odor of neoprene made his stomach turn and his head pound.

"You don't look very happy," Marco said.

Gunner took a deep breath. "I'm not up for this. We went way too late last night."

"How did you get conned into diving?"

"I made the mistake of bragging about how good the reef was in this location. Bykov immediately jumped at the opportunity to spear some fresh grouper for our dinner for tonight. He insisted I take him down and show him how to do it." Gunner grimaced as Marco struggled to get the left arm into the suit. "Are you sure this is my suit?"

"Yes." Marco laughed. "I admit the suit looks a little tight. When was the last time you worked out?"

"Fuck you." Gunner smiled as he slipped the suit over his shoulders while Marco finished zipping him up from the back.

Marco tapped him on the shoulder. "There you go."

Gunner walked to the edge of the platform, where a dozen air tanks were secured against the wall.

Bykov had his tank strapped on and was busy checking the air from his mouthpiece while another crew member was adjusting the weights around his waist. He looked at Gunner and smiled. "Good morning. Looks like a good day…" He paused, staring at Gunner. "…for using this." He lifted a speargun powered by a compressed air cartridge.

Gunner returned the stare as he slowly placed his hand on the rubber sheath of his diving knife. "Agreed." Gunner's headache and the dullness from his hangover were instantly gone. All of his senses went into overdrive. "This could be a good day for a lot of things."

Marco sensed the change in the air and stepped in front of Gunner. He pretended to adjust a strap on Gunner's chest to secure the tank on his back.

"Is there something going on here?" Marco whispered. "Did something happen last night that you're not telling me?"

"Nothing I can't handle." Gunner pointed to the rack on the wall. "Can you hand me the Hawaiian sling?"

Marco picked up the long metal spear that was inserted into a wooden handle attached to two thick rubber bands. To operate the sling, a diver would point the spear at the target and pull the end of the spear using the two rubber bands. When released, the spear would be propelled forward with surprising speed and accuracy. It was an old-school device widely used before compressed air cartridges-powered spearguns.

Marco glanced at Bykov, examining the powerful speargun. "I think I should throw a tank on and join you."

"No," Gunner said without taking his eyes off Bykov. "Best I make this dive alone."

"I don't like it," Marco whispered as he finished adjusting the weights on Gunner's waist.

Gunner and Bykov inched to the edge of the platform in their flippers.

Gunner motioned to Bykov and said, "Once we get underwater,

we'll head to a reef that's about fifty feet down. Follow me, and I'll show you where the grouper like to hide in large holes in the reef. You can pick one out and spear it. I suggest you stay with fish weighing less than fifteen pounds. Bigger ones put up quite a fight. I'm sure we'll see some lobster. If you'd like, I could spear a couple for appetizers."

Bykov nodded. "I'll follow your lead."

They placed their hands over their masks and stepped into the ocean. Once underwater, Gunner watched Bykov adjust the buoyancy compensator on his tank to descend, then gave him a thumbs up and started to swim toward the reef. The water was crystal clear. The colors of the reef were brilliant in the sunlight. The red fan, staghorn and brain coral were filled with schools of tiny, multi-colored fish floating in the gentle current. Fluorescent parrotfish nibbled on the coral, and clownfish darted in and out of their hiding places. A large green sea turtle swam below them.

As they neared the bottom, a dark shadow passed overhead. He glanced up at a huge, five-foot barracuda gliding within several feet, its mouth filled with long, jagged teeth. Gunner stopped for a second. This was one of the largest barracuda that he'd seen in these waters. He wasn't worried because they were more of a pest than a danger, even when spearfishing.

Gunner waved his hand to get Bykov to see the barracuda. Bykov nodded. Gunner turned and continued toward the reef with Bykov close behind. They swam slowly along the reef's edge, searching the holes in the coral for grouper of the right size. Gunner stopped and floated without moving next to a large black cave in the coral. He glanced over his shoulder and noticed the barracuda was still following them closely.

Gunner motioned for Bykov to come closer and pointed at two groupers floating inside the mouth of the cave. Bykov nodded. Gunner pointed his spear to the fish on the left. It was a perfect size for dinner. Bykov shook his head and pointed at a thirty-pounder on the right. Gunner shook his head and gestured no—too large. The grouper on the right was at least thirty pounds. They could hear grunting and burping sounds from the groupers as they sensed the divers in front of their cave.

Gunner pointed again to the smaller grouper, but Bykov was adamant. He wanted the big one on the right. Gunner knew that as soon as Bykov speared the grouper, all hell would break loose on the reef. This would be a hard struggle and would likely attract the black-tip sharks that are always lurking around for sick or wounded fish.

Reluctantly, Gunner signaled Bykov to shoot the larger grouper. To his surprise, Bykov pointed his finger at Gunner to spear the fish. Gunner shook his head and pointed at Bykov to go ahead, but again to his surprise, Bykov was insisting that Gunner spear it.

Grudgingly, Gunner swam close to the opening and aimed the sling at the larger fish. He pulled back the two rubber bands and released his fingers. The spear went through the middle of the grouper and exploded inside the cave. Gunner struggled to retrieve the thin rope connected to the spear so he could pull the fish out of the cave. He needed to do this quickly to have any chance.

The fish took off, wiggling frantically as it tried to shed the spear from its body. Gunner reeled in the rope until the fish was close enough to grab the end of the spear. Once he had a good grip, the battle was just beginning. The big grouper was enormously powerful for its size and swung the spear and Gunner in circles.

Gunner started slowly to bring the fish toward the surface when he saw the large barracuda shoot past his shoulder and hit the grouper right behind the head. The barracuda clenched its jaws on the fish and thrashed violently, trying to tear the grouper off the spear. Gunner was barely able to hang onto the end of the spear. He looked at Bykov floating several feet from the death struggle, still thirty feet below the surface. Gunner took one hand off the spear for a second and pointed at the barracuda, hoping Bykov would spear it.

Bykov swam close enough for Gunner to see his eyes inside his mask. Bykov slowly raised his speargun, but instead of aiming at the barracuda, Bykov pointed his speargun at Gunner's chest. They locked eyes, suspended in water and time, as they confronted the game, the charade they had been playing since the start of the trip. No one else was around—just the two of them.

Gunner waited for Bykov to pull the trigger. At the last second,

Bykov shifted his aim and released the spear, which landed just behind the eye of the barracuda. Now it was Bykov who struggled as the barracuda released its grip on the grouper and tried to shake off the spear.

The battle only lasted several seconds before the barracuda went limp. Gunner was still holding his spear. A large portion of the grouper's head was gone, and it had stopped moving. Gunner and Bykov looked at each other again for a moment. Finally, Gunner pointed to the reef's floor, where three reef sharks had begun circling. They were excited and agitated by the wounded fish.

Gunner pointed toward the boat. Bykov nodded.

Bykov surfaced first, and the crew was waiting to help them onto the dive platform. One of the crew grabbed Bykov's fins and the spear with the barracuda attached. Bykov climbed the steps up to the platform. He took off his mask, sat on the edge of the dive platform, and watched Gunner floating in the water below him. He unbuckled the straps holding the tank and smiled.

Gunner swam close to the steps and handed his spear to Marco. He followed the same routine as Bykov and finally sat down next to the Russian as he removed his mask. Neither said a word nor did they look at each other while staring out over the ocean.

After a long minute, Gunner said, "You have quite a story to tell at dinner. That was a huge barracuda."

"I don't think we have an ending to the story yet. Do you? Isn't life interesting?" He grinned. "Always full of surprises." Bykov continued to stare straight ahead for a few seconds, then looked at Gunner out of the corner of his eye. "I was right, wasn't I? We'll have to do this again." He stood and added, "See you at dinner."

* * *

Two hours later, Gunner watched an old fishing boat slowly motor into the deserted bay where they had anchored earlier that afternoon. It was a rusty, dirty boat about forty feet long with an open cockpit and a large cutty in the middle. Black smoke billowed out of its noisy engine. Gunner watched the boat from the bridge until it cut the power and slowly drifted about seventy-five yards away.

Gunner called Marco on the ship's phone, "Where are you?"

"I'm in the boat bay working on preparing the submersible for tomorrow. What's up?"

"I need you on the bridge now."

Gunner looked at his watch. The guests were relaxing on the outside deck on the fourth level before dinner. The sun would be setting in a half-hour, and Gunner needed to take care of this new situation before dark. He picked up a pair of large field glasses off the counter.

A few minutes later, Marco stepped into the bridge and looked in the direction Gunner pointed.

"What's going on?"

Gunner kept his eyes pressed against the lens of the field glasses. "Pick up the other pair and tell me what you see."

Marco grabbed the binoculars and looked at the boat off the port side of the Destiny. "I see three scruffy-looking men in the cockpit and one more on the bow drinking a beer."

"What else?"

"Not sure, but that's one ugly, beat-up boat. Looks like an old lobster boat we used to see on the east coast of Maine." He kept the glasses on the boat for a moment. "Wait, another man is moving around inside. That makes five."

Several minutes later, they heard the noise of a high-speed boat approaching from the opposite direction. They quickly swung their field glasses toward the north end of the island. A large speed boat emerged from around the point and headed into their bay. As it got closer, they cut the engine, and the boat went into a slow glide about a hundred yards away. Gunner focused his field glasses on the second boat.

Marco stared for a few moments. "They look like locals—different from the other guys." He squinted. "Hey, look. The guys in each boat are waving to each other."

Gunner didn't respond as they watched the exchange between the two boats. "Check the man with the beard on the bow drinking a long-neck bottle of beer. He's dressed slightly better than the other men, although they all look rough."

"I see him talking on his cell phone," Marco said, holding the binoculars. "Are you thinking what I'm thinking?"

"Watch the guy just inside the cockpit. I saw a flash of metal."

"Shit," Marco said. "The big man in the bow of the other boat is talking on the phone?"

Gunner set his binoculars on the counter. "I saw the same two boats following us out of the harbor in St. Thomas. This is no coincidence. These men aren't tourists.

"Fucking pirates!" Marco blurted out. "What're you going to do? There isn't any island police way out here."

"Meet me in the lounge in a few minutes. Bring my large field glasses." He pointed at the guests below. "Calmly move all the guests inside the lounge, but do it quickly. We don't have much time before we lose light."

Gunner went back to his cabin, unlocked a tall cabinet in the closet and stared at three different guns—an AK-47, a 12-gauge pump-action shotgun and a 44 Magnum handgun. A tall, black metal case stood in the corner. He pulled it out, locked the door and walked quickly back to the fourth-floor deck. He stood outside the lounge and watched Marco trying to calm the guests. Rizzo was upset and refused to follow the group inside until Marco whispered an explanation.

With the guests in the lounge, Gunner walked to the south side of the deck and set his case on the floor. He opened it and started to assemble a rifle packed in foam. The last piece was a large scope, which he snapped in place and began to adjust. When he was ready, he looked at Marco inside the lounge area with the field glasses. The guests were watching Gunner holding the rifle in his arm.

Gunner glanced at Marco and pointed to his own eyes and then to the pirate boat to their immediate south. Marco nodded and raised the binoculars to his eyes. Gunner set the rifle on the railing and peered into the scope.

On the boat, the man who seemed to be in charge was still on the bow talking on his cell phone and holding a beer bottle in his left hand. Gunner wiped the lens of the scope one and then settled into the rifle. *Like riding a bicycle*, he thought. He paused for a second and took a deep breath. The heat from the late afternoon sun created small beads of sweat on his brow. The taste of the salty sweat on his upper lip combined with the faint residue of gunpowder from the barrel was like a drug. It brought back instant memories—but not now; he had to concentrate.

He made two small adjustments to the scope and then held the rifle without moving for several seconds while forcing his breath and heart rate to slow. He imagined this state of consciousness to be like that of the great Zen masters in extreme meditation. On one hand, everything became calm and quiet, with no sounds, no distractions from anything but the object on which he focused. Yet, in a unique paradox, he felt intensely alive, his senses acutely aware of everything.

As he exhaled one last time, he gently squeezed the trigger. The beer bottle in the left hand of the leader exploded. The gunshot made everyone in the lounge jump, and some of the women screamed. The man on the pirate ship dove into the water on the opposite side of the boat. Gunner held his rifle in position for a moment and then moved his aim to a new target in the stern cockpit. Gunner could see the men scrambling around the back of the boat—everyone but one man, who was looking at Gunner through his binoculars.

Gunner grinned and pointed at the man, clearly indicating that he was next. The engines of both boats started, and the pirates scrambled to lift their anchors. Gunner swung his rifle to the second boat. Two men sitting in the stern dove into the cockpit as a third man ran to the bow. From the bow, the man frantically pulled on the chain to retrieve the anchor. Gunner fired a second round that shattered the anchor chain six inches from where the man's hand gripped the chain, thus freeing the boat to leave.

Gunner turned his attention back to the first boat, but the boat had already turned and was speeding in the opposite direction. Gunner watched the second boat round the corner of the island and then calmly disassembled his rifle as Rizzo ran out of the lounge.

"Holy shit!" Rizzo yelled.

Gunner didn't respond, just continued to pack his rifle.

"Holy shit, holy shit," Rizzo kept repeating.

"They won't bother us again."

"Marco said you shot the fucking beer bottle right out of the guy's hand."

Gunner shrugged.

Rizzo continued to stare at Gunner.

Gunner closed the gun case and looked up. "Tell your guests I'm sorry for disrupting their happy hour, but the danger is past now. This won't happen again. Also, tell Marco to let everyone back out on the deck to enjoy themselves. I need to freshen up before dinner."

Gunner stood up and slapped Rizzo on the back. "Nothing like a little excitement before dinner. This will give your guests an interesting story to tell their friends back home."

"I'll have your gin and tonic sent to your cabin. Shit, that was the most incredible thing I've ever seen."

"See you at dinner."

* * *

Gunner skipped the happy hour because he didn't want to rehash the pirate incident with the guests. Dinner was already in process when he arrived.

"Sorry, I'm late."

Rizzo pointed to an empty chair between Nika and him. The table was set for Bykov and his entourage. They were loud and drunk.

Rizzo tapped his glass and stood. "I want to raise our glasses to Gunner. He was amazing today. We're lucky to have the finest captain in the world and…" He paused and tapped Gunner's shoulder. "…an outstanding shot. I've never been threatened by pirates."

They all applauded and raised their glasses toward Gunner.

Halfway through dinner, Bykov asked, "Was that an M21 rifle you used?"

Gunner nodded.

"I prefer the Russian Dragunov SVD."

Gunner stopped eating. Bykov smiled as if they were sharing an inside story.

"I don't care for the Dragunov."

"Why? Maybe because you'd have to admit we make a better sniper rifle."

"No." Gunner's eyes narrowed. "The Dragunov may be slightly better long-range because of the greater muzzle velocity, but the M21 is far more accurate mid-range."

"I was told the M21 jams too often."

"Don't believe everything you hear."

"Is that the rifle you used in Vietnam?"

Rizzo changed the subject. "Are we playing poker tonight?"

Gunner and Bykov stared at each other like two boxers in the middle of the ring.

"I look forward to it," Bykov said.

Gunner looked at Nika. "Bykov, how do you and Nika know each other?"

Nika tapped Gunner on the hand. "Let's not ignore our other guests." She waved at Palmer. "More champagne for the table."

Gunner's phone buzzed, and he saw Bonita's number. He stepped out onto the deck. "Hi, Bonita. What's up?"

He could hear her crying.

"They killed him," she sobbed.

"Killed who? What are you talking about?"

"They murdered Cody. The police found him floating in the bay with a bullet in his head."

Gunner was stunned. "Who did this?"

"The Russians. They were in Cody's office earlier today, and I could hear them arguing. These are the same guys that came from Miami and opened the new nightclub, the Wahoo. I overheard them yelling about some kind of shipment. They stormed out, and when I asked Cody what was happening, he told me to shut up."

Gunner shook his head. "Did you tell the police about the meeting?"

"No, I wanted to tell you first."

"Don't say anything yet. I need some time to think."

Bonita continued to cry. "Oh, Gunner…"

"I know. We always worried something like this would happen." Gunner ran his fingers through his hair. "I can't do anything right now. I have to deliver the ship to Aruba. I'll call you when we arrive. In the meantime, don't talk to anyone about this." He took a deep breath. "I'm sorry, Bonita. Listen, everything will be all right. I promise."

Gunner walked back to the dinner table and sat down. Rizzo leaned over and whispered, "What's wrong? You look upset."

He reached for his drink and gulped half the glass. "I'm fine. No worries."

He tried to control his voice and asked, "Bykov, tell me about your business. Do you have any investments in the States?"

"A few in New York."

"What about Miami?"

"I love Miami. I helped some friends open a successful nightclub there."

"Have you thought about expanding?"

"I'm always looking for good opportunities. Do you have a suggestion?"

"I would seriously consider Santo Domingo. I have a marina near the city, and the Dominican Republic is booming."

"Funny you should mention it. I already invested in a new club in your town."

"With the same guys that operate the Miami club?"

"Yes, why?"

"Just curious." Gunner stood. "I have to make the evening rounds on the ship. I'm sorry, but we'll have to arrange another time for poker."

Once Gunner reached his cabin, he called Jett with the news about Cody.

"Oh, shit," Jett said. "Who did it?"

"The Russians. They're using go-fast boats to run drugs to Miami from the Dominican Republic. Cody was selling them the boats. I told him to stop. I also found out tonight that Rizzo's partner is an investor in these guys."

"What are you going to do?"

The phone went silent for half a minute. "Have to go. Hug Addie from me."

"Gunner, wait. You didn't answer my question."

"Yes, I did."

* * *

That night Gunner's nightmares were worse than ever. He tossed and turned, but he couldn't get Cody out of his head. He cursed the time they spent in Vietnam. Cody was never the same after they returned home and turned to drugs. Neither was he, but he learned to cope.

Gunner thought about all the suffering Cody had endured. At least now, he was not in pain anymore. He also mourned the loss of Vin to the Columbians. He realized that he was back in a war zone again.

Eventually, he drifted off to the same recurring dream that had haunted him since he'd returned from the war.

* * *

The incessant Vietnamese rain slowed enough for Gunner and Vin to calibrate the shot. Vin ran the numbers and gave Gunner the measurements. Gunner shouldered the rifle and began his usual routine by adjusting the scope. It wasn't any different from what other professionals do in preparation to excel at the highest levels in sports, business, and other life challenges—only in this case, he was preparing to kill someone tonight.

Vin repeated the coordinates—wind, range and angle of elevation could change from their position. They had perfected this procedure without words hundreds of times. They used a combination of sign language, gestures and other signals to communicate without speaking. Sometimes, for safety reasons, they would go weeks without uttering a word.

Gunner liked the solitude of the jungle. He was in his element, his natural state. He was in control. Life was reduced to one truth— survival—so simple, so pure. No bullshit. No hidden agenda, no excuses. Gunner would enter a different world when the moment came to kill or be killed. The external world disappeared, and his intense focus would transcend fear.

Their mission was to harass the distribution of weapons and supplies traveling into South Vietnam from the north. Their strategy was to hide in the jungle during the day and hunt on the trails at night. On this evening, they found a position fifty yards from one of many trails the Viet Cong used for transporting goods. It was a rare opening in the dense jungle and allowed a clear shot from their hiding position. This was the second night of their hunt in this location. The first night in this location was a bust because of the constant downpour.

Gunner and Vin were exhausted. They had laid camouflaged and motionless for over thirty-six hours. This was the third week living in the jungle as a two-man sniper team. After they finished tonight, Gunner was meeting his buddies, Jett and Cody, in Saigon for a week of R&R.

Soon, they heard muffled voices and clanging military equipment but couldn't see the combatants. Vin poked Gunner in the arm and pointed. A column of Viet Cong was walking single file down the trail. Gunner pushed the stock of his rifle tighter against his shoulder as he peered through the night scope. The men looked like ghosts moving slowly across the clearing. The rain had finally stopped, and other than water dripping off the trees and foliage, the jungle was eerily silent.

Gunner wiped the sweat out of his eyes and checked the silencer on his rifle. Satisfied, he settled back into a shooting position and nodded to Vin, who wiped the condensation off the night binoculars and signaled his calculations before he nodded. Like passing a baton in a relay race, everything was now up to Gunner. He alone would decide which target would live and which would die.

Vin motioned that seven Viet Cong were trailing behind the others. Typically, Gunner would wait until he saw the last person in the group and start the killing there. At that point, they'd usually pick up their gear and disappear into the jungle.

Vin didn't take off his night binoculars but signaled seven porters. He gave another signal to wait until the last combatant emerged from the trail and stepped into the clearing. Gunner quickly figured that six people would still be open after he dropped the last one without noise. He blinked twice to keep the sweat off his eyes, took a deep breath, and placed his finger on the trigger. This was the Zen moment. No judgment—that would be up to some other power later, in some other universe.

Vin dropped his glasses and looked at Gunner. He sensed something wrong. Not once in a year of working together as a sniper team had Gunner hesitated. Vin and Ginner were closer than brothers, closer than a husband and wife.

Maybe it was exhaustion, maybe fate, but tonight was different. On any given shot, all Gunner saw inside the scope was an image of a person, then he'd pull the trigger, and the image would be gone. Then he'd move to the next one, and so on. No connection, no anger or remorse, only a job to do.

Sleep used to be his refuge, the one place where he could escape from himself and the things he had done. Now he dreaded every night. The ghosts always know where to find him—every person he had killed. That's why he preferred to hunt in the dark. If he stayed awake, they couldn't bother him.

Gunner pressed his cheek to the side of his rifle. He loved the feel of the wood stock, the faint order of gunpowder in his nostrils and the smoothness of the barrel and trigger. Vin poked him again and pointed.

Gunner shrugged and nodded. Vin put the glasses back to count the kills.

Gunner slowed his breathing to a level so light it wouldn't move a feather. Then he focused the crosshairs on the head of person number one, the last one on the trail, and gently applied light pressure to the trigger. As quickly as the first one fell, Gunner rapidly moved his scope to the next target and dropped as many as possible before they scattered into the jungle.

Gunner had made this kind of shot over a hundred times with the same results—except for this one. Something was wrong.

As Gunner pulled the trigger, it seemed like an eternity before the bullet hit its target. The rain had fully stopped. A full moon broke through the clouds and briefly lit up the clearing. At the exact moment he pulled the trigger, the person on the trail turned her face to him and looked directly into his eyes, his soul, as the back of her head exploded. Gunner guessed she was in her late teens or early twenties with almond eyes and a small scar on her left cheek.

It was not possible, but she knew. And worse, he understood that she knew. Gunner dropped the rifle and ran. He ran all night.

Gunner woke from the nightmare covered in sweat. He missed Vin and was so angry that he had been killed on Bimini. He was determined to identify the killer, but his idea of justice would have to wait.

* * *

The next morning, Palmer served breakfast to Rizzo, Nika and Bykov. Between trips to the kitchen, she could hear snippets of their conversation about the shipment they were meeting in Aruba. She had to figure out a way to communicate this information back to Bob at the DEA. After cleaning up the breakfast table, she walked back to her cabin. At the end of the hall, she bumped into Marco.

"Marco, is there a way to call someone from the ship while we are traveling?"

"We have ship-to-shore satellite access, why?"

"Could you let me make a call? I'll make it quick."

"Sure, you can call from the bridge."

"Umm, is there anywhere else I could call from? I need a little privacy."

"You can call from my office. Meet me there in ten minutes."

Palmer stopped at her cabin and grabbed a pen and tablet. On her way to Marco's office, she saw Nika talking to Bykov on the deck below her. They were speaking in Russian, which made Palmer curious. They couldn't see her, so she listened.

"Is everything set?" Bykov asked in Russian.

"Yes. I discussed our plan with Castillo while he was on board the yacht. He's a go."

"And Ortega?"

"Castillo is taking over the organization after the first shipment goes through. At that point, he thinks we're 50:50."

"Perfect."

"What about Rizzo?"

"My people will be waiting outside the restaurant while we have dinner with Rizzo and Castillo. This will be over in seconds." Bykov looked at Nika's face. "What's wrong?"

"What about Gunner? He could be a problem."

Before Bykov answered, a group of his entourage ran up and started talking. After the group moved on, Nika kissed Bykov. She continued speaking in Russian, "In twenty-four hours, you'll be the richest and most powerful man in the world."

Palmer felt her chest tighten. This was critical information to get to her boss, but she had a huge dilemma. She wanted to warn Gunner, but if she did, she'd blow her cover. Palmer waited until Nika and Bykov were gone before she went to Marco's office.

"Thanks for letting me make the call."

"Sure, just dial the number as you would normally. I'll be outside. Let me know when you're done."

She made the call to Bob. "The shipment is on. They're having a celebration dinner at the main restaurant overlooking the harbor."

"Will they all be there?"

"Yes—Rizzo, Castillo, Bykov and Nika. You can arrest them at the dinner."

"What about the captain?"

Palmer hesitated. "Yes." Palmer went on to explain the plot that Nika and Bykov had concocted to betray Rizzo and Castillo.

"You like this guy, Gunner."

"I do. You should hear how many people adore him. It makes me sick that I'll be the reason he spends the rest of his life in prison."

"I could write a book about the number of 'good' people I've put in jail. Money and power can really screw people up."

"That's the confusing part. I don't think Gunner is motivated by either."

"Who knows why good people go bad. It's not your role to figure that out."

"I hate this part of the job."

"I know. We'll be ready in Aruba. Once this is over, you can take a nice long vacation."

Chapter Eleven

They arrived in Aruba the next day. Gunner positioned the Destiny in the harbor for a great view of the boardwalk and restaurants, as well as the container ship docked in the staging area. Several flatbed trucks were lined up as the dock operators used cranes to lift the containers off the ship and load them onto trucks.

Rizzo was bouncing around the bridge, pointing to the cargo ship. "Look, they're already unloading product to the dock."

"Congratulations," Gunner said.

Rizzo rubbed his hands together. "I can't wait for dinner tonight. Did you connect with Rayaan, the harbor master? We don't want customs around our ship."

"There won't be a problem, but I'll check as soon as I secure the ship."

"Our celebration dinner starts at the restaurant at nine sharp. See you onshore."

Gunner left for the bridge and bumped into Palmer.

"What are you up to?" he asked.

"Nothing," she said, avoiding eye contact.

"What's wrong? You look upset."

"Didn't sleep well."

"Me neither." He smiled. "Quite the pair, aren't we?"

Palmer didn't trust her voice, so she just nodded.

"Stick close to the ship tonight. This isn't a good part of town."

"I can't. Rizzo wants me to be his assistant at the restaurant."

Gunner frowned. "Don't do that. The restaurant staff will have everything he needs."

"It's not my choice."

"I'll talk to Rizzo."

Gunner found Rizzo lounging at the pool with Nika and Bykov. The celebration had already begun with two buckets of champagne on ice. Rizzo clapped his hands and insisted that Gunner join them.

"Thanks, but I can't. I have a long list of things to do." He stepped closer to Rizzo. "Can I talk to you for a minute?" He glanced at Bykov. "In private."

Rizzo pulled Gunner a few feet away and spoke in hushed tones. "What's up?"

"Palmer said you wanted her at the restaurant tonight. I need her to stay on the ship."

"You have a staff of thirty crew."

"You should take Zoie instead. She's better."

"Better at what?" Rizzo shook his head. "I like Palmer. End of story." He walked back to the pool without waiting for Gunner to respond.

Fuming, Gunner returned to his cabin and called Rayaan.

"Are you set?"

"Yes."

"When is Castillo transferring the product to Rizzo's ship?"

"Later this afternoon. We're almost done unloading the containers into a warehouse next to their ship."

"Good. What about Castillo? Has he been inspecting the cargo?"

"No, but his men have been monitoring the transfers. They only opened a few containers to check the contents. Same with Bykov's team. They've tested several containers."

"What about Jett? Is he here?"

"He arrived last night."

"Do you have that vest I gave you on my last trip?"

"In my car."

"Put it on before you come to the restaurant." Gunner stared out the window overlooking the harbor. Rizzo's ship was tied up to the pier a short distance from the open-air restaurant where they planned to meet Castillo and Ortega for dinner. "See you tonight."

At dusk, Marco was busy helping all the guests board the tender boat used to shuttle everyone to the restaurant when Gunner arrived in full uniform and pulled Marco aside. "Is everyone ashore?"

"The guests are, but I have two shuttles still to run for staff."

"Good. I want to send Zoie instead of Palmer. I need her on the ship tonight."

"She's already ashore. She went in the shuttle with Rizzo, Bykov and Nika."

"Goddamn it!"

"What's wrong? I can send someone to get her."

"No, forget it." Gunner marched off and returned several minutes later to board the shuttle.

"Marco, thanks for being such a great first officer." Gunner put his hand on his friend's shoulder. "We're a good team."

"I know." Marco looked puzzled.

"Oh, one other thing. You remember my good buddy, Jett?"

"Of course."

"He's in Aruba on vacation for a few days and is going to stay with me. He'll board tonight while I'm at dinner. Can you make sure that he has everything he needs? He'll explain when he arrives."

"Sure. Good luck at dinner tonight."

Gunner took a seat in the shuttle along with the rest of the staff, and they motored toward the pier.

* * *

The party was underway by the time Gunner arrived. The tables were filled with appetizers, bottles of expensive wines and spirits. Gunner made sure Rizzo was seated at one end of the table and Castillo and Bykov at the other. Palmer stood behind Rizzo and gave Gunner a tiny wave as he approached the table.

Rizzo pulled out the empty chair next to him and pointed at Gunner. "Sit here." Rizzo slapped Gunner on the back. "Good job. We have a lot to celebrate."

Gunner glanced at Palmer and noticed she was shifting side to side nervously.

Rizzo went to the restroom, so Gunner motioned for Palmer to come over. "Are you feeling okay? You don't look well."

"I'm fine. Could be just a cold."

Rizzo returned to the table and patted Gunner's arm. "I have ordered a surprise for you. You'll see later."

Gunner smiled thinly. "Great. This night will be full of surprises."

As the guests finished their appetizers, Gunner noticed that neither Perez nor Ortega had arrived.

Gunner whispered to Rizzo, "Where's Ortega and Perez?"

"I don't know. Running late, I guess."

"Carlos," Rizzo asked. "Where are your partners?"

Castillo smiled. "They will not be joining us. Unfortunately, Perez had a family issue and returned to Venezuela, and Ortega had to return to Mexico for some pressing business. I guess you're stuck with me." He glanced at Bykov sitting next to him. "And Bykov."

"No worries, just fewer people to share with tonight," Rizzo said.

"That's what Bykov said to me," Castillo replied.

At nine o'clock, Rayaan entered the restaurant from the boardwalk and handed Gunner a note. Gunner frowned and handed it to Rizzo who stared at the note, and then threw it on the table.

Palmer noticed Gunner tense and push his chair slightly away from the table as Rizzo played with his glass of wine.

Rizzo made eye contact with one of his bodyguards lounging in the background of the patio. The man immediately stood, took his hands out of his pocket and elbowed the man next to him.

"Seems we have a problem," Rizzo announced to the table.

The chatter stopped, and everyone turned to Rizzo, who said to Castillo, "I was just informed that the quantity of cocaine you loaded onto our ship is short and half the quality you promised."

Castillo set his glass on the table. "Are you accusing me of cheating you?"

At the same moment, Gunner nodded to Rayaan, standing off to the side. Rayaan put his hand in his pocket and pushed a button.

Two simultaneous blasts shook the patio as Rizzo's container ship, and Castillo's warehouse exploded. For a moment, everyone was motionless—stunned at the conflagration.

Gunner reacted first, and dove for Palmer as the bodyguards for Castillo, Bykov and Rizzo drew their weapons and began to fire at each other. Gunner knocked Palmer off her feet and yelled, "Stay down." He pulled out a gun and aimed at Bykov, but the Russian ducked behind a counter.

Gunner glanced at Rizzo, who was on the ground with a bullet wound in the middle of his forehead. Then he moved quickly behind a portable bar and motioned for Rayaan to run for cover. The gunfire came from all directions.

As Gunner peered around the room for Bykov, he saw Castillo go down, his white shirt covered with blood from a chest wound. Rayaan crouched twenty paces away, waving his pistol to get Gunner's attention. He pointed toward a counter that was used to stage food deliveries from the kitchen. Rayaan mouthed, "He's still behind the counter."

Gunner took a deep breath, the same breath that he'd learned to take before he pulled the trigger in Vietnam. Everything went into slow motion as he leaped up and ran toward the counter. He only made it five steps before he was shot and fell to the floor.

At the same time, Palmer rushed from behind Rizzo, grabbed Gunner's pistol and began firing. Reaching the counter, she aimed at Bykov on the floor. She pulled the trigger, but the gun was empty. Bykov pointed his pistol and pulled the trigger. The impact of the bullet twisted Palmer off her feet. Bykov smiled and stood over Palmer, ready to finish her, when his skull exploded. Rayaan looked in the direction of the gunshot and saw Jett pointing Gunner's sniper rifle on the railing just outside the bridge of Rizzo's yacht.

At the same moment, the patio was overrun by Interpol and DEA agents. The gunfire lasted only another minute and then was over. Rayaan ran over to Gunner, who was sitting up, holding a bloody napkin to his head. Rayaan pulled the napkin away. "Gunner, you're one lucky sonofabitch. You now have a new part in your hair."

Gunner pushed him away and stood. "Where's Palmer?" They saw her lying face down next to Bykov. She was unconscious but still breathing. Bob Davis rushed over and flashed his badge. "DEA, she's one of us. We'll take her." Two agents picked her up and carried her toward a van parked on the boardwalk."

Rayaan and Gunner sat down on the floor with their backs against the bar.

"Fuck these guys," Gunner said.

They surveyed the chaos as agents finished arresting the bodyguards who were still alive. Tables and chairs were scattered everywhere. One agent was covering dead bodies the white tablecloths.

A bottle of Bykov's favorite Russian vodka lay on the floor next to them. Gunner unscrewed the top and took a large swig. He handed it to Rayaan. "Ironic, isn't it?"

Rayaan did the same thing and wiped a dribble off his chin with the back of his hand.

Gunner pointed at the two fires still blazing in the distance. "Rayaan, you did good tonight."

"I want to thank you. This is the end of the cartel."

Gunner shook his head. "This won't stop things."

"It will for a while. The Dutch Caribbean authorities have taken back the government tonight. They plan on arresting hundreds of corrupt officials, military and policemen." Rayaan sighed. "This has been a nightmare. We finally have our country back." Finally, they slowly stood, and Rayaan hugged Gunner. "I love you."

They stared at each other.

"I know." Gunner grabbed a clean napkin off a table. "I need to go check on Palmer."

"Hey, tell Jett nice shot on that bastard, Bykov. He saved Palmer's life."

Gunner stopped. "What do you mean?"

"When you went down, Palmer ran through a hail of bullets, grabbed your gun and started firing at Bykov. You should've seen her. It was like one of those army movies where a soldier snaps and walks toward the enemy firing nonstop." Rayaan pointed at Gunner's chest.

"It's a miracle that she survived. Just as she reached Bykov, she ran out of bullets. Bykov was going to shoot her in the head when Jett blew his brains out. Gunner, she saved your life."

Gunner shook his head. "She's a good girl."

"What a night. I'm going to go home and hug my wife and daughters. Also, bring Marco and Jett to our house for dinner tomorrow."

As Rayaan walked away, an agent approached Gunner. "Are you hurt?"

"I'm fine."

The man dressed in black special forces gear touched a button on his chest and said, "Yes, I got him. He's safe." The man waved at someone standing a few feet away. "We need to get him out of here right away."

"Wait a minute. I need to get to the hospital and check on someone."

"If you're referring to Palmer, they say she'll recover. She has wounds to her right hand and shoulder. I have orders to get you to a safe place immediately. No one else on this operation knows you're with us. We need to keep it that way." The man waved at a black suburban and pushed Gunner inside.

* * *

The next day, Gunner approached an agent guarding Palmer's hospital room. The guard saw him coming, took his hands out of his pockets and blocked the door until Gunner flashed CIA credentials.

"Relax. How is she feeling today?" Gunner asked.

The guard shrugged. "I just started my shift. The doctors don't tell me anything." He jerked his thumb at the door. "She's had a lot of visitors over the last hour."

"Do you know who they were?"

"No, but they like black suits."

Gunner knocked on Palmer's door and poked his head in. Palmer was sleeping, so Gunner pulled up a chair next to her bed. Her right hand was bandaged, and her right arm was in a sling.

Palmer slowly opened her eyes and stared at Gunner.

"How are you feeling?" Gunner asked.

"I'm so angry with you."

Gunner rubbed his hands on his thighs. "I know."

"You are an asshole."

Gunner pulled his chair closer to her bed. "Are you in much pain?"

"Don't change the subject."

"I couldn't tell you. It was too dangerous."

"So, when did you know I was an agent?"

"Can I get you something? Water? Ice?"

"You knew from the beginning?"

Gunner nodded.

"Let me rephrase what I just said, 'You are a *fucking* asshole!'"

Gunner smiled. "I want you to know that you are a *fucking* great undercover agent."

Palmer shook her head. "Please give me the short version because I want to hit you."

Gunner sat back in his chair. "I've been with a secret branch of the CIA after I returned from Vietnam. I was so angry at the drugs ruining my buddies in Vietnam and all the drugs that were shipped back to the States. I lost one of my best friends to an overdose of heroin. We only had two weeks left before we finished our tour and could go home. I vowed revenge but didn't know how I could make a difference.

"I had developed an extensive network as a captain sailing around the Caribbean. The Columbians were beginning to increase the drug flow into southern Florida, so I approached Jett with my idea. He used to work in Army intelligence in Vietnam, and he connected me with the CIA. I convinced them I could gather information on the drug pipeline flowing from Columbia through the Caribbean. As a captain sailing around the islands, no one would ever suspect me. It was the perfect cover.

"Three years ago, we heard vague rumors about the potential of the Italian mafia and the Columbians colluding to form a mega-cartel. It was not an accident that I sought to work for Rizzo on the Destiny.

I'd been working on his yacht, gaining his trust and passing on critical information to my contacts in Miami."

Gunner gently touched Palmer's arm. "I'm sorry that I couldn't tell, but my group is operating outside the normal DEA or CIA agencies."

"Was it all pretend?" Palmer's eyes welled up. "Was any of what happened between us real or not?"

Gunner leaned close to Palmer. "What do you want it to be?"

"I don't know."

They sat for a few minutes, not speaking. Finally, Palmer pointed at the bandage above his forehead.

"Just a scratch." Gunner pulled up a chair. "Here's the update. Rizzo, Castillo and Bykov are dead, and Nika is in custody. She'll spend the rest of her life in prison." Gunner grabbed her good hand. "I wanted to thank you. Rayaan told me that you saved my life."

"Then we're even because you saved my life on the yacht with your kindness. I was drowning in self-pity. You gave me the courage that maybe, just maybe, I can let myself dream again."

"You sell yourself too short." Gunner paused. "I've wanted to ask you something since we met. Why did you become an undercover agent?"

Palmer sighed. "Revenge." She repositioned her arm in the sling. "Heroin killed the only person I ever loved."

"Well, congratulations. You accomplished your goal."

"It's odd. After everything that happened, I thought I would be celebrating. Instead, I just feel relieved."

Gunner changed the subject. "How's your hand?"

"The surgery was kinda successful, but I'll never have full use of it again. The DEA offered me a desk job, but I think I'll leave the service. This will be the third time I survived. Two assassination attempts and now this. I'm tired of living undercover, wondering who would betray me next." Palmer looked out of her hospital window. She could see the ocean and the ships anchored in the bay.

"What's next for you?" Palmer added.

"I need to put my feet on land for a while."

"Thank you for everything you've done for me."

Gunner laughed. "You have it backward. I should be thanking you." He played with a piece of fuzz on his black pants. "I understand you're flying back to the States tomorrow."

Palmer nodded.

"It's been quite a ride."

Palmer dabbed her eyes. "Will I ever see you again?"

"That's up to you."

"Of course, I do." She reached out with her good arm. Gunner leaned over and hugged her. "I have some business to take care of at my marina. Cody was murdered, and Bonita is returning to Miami, so I'm selling it."

"I'm so sorry about Cody."

"It wasn't a surprise. I knew he was in trouble. I tried to help him, but…"

"Gunner, you have to stop carrying this rock. Jett told me you've been his guardian angel his entire life. There was nothing you could've done to change Cody's destiny."

Gunner simply shook his head.

"What are you going to do after you sell the marina?" Palmer asked.

"Not sure." Gunner moved a strand of hair away from her eyes. "Will you go back to Washington?" he asked.

She nodded. "Yes, Bob wants to debrief me before they let me retire."

Gunner took a deep breath. "I have an idea. When you can travel, I'll send you a plane ticket to Virgin Gorda. It will be a nice vacation for you."

"Will you be there?"

"Wouldn't miss it."

Gunner leaned over and kissed Palmer on the lips. "See you soon."

Chapter Twelve

A month later, Palmer was with Addie in a lounge chair next to the pool. "When does Gunner arrive?" she asked.

"He called last night and said he'd be here tomorrow. The sale of his marina closed, so he's sailing the Rainbow here. How did you leave things with Gunner?"

"I don't know. I had to unwind from the agency, and he needed to sell the marina. He suggested we meet here once we settled our respective business issues."

"Have you thought about your future?"

Palmer took off her sunglasses. "Yes and no. I'm not sure there is a future with Gunner."

"Why not?"

"Because I'm afraid. I don't know how to explain it, but I think I'd be a disappointment to Gunner. Look at me. I don't have anything to offer. Why would he want me? Not sure I'm even capable of having a meaningful relationship."

"Then why are you here?"

Palmer closed her eyes. "Because for the first time in my life, I feel at home when I'm with him. I spent my childhood in shame for causing my parents to die in a car accident—and wanting to love and be loved." She stopped. "Does this make any sense?"

"Do you love him?"

"Yes."

Addie reached over and touched her hand. "I know Gunner.

Despite his aura of confidence, he's insecure about his self-worth. That's why he's avoided long-term relationships. Rejection from his birth parents and indifference from his adopted parents warped his view of himself. He can give his heart to me and Jett, but he can't seem to let go and try to love again." Addie smiled. "Until he met you."

Palmer sat up and looked at Addie. "But am I enough?"

* * *

Palmer woke early the next morning to watch the sunrise. The sky was clear and the sea calm. As she stepped onto the patio, she saw the Rainbow anchored fifty yards off the beach.

Palmer jumped at the voice behind her. "You're up early."

Gunner emerged from the living room just off the patio.

Palmer rushed over and hugged him. "I've missed you." They pulled apart and looked at each other.

"When did you get in?"

"At dawn. How's your hand and shoulder doing?"

Palmer shrugged. "Fine."

Gunner motioned toward the beach. "Should we take a walk?"

They strolled the beach for an hour, trying to find a way to talk about the important things. They laughed and held hands but couldn't find a way to bring up their feelings. Finally, they arrived back at the patio.

Palmer drummed up her courage and asked, "Can we talk?"

"I thought we were talking for the last hour."

"No, I mean *talk*."

"Sure, but I want to show you something first. Follow me."

He led Palmer to the top of a hill about fifty yards from Addie's house. Jett had finished framing the house. Gunner took Palmer's hand and walked her through each room until they reached the patio overlooking the ocean.

"What do you think?"

"Amazing. What a view. This is even better than Addie's patio."

They sat down on the edge of the unfinished deck.

"How did the sale of your marina go?"

"Good. Bonita says hello."

"I've been doing a lot of thinking over the last two days," Palmer said.

"This place will do that for you."

"You once asked me what I dream about. I lied to you. I made up the story about wanting to become a captain because I thought it would gain your trust and lead to information that would be valuable to the DEA. I'm sorry. Can you forgive me?"

"So, you believed I was a bad guy?"

Palmer squirmed. "Something like that."

"Don't go there. It was your job. I wanted us to be friends as much as you did."

"I woke up this morning feeling like I'd been reborn—like I'm starting over. Since I met you, I stopped thinking about my shitty past. And for the first time, I started thinking about the future."

"I had the same feelings as I sailed the Rainbow over here." Gunner moved a little closer. "Since we're starting over, tell me. What is your dream now?"

Palmer smiled. "Simple—to have a place to call home with the people I love. I've never associated love with the word 'home.'" Her voice trembled. "Until I met you, Jett and Addie." She looked at Gunner and touched his hand. "I'm so happy for you. You found something in Montana you've been searching for all your life. You finally have a family."

"If you could do anything you want, what would it be?"

She blushed. "I want to write a novel. I used to write in college."

Gunner smiled. "That sounds awesome as long as you don't include me in any of your novels."

Palmer laughed. "This past year has given me enough material for five books."

Gunner grabbed her hands and faced her. "I may not be your pot of gold at the end of a rainbow, but we could make a life here. Jett's almost finished this house. We could move in very soon." Gunner continued to speak so fast that Palmer didn't have a chance to respond. He stopped speaking. "Maybe you could find your happy place with me."

Palmer fell into his arms. "I love you."

"I love you too. But I have to tell you something else."

Palmer froze.

"I can't father a child. I was wounded in Vietnam and—"

Palmer touched his lips with her index finger. "Stop. It doesn't matter."

"Are you sure?"

"We can make this our home."

A squall passed over the beach, dropping a brief sprinkle of water. As Gunner and Palmer rocked back and forth, holding each other, Palmer suddenly pulled away and pointed. The sun had reappeared, forming a perfect rainbow that ended directly over Gunner's sailboat.

"She's so beautiful," Palmer said.

Gunner nodded. "My first love."

"Would you ever sell her and upgrade to a newer boat?"

"Never."

"What if someone made you a large offer?"

"No."

"There must be some price."

"She's priceless."

Palmer squinted. "What's priceless to you?"

"Seven and a half million."

Palmer threw her head back and laughed. "You're a funny man."

"I've been told that before." Gunner smiled, thinking back to Eze and his negotiations with Rizzo.

"What do you mean by that?"

"Did I tell you that Jett and I are building housing for the islanders that lost their homes during the last hurricane? No? We're hiring dozens of unemployed people and training them with skills they can use to get future work. Also, Paz and Addie are planning a marine center with a world-class aquarium. We're partnering with the National Marine Biology Institute to conduct research and provide education for biologists around the world. Maybe this will bring more jobs and tourism to the island."

"Amazing! But how are you paying for all this?"

"I have resources." He stared at the Rainbow rocking in the waves. "Sometimes, nothing is what it seems, but for a good reason."

Palmer looked confused but changed the subject. "What are you doing tomorrow?"

"I'm having the Rainbow transferred to a large shed at the local marina. I need to replace the keel. It was damaged on a coral head when I left the Dominican Republic to travel here."

* * *

A year later, they were sitting on the same deck admiring the sunset.

"I forgot to tell you." Palmer nodded toward the house. "You received a letter today from your adoption agency back in Maine. I left it on the kitchen counter."

"What did it say?"

"Didn't open it. I assume it has to do with your family in Montana."

Gunner walked back to the house to retrieve the letter. Fifteen minutes later, he sat down, holding the envelope.

"What's wrong?" Palmer asked. "You look upset?"

Gunner showed her the letter and a photo. "A couple of months ago, I sent a letter to the director of the adoption agency thanking them for connecting me with my family. I also gave them an update that we got married, I quit my job and that you're writing your first novel." He held the letter up in the air. "I wasn't expecting to get a response."

"What does it say?"

He handed it to her, and she read it.

Dear Gunner,

Thank you for your kind note. We are so happy that the meeting with your family was a success. Not all reunions end that way. Also, congratulations on your marriage to Palmer. I'm writing because we have a terrible situation. We have two young children, ages four and six, whose parents were killed in a car accident. We've tried to place them in adoption but now have run out of time. The state requires that we place them in the foster care system, which means they will be separated. It's so heartbreaking. We were wondering if you knew of anyone that might consider adopting them so they could stay together. We included a photo and some background information. Let me know if you have any recommendations because we only have a month before we have to split them up.

Gunner looked at the photo and handed it to Palmer.

Palmer smiled as she slowly touched each face in the photo with her index finger.

Gunner stared at the Rainbow anchored just off the beach. "What do you think?"

She held the photo to her chest and stared at the ocean for a moment. Then she reached over and grabbed his hand. "Make the call." Wiping tears from her face, she said, "You are going to be an amazing daddy."

Acknowledgments

Gratitude. Amazing how nine letters can have such meaning. This is the first word that I think of when I reflect on the journey of writing this novel. The team at Calumet Editions made this project possible. Ian, Gary, Beth and Josh have unique skills that added tremendous value to my project. They are always generous, not only with their expertise but more importantly, with their friendship.

I'm grateful for a dozen friends and family that I pestered throughout last year with various drafts of scenes and chapters. They never failed to smile and provide encouragement to keep writing even though most of what I wrote was not very good. Writing this novel is similar to my poor golf game. I swing and swing and every once in a while, I hit the sweet spot. Same with my attempt to write this story. Now and again, I would get lucky

About the Author

Pete Carlson's debut novel, *Ukrainian Nights*, won the Finalist Award in the General Fiction category of the highly prestigious Eric Hoffer Awards 2020 program. His second novel, *Tearza*, was published in December 2020 and won the Finalist Award Colorado Authors League 2021 and the 2021 Midwest Book Finalist Award from the Midwest Independent Publishers Association.

Made in the USA
Las Vegas, NV
04 November 2022